The Joan Cra

by Peter Jo

Copyright 2013

For Tracy Hamby
and a very special thanks to all the Joan Crawford fans
who hung on until the very end

More PJS novels at, http://peterjosephswanson.weebly.com/

Chapter one

    The first day of shooting, June 30 1969, was exhausting for sixty-six-year-old Joan Crawford. She was sick with a bad cold and it already caused her to lose five and a half pounds. That was in addition to her steak-cube diet—the cubes kept in the compartments of candy boxes to help make it seem more fun.
    The first scene on the production schedule hadn't been shot yet. They were still setting up outside on the moors of England. Just as a weary Joan was about to pass out on her cot she heard something small and metallic rattle at the trailer door. She opened her eyes and first saw the door reflected in the main makeup mirror. She didn't see anything so she opened the door, stepped outside, and because of the thick fog she didn't see the moors at all. She didn't see anybody. She smoothed her bold orange and green silk robe over her tiny belly. "Hello?" She repeated louder in a phony heavy cockney accent, "*Ahllo*!" She thought she smelled fingernail polish remover but when she turned she saw fresh spray paint.
    MONSTER was spray painted in red across the front of her dressing trailer.
    "You got the wrong trailer!" she said to it, walked back inside, slammed the aluminum door, coughed, and collapsed on her narrow bed again. She closed her eyes, ran her fingertip along the tubing on her robe, but then opened her eyes just to look again at the riotous

orange and yellow mod wallpaper that looked like cartoon flowers. She wondered why they had to paper every wall in England.

The director, fifty-three year old Freddie Francis, knocked and rushed in after he was invited. "Miss Crawford, are you alright?"

She sat up and grabbed her large glass with the Pepsi-Cola logo on it. "Call me Joanie. I insist." Ice cubes clinked as she took a sip from her vodka. "Do I clash with the wallpaper? Look at my gown against this wallpaper! What does one wear for this wallpaper? I can only allow black and white photos in here." She redid her dusty-pumpkin lipstick.

Freddie looked exasperated but didn't look at the wallpaper.

Joan made a dismissive gesture to the door. "Yeah, I saw what was painted out there. They got the wrong trailer. And Trog doesn't get a trailer. Only I do." She smirked then grandly pushed on the side of her dyed blonde hair.

"What tosh!" Freddie glanced nervously toward the door. "I was hoping you hadn't seen it yet. It's fresh so it can be easily removed. We'll have it removed within the hour. I'm so sorry that happened. Some hooligan was taking advantage of the cover of such thick fog. It's an unusual fog for summer—it's like a horror movie out there."

Joan raised her voice. "I don't do horror! I do drama…with moments of suspense!"

"Of course! I was just suggesting that it's a shame the script didn't call for thick fog. But if we tried to film it then the sun would suddenly pop out and it would all burn off in no time and then the shots wouldn't match."

As he talked she was pulling a glass bottle of Pepsi out of a metal ice bucket. She opened it and handed it to him, then interrupted, "Here. This is better than barley water. You have the most adorable accent. I love being back in England. I love everything British. Hail Britannia ruler of the waves." She flashed him a full wide smile of gorgeous porcelain teeth.

Freddie took a sip of Pepsi.

She blew her nose and asked, "Why are you carrying a monkey mask around? Don't tell me you're going to throw a monkey man into the picture now, too. Don't tell me they're going to fight in the end. Trog VS Kong? That's not in the script." She looked aghast.

Freddie put the flimsy rubber monkey mask on. "It looks lousy, huh."

Joan mockingly puffed out the side of her mouth to agree, and swore about it.

He took it back off. "I told the producer we should have a backup incase anything happened to the trog mask. This is the best that the prop department could come up with." He looked at the monkey mask in disgust.

Joan put her hand over her eyes. "If you use that you'll need to also add a fog machine so we can't see it at all. Or film right now before all our real London fog blows away. This fog is really all just blowing in from London, right? London is really a big fog machine."

Freddy set the ape mask down and looked at it sadly. "Yeah, this one just doesn't have the same *je ne sais quoi* as the trog mask." The backup looked *totally* different. "It's wonky. We'll try to keep the good mask in one piece. It's really well made. This whole movie is based on having that one mask. We're so lucky we got a hold of it."

Joan picked up the replacement ape mask and looked at it. She suddenly looked depressed enough to cry.

Freddie said, "Just rest, Joan. Save your voice. You sound knackered."

She lit a cigarette. "This'll help sooth my voice. Lucille Ball said tobacco was soothing. She said once on television while I was watching. So it must be true. She acts like a know-it-all, anyway." Joan gritted her teeth and her eyes wrinkled.

"I'd love to hear all about what you think of Lucy, someday." He raised his eyebrows while watching her smoke. "Soothing?"

"It's a cigarette." Joan gave it a pert nod. "It's made out of leaves. Leaves are always so healthy, we can only pray. I'm smoking a salad. That's what I've always believed. And like a salad of leaves they help with the diet. That's what I've always counted on. A natural herbal diet. They said so at the drugstore when I was a kid. That was before the government stepped in and ruined all the fun with statistics. Drugstores used to be so much fun, so full of miracles. They had beauty cream back then that promised to erase all wrinkles, made your hair grow in thick, and made your teeth white as snow—just from one beauty powder. But I didn't need that then. I wish I had some of that stuff now." She coyly blew smoke off to the side, haughtily shaking her head a tad, to flirt, to beg him to insist she still looked young.

Freddie took the ape mask back and started to back out of the trailer but stopped at the door. "Don't worry about a blooming thing. Everything is well in hand. We'll find who sprayed that on your trailer and have them put in jail!"

She pretended to pull a bit of tobacco off the tip of her tongue just out of habit from the days before filters, and narrowed her eyes to show she was dead serious. "Me worry? I've wasted my life worrying about the wrong stuff. I know better now." She looked at the lipstick stain on the filter of her cigarette and then continued talking as she redid her lips with a new shiny orange color. "This film smells like success, I can smell it like… like I can smell spray paint now. This is a very different part for me and I'm excited by that. I want the Joan Crawford of this year to be a building block for the Joan Crawford of next year. I haven't even begun to be what I want to be. I haven't done anything professionally yet in all my life that I'm completely satisfied with."

He nodded.

She continued, "Success is thick in the air. I'll be on top again." She opened her eyes wide and chortled playfully. "Funny I had to return to England to get on top of Hollywood but the times have changed. I'm Joan Crawford, I change with the times like nobody. I'm ready for the seventies."

He nodded.

She gestured down at the loud robe she was wearing. "It's a shame I can't wear this Ohrbach in the movie to give the audience what it wants…the most festive fashions of the year."

Joan was wearing several of her own simpler dresses in the movie, out of her own closet from home, with a lab coat dyed azure to match one of the dresses, so she would still look very nice. For the moors she would wear an off-white casual pantsuit that she was annoyed with—as *Joan Crawford* she would otherwise never be seen in public in any kind of pants.

Joan continued, "But I know it isn't that kind of picture, I'm an energetic scientist running about and even poking into caves."

He nodded. "Rest. We'll let you know when the sun is low and we can shoot." Freddie looked out the window. "As soon as the sun comes out it'll burn off this fog. The forecast says that should happen any minute."

"Forecasts. We could wait for the sun all week then. Let's just shoot it no matter what's going on out there, just to get it in the can."

"It may come to that." Freddie said. "You have four hours and then we'll shoot rain or shine."

"Is the Pepsi ready out there?"

He nodded.

A showy Pepsi concession stand was set up nearby at the cave set. It would not only serve up refreshments for the crowd that would gather for the angry mob at the film's climax but also appear in a shot for a flash of advertising.

She said, "Bless you. Don't worry, I'll get it all for you on the first take. I hope we do see a peek of sun. That low angle light will look great on me. I'll glow like an angel. I'll give my fans the Joan Crawford they want. A movie star." She grinned wearily. The morning spent doing interviews with the press had drained her. "Call Frenchy. I want to start early." Frenchy was the one-woman hair and makeup department Joan had worked with for decades. Joan patted the back of her hand against the front of her neck. Then she rolled her grand expressive eyes in worry. "Just a little powder to bring all this makeup back to life. I don't want any of it to shine. I don't want to look like a melting candle."

Freddie flattered her, left and found Mark the production manager where the snacks were being served in camp under a small drab canvas tent. Freddie put down his full bottle of Pepsi and glared at Mark's scone as he said to him, "Joanie's caravan has been vandalized. Why aren't you out looking for who did it? Go!"

"Don't have a wobbly. I've just poked into everything and didn't see anything. But with this fog you can't see anything a stone's throw away."

"Look for the spray paint can, too."

Mark said, "I poked my nose into all the dustbins. Whoever would spray paint like that on a movie star caravan like a bloody vandal is going to hide their can better than that no matter how crackers they might be."

Freddie frowned. "*Who* would do something like that to Joan Crawford? We all love her! It's great to have a star like her on a picture like this. She's been a star again and again since the silent days. She's fantastic. She's a trooper...a good sport. She's a corker!"

"Think this will be her last movie?" Mark asked.

Freddie rubbed the side of his nose. "She thinks it's a comeback. She's had so many before, so many that she's now on her 81st movie, and that's just for the big screen. She's just bloody amazing!

But she's fifty-nine years old now, sure. That's what she told me." He looked doubting, then smirked. "How many sticky wickets can she squeeze out of one career?"

Mark grinned sadly. "And how old will they let her be to push Pepsi? They're pushing the stuff as the drink for the young. She don't look like that anymore to me. Fifty-nine is old as the bog in Hollywood. Are you sure that's her age?"

Freddie gave a crooked grin. "That's what she said but I really know bugger about all that. I think she looks knackered for fifty-nine but then she used to sun herself so much and the Hollywood sun is a desert sun. Very hard. You have to be a cactus to survive that. She could be fibbing about her age—they do that in Hollywood, too. I think if she did that many silent films she has to be older than she says. She wasn't a flapper when she was six." Freddie nodded sadly. "That makes her a little old lady anywhere. I'm glad I'm an old director. Nobody looks at my wrinkles in that way like it means I can't do my job anymore. I can be a little old man and just get more respect. What'll Joan do when they all decide she's far too old for this stuff and they stop taking her phone calls? It's a very cruel business for everybody who's in front of the camera." He shook his head sadly.

Mark shrugged. "Tele?"

"Yeah, there's always the gogglebox. TV is the graveyard for old stars."

"Why are we sad on the first day of shooting?" Mark looked around and took in the layout of the camp like ghostly shapes in the fog. "We're supposed to be thrilled."

Joan Crawford walked up to them looking tinier than usual. She was wearing flat shoes, being out in a field. She turned her head away from him, coughed and then said, "There you are. This fog is so thick I had to follow voices. Why aren't you enjoying a Pepsi? God knows I had enough brought out here." She chuckled at herself.

Freddie smiled politely and picked his bottle back up. "Yeah, I need a Pepsi. I need refreshed after this long day. And it hasn't even started yet."

Joan winked at him. "I'd make you have drinks with me in London after we shoot, to refresh you some more, but I'm going to have to give you a rain check on that until I shake this damn cold. I don't know what it's up to anymore. It started as a head cold and turned into a chest cold and now it's a head cold again and my ears are ringing. But I'm not sure. I just know it's evil."

"Why aren't you resting in your caravan?"

Joan looked back towards it, the only star trailer the film could afford. Everybody else was using tents and cars to prepare for the sunset shoot. "I don't have a telephone. I'm so lost without one. Who knows what job offers I have piling up in New York right now. I'm really roughing it, huh. I'm not complaining. I just wanted to see where everybody went."

Freddie assured her, "We'll all be right here at camp. Don't worry. Lock your door and rest and we'll let you know when we shoot. I'm sure the fog will clear away in no time."

"How is my hair and makeup going to know that I need her?"

"We've already sent for Frenchy. She might be there now waiting for you."

"Bless you, Freddie. I'm in good hands with a director like you. You're a master director. I'd kiss you now but I don't want to give you what I have." She blew elegant air kisses.

"I had my shots."

"No. My color." Joan puckered her orange waxy lips and then left them.

The forty-five-year-old producer, Herman Cohen, walked by, grinning, thrilled to have Joan again. "Seen Joanie?"

Mark pointed. "She just headed off to her tailor. Just two seconds ago."

Herman looked surprised. "She's up and about? That's remarkable. I thought we killed her with so many interviews in London. Boy she's a trooper."

Mark made a bitter face. "I hope we're not outside here all week. I hear Hollywood stars are difficult."

"Maybe the new ones. Joan's a pro and having her will actually help keep us moving along on pace. My last film with her came in on schedule and under budget. I expect this one to go that way, too. She's like clockwork." He hurried off. He caught up with her before she got to her trailer, and took her arm. "Let me help you through this fog so you don't end up at Winsor Castle."

Joan chuckled at his joke. The castle was in the town nearby.

Herman added, "Were you lonely again? I'm sorry. We thought we were leaving you to rest."

Joan dramatically pouted.

Herman gave her arm a squeeze. "Let me put you to bed and tuck you in. You need a little kip, a bit of a nap, before we shoot again. I want you to shake this flu you have. Now that I've got you for another picture I want to make sure I take good care of you."

"I'm in good hands."

He said, "I wouldn't be here again without you. Without you, my career would probably have been all over a few years ago."

"Bless you. If we all pull together we all just might get somewhere."

They stopped in front of her trailer to watch two men washing off the graffiti from it, with gasoline. "I'm so sorry this happened. I wanted everything to be perfect for you."

"Oh, you're far too cheap a producer to keep that promise." Joan poked him playfully in the belly.

"We'll find who did it and string him up."

"Or *her*. It might be Marlene Dietrich jealous of my new part. She doesn't have one and I do. She just sings anymore and she sounds like she's doing that from a coffin in a very deep echo chamber."

Herman chuckled. "She's in Paris these days."

"Then she's plotting her revenge from there."

"Why would she be thinking about you right now?"

"You know she's still mad. Ever since the press went bananas about how good I looked in circus tights, actually putting in print that my legs rivaled Dietrich's. You just know she's damn mad about that since her legs are all she has. I've been waiting for a drunk phone call since."

"Your legs make a lot of the new stars jealous, too. Still."

"She'd swim the channel for a good part. These days we all would, those of us who built Hollywood in the first place. Now we fight for parts like you wouldn't believe." They stepped up into the trailer and sat on her cot. "And this is a great part. I like variety. I've never played a lady scientist before. This'll show I still have range. Ole Joanie was never a one trick pony. Look at how Bette Davis turned out. Now she only flounces and talks like a drunk drag queen hell bent on not slurring, when she doesn't screech. She was never good at playing kind and gentle people, anyway. She was never kind."

"Calm down, Joan. You need to rest. Bette is an ocean apart from you now so let your argy-bargy with her rest for a few weeks."

"Argy-what?"

"That fight you're having."

Joan noticed the main makeup mirror was cracked from side to side. "Oh look! That wasn't like that before! When did that happen?"

"Bad luck! A curse!"

"Nonsense. It's just a flimsy trailer. What can you expect. And the road here was so bumpy. But I didn't even notice it until now. Maybe Stanley Kubrick is still mad at us for stealing his mask. Maybe he did it! He threw a curse! I keep waiting for him to pop by anyway to meet the great movie star. Me. He does want to meet Joan Crawford while I'm in England I hope, if he likes the movies as much as he says he does. Or maybe he'll just come by to try and get his mask back. Keep an eye out for him. Keep him away from Trog!"

Herman shook his head. "Don't worry about that."

"He's been trying to destroy everything left over from his space movie so it can't all show up again in other people's movies. He's so wasteful. The studios used to warehouse everything for years to reuse."

Herman pushed Joan's head down onto the pillow and insisted she rest, adding, "I didn't steal anything from Kubrick. I paid good money for that mask."

She slapped his hand away. "My hair! I'll rest sitting up so my hair doesn't have to be completely redone. And I don't think buying stuff on the black market counts. Kubrick didn't get a penny. What if he wants his mask back and we aren't done with it yet?"

He pushed her down again. "The back of your hair can take that pillow for an hour. It's only pulled up so high in the front, so…"

Joan touched her face above her ears. "My face tapes!"

"Keep squirming and fighting me and they'll pop loose, sure."

Joan relaxed and finally said, "Bless you. I'll be a good girl and do what you say, you're the boss. I'll have my strength back and I can carry that little girl all over the moors."

"Chloe can walk on her own two feet if you're too weak. I don't know why girls have to be carried when they're being rescued."

Joan sat back up and looked at her lipstick stain on her cigarette filter before sucking on it again. "It just looks right…it'll look good having me carry her out of the cave as if I'm a hero since I'm the Hollywood star. But I can't crawl and carry at the same time. Your exterior cave set is rather tiny. Couldn't they put a bigger cave opening out there? If we were in LA you'd think we'd found Trog in a pothole. Here it looks more like we're all parading in and out the backdoor of a gnome's house. Just a foot taller and I wouldn't have to stoop to go in and out…I'm so tiny as it is. Then I'd only have the worry of not cracking the little's girls head on the side of the door as I carry her out." Joan shuddered. "Oh poor Chloe! That would be a horrible thing to do to such a sweet little girl. I'll have to make sure I don't crack her head on the side as I make sure I don't rip my hairpiece off on the top."

"We'll work something out to get you through that little hole gracefully. We'll put a few cops in the way, between you and the camera, and then as they back away we see you…we see you just stepping away from the cave opening with the little girl in your arms. People will just assume you're stepping through."

"Clever!"

"You'd put your back out carrying her out all the way through, otherwise."

"Good idea. I'm glad we're working together again. You always have good ideas. You always make things work. You and our director sure know how films work."

Herman said, "I'll tell your hair and makeup to come by in an hour."

"Frenchy already knows to pop back." Joan looked off in dreamy thought. "It'd be nice if I could show Chloe the dollhouse in Windsor Castle. I read about it in a brochure at the hotel. Seeing something like that is always more fun with a child. And it'd be nice if Chloe had memories of Joan Crawford that just weren't about monsters. A little girl at that age is so impressionable. An outing with her would be fun. We can only pray we have some extra time for fun."

"Maybe you'll have time later in the week when we film with the other actors. Your driver knows the way to Windsor Castle. He may be a few cups shy of a tea service but he can do that much."

"And maybe I can stop by the flower shop in the village." Joan glared at the small empty table. "Where are my flowers? Joan Crawford always gets flowers in her dressing room no matter what that dressing room may be."

"I ordered them. I'll check on why they didn't come. Please don't feel slighted."

Joan gently rubbed a knitting needle on his cheek. "This time I'm not feeling slighted. I know you are a dear. This time I worry about the girl at the flower shop. Vanessa Winklehorn is her name. She's been writing me since I first came to England to film the last picture we did together. She's a very kind fan. Maybe there's another flower shop around here. Maybe you didn't order from her flower shop at all. So maybe it's silly that I'm having such a horrible feeling about Vanessa right now. You know me. I have a psychic connection to my fans…and they to me."

Herman said, "It's a small town. A village. There's only one flower shop. And it's also a gift shop and I think they also hire out bicycles. When I call the flower shop I'll ask for Vanessa and see if they won't let her deliver the flowers to you personally. That would be thrilling for her. It would be fun for you to meet her, too, if you've written back and forth. I wonder why it hasn't been done already. I put in the order, myself, when we first hired the trailer."

Joan stabbed a ball of tan yarn with her needles. "Bless you. You're such a dear. And I love my fans. I dream about them. I have no idea what Vanessa looks like but I had a dream that she was a sweet young thing and then she was murdered horribly. I was suddenly Miss Marple but I had no cue cards so I couldn't solve anything until a mummy, who said she was *the chosen*, came out of a box and strangled me, waking me up. Dreams are always so stupid so I didn't think anything of it. But now it's all coming back to me." Joan shivered. "I remember it and I'm worried about her now. It was a horrible thing to dream about one of my lovely fans. I don't think I've ever had a dream like that. I wonder what that means. And why would I dream about a mummy strangling me? What is the symbolism of that? Maybe it isn't symbolic at all. Too often I just dream that I'm trying to sign autographs but the pen has no ink. That's so horrible! That's not symbolic. It could happen!"

Herman said, "I'll check to make sure Vanessa is okay. I'll tell her you think of her too. You two must meet! I'm touched that you feel so deeply about your fans."

"I think it was Gloria Swanson who told me that we become psychic about what we think about most. I think about my fans morning and night and for the many hours in the day that it takes me to respond to all my fan mail. I must thank Vanessa for being such a dear fan. I hope we meet soon. I must assure her she's on my

Christmas card list so she doesn't worry that she's forgotten. It's horrible to feel forgotten!"

"I'm on that list too." Herman grinned. "How do you afford so many Christmas cards every year?"

"Pepsi pays for the cards and postage. Not that I don't work for that money. Not that Pepsi should ever take fans for granted. Without fans we're nothing. Joan Crawford fans are what made me and Pepsi what we are today. They kept me *Joan Crawford* over all these decades. When Hollywood kept throwing Joan Crawford away it was the fans that kept pulling her out of the rubbish pile and putting her back on the throne. The movie throne."

"Yes, you're the queen," Herman said. "We should get some publicity shots of you at the flower shop surrounded by all those flowers….and, also, even better…shots of you at Winsor Castle as the queen! That'd make some shots people can talk about. The queen at a castle. Wear one of your mod turbans."

"I'm not a real queen. I wasn't born this way. I was born dirt poor and had to live at school and earn my keep by getting all the smaller children ready for the day and putting them to bed again at night, bathing and dressing and talking to them like they were somebody. For many of them I was their only mother. A real queen doesn't grow up like that."

Herman said, "Well, you're a queen now. Cinderella style. But the prince you married was the other half of yourself. You became your own husband."

Joan chuckled. "I like that…until it's time for a *man*…" She smiled at him but still worried about Vanessa at the flower shop. In her imagination she only pictured flowers on graves and not in her dressing room. Annoyed by her ghoulish thinking, she grabbed a tube of lipstick and rubbed it on her lips, a paler color than she'd had on before. She faced the cracked mirror on the wall. She decided to look in a smaller mirror to the side of it. "Pretty. This would be a better color for the court scene. When I have a speech like that the lipstick color has to fit the serious theme just perfect. Then I'll wear a very red lipstick for the interview I have later with *McCall's Magazine*." She pushed on her skin between her eyebrows, annoyed by the worry lines. "And please find Vanessa Winklehorn. I love to meet my fans. I'm worried about her now. I'm feeling psychic about my fans right now, strongly, and it's only bad feelings today. And…should I be worried about *MONSTER* spray painted across my trailer? What does that mean? I don't know what things like that mean in England, if they're as threatening as they might seem in Hollywood. But then Hollywood is a bunch of crybabies and brats. In New York they call spray painting like that *art*."

Herman said, "Don't worry about a thing. And I'll get this mirror replaced as soon as possible."

"Let it go. I have many mirrors. I won't be in here long. Let's not slow down this shoot for vanity that doesn't show up on film."

Chapter two

Joan went to her hotel, Hornfield Court. It was an ornate stone country house built in 1860 overlooking the Thames River. Against the dramatic backdrop of distant lightning and thunder, Joan washed off her makeup. Her lipstick had grown slightly larger on her mouth over the course of the day and left a perky stain on the skin around her lips. After she added a shiny layer of cold cream to her face she spent time looking at all the antique furnishings and decorations in her room. A foot tall black stone Egyptian cat made her nervous. She called the front desk and asked about it.

"It's a few thousand years old, they say."

"I could swear I just heard it purr."

"I doubt any sound came from that." He laughed nervously.

"It's just staring at me."

"It's marvelously done, isn't it."

Joan was amazed. "That old and it's just sitting here in a hotel room?"

"There's antiques all over an old nation like ours. And even older things from even older countries that we took them from. Like Egypt."

"Really?"

"Egypt was such a fashion, here. A rage. Many people went to Egypt and bought up all the antiques that they could. Or excavated and opened tombs. They got the stuff very cheap. So that cat may be thousands of years old but it didn't really cost anybody all that much, I'm sure. I'm sure it came from some great adventure, or some honeymoon."

"It should be in a museum," Joan said.

"Someday maybe it will be. You wouldn't believe how much of ancient Egypt is scattered about in the old homes of England."

After Joan finished chatting with the front desk she put the stone cat where she couldn't see it anymore in a closet. She didn't like it staring at her. "I always liked doggies best."

She sat up in bed and knitted. She didn't like the image of herself that came back to her from a tall cheval floor mirror. She thought she looked frail and old. Without makeup, her eyes looked bald and had dark circles under them.

She took a bolstering sip of vodka and thought about how she disliked the change that had occurred in Joan Crawford since *Mildred Pierce*. Male stars had always hogged the movies and it had gotten much worse with the rise of war movies. To play the average female role she had to be young and always looking sexually ripe. Men wanted lovers the age of their daughters. Her career had gone on for so long that she was past those years. She had been too old for decades now. After *Mildred Pierce* her face got hard looking, her voice and eyes ominous. Now her face was softening again but in grandmotherly pouches and bags. She put her knitting down and had the same cry she'd had over that lost Joan Crawford since *Mildred Pierce*. She'd cried many years by now—*Mildred Pierce* came out in 1945.

Crying made her think about Judy Garland. She had died just a week ago. Everybody knew she was doing badly, but still, in Joan's mind's eye she couldn't help but always see Judy as that young MGM star. MGM had gotten rotted and old by now. Many of its stars had just worn out and Judy was the worse casualty of the lot. JFK had once told Joan that Judy used to sing "Somewhere over the Rainbow" to him over the telephone. Joan wondered if Judy had kept it sweet or spontaneously changed the words to make JFK laugh. Judy would usually do anything for a laugh with quick wit.

Joan smiled through tears as she remembered how she first met Judy at her own kids parties. Judy was the only kid there who appreciated everything. That was because MGM was starving her, and as with Joan, Judy had never been close to her real mother and barely knew any father. So they were more than just MGM colleges. Joan had become like an adopted studio Mom to Judy, helping her navigate studio business and life business. Judy knew she could always visit Joan's house to raid her refrigerator to make sandwiches. Joan and Judy had stayed close for decades after, often dinning out together. The candid photos that the press snuck of them often showed them laughing raucously.

Joan cried into her pillow until she fell asleep. She dreamt that the cat statue told her, "Judy got lost in the witch's tower. She got lost at the mirror's view. She looked away from the mirror to the actual window and saw that there was nothing. Out flew the yarn and floated wide. The mirror crack'd from side to side."

"The curse is come upon me," cried Judy Garland in her dressing room. "I was cursed but now I'm free. The spinning wheel I spun all day was never spinning just for me."

The stone cat told Joan, "You will get lost if you aren't wary. But you will live forever if you escape the tower and escape the woods and enter the desert. In the desert you will find the sun and clarity. You will find the magic of ancient thoughts." Then the cat licked Joan's face until her face became a rubber Halloween mask. Judy was singing, "Somewhere Over the Rainbow" however there was no rainbow. The woods were too dense and the desert too dry. Joan dreamt that she woke up screaming. She was screaming as she was trying to get out of the dressing room mirror that she was stuck in. However it was only reflecting loud orange groovy mod wallpaper.

* * * * *

The next morning Joan woke up, hacked and coughed and lit a cigarette and sipped her room service coffee, then she dialed up Bill Haines. He had been her best friend from Hollywood since the 1920s. He had helped start her out in the silent days before MGM had even given her the name Joan Crawford. After chatting with the operator about paying for the long distance call, she got through to him.

Bill said, "What happened?"

"How's my favorite fairy dust? How's your hubby, Jimmy? How are my favorite Hollywood homosexuals?"

"Oh! Cranberry! It's you!"

"I swear they wallpaper everything in this country. This room has very lovely wallpaper. Lovely vines and roses. So pink. Some of this wallpaper is delightful! I dreamt last night about wallpaper, I think. The wallpaper in my caravan looks like it was picked by a rock band. That's what they call it here, a caravan, as if I'm a gypsy.

I suppose I am. I have no real home." She noticed that the stone Egyptian cat was back on its table staring at her. She glared back at it.

"What are you talking about?"

"Sorry I was just putting on my lipstick. And I was sleepwalking with the art, or gnomes sneak around this place and put things all back in their place, in the night."

"I heard what you said, I just could figure it out."

"You're an interior designer so I thought I should tell you that about the wallpaper. And you know very well I'm in England now making *Trog* and so far so good. The weather shaped up for us just in time. I just wanted to tell you everything. They wallpaper everything. If only you could see all the wallpaper I've seen in the last few days. I don't know if I'd call it fascinating…maybe a curiosity?"

"You make no sense when I first wake up. Oh that's right. You took me by surprise. *Trog*." He loudly yawned. "Why did you send me a copy of the script? You're really going out on a limb this time."

"That's where the fruit is—the end of the limb."

Bill groaned. "Are you trying to kill me? Or is this a joke. Did Gloria Swanson write this from her Ouija board and it's all a joke between you two? Please send me the real script for your movie. It can't be this one."

"It's a perfectly fine film about science written by three intelligent men."

"It was written for a man."

"So the role has balls. It will especially be fine after I star in it. You know that by now I can make anything work. People will see a Joan Crawford show. That's all they care about. They love my famously intense eyes and vocal delivery that would frighten Medusa. And the kids get what they will consider a monster. Double the crowd. And it comes out in 1970. It'll be such a modern year. I'll be ready for the seventies!"

"You're just indefatigable."

Joan snorted into the phone. "The way you say that you make it sound like a bad thing."

Bill said, "And along the way you've become quite the horror movie queen. Is that what you really meant to do with your life?"

"I don't do horror! I do drama…with moments of suspense! I am still a serious actress! I am still Joan Crawford!"

"I think William Castle is schlock." Bill moaned. "Two in a row with him, oh dear. And now Herman Cohen, two in a row. Horror!"

"The kids love it. What do you have against kids having fun at the movies? Why shouldn't they get Joan Crawford quality drama. And so what if the drama has moments of suspense!"

Bill moaned. "I guess I'm too old for that anymore. I'm seventy now. You aren't too far behind me. What are you these days? Forty-nine again?"

Joan pretended she hadn't heard that. "The press in England especially loves me. They called me 'Her Serine Crawfordship.' They gave me a title!" Joan grinned at the memory. During her last film she was up at five and at Shepperton Studios by six to cook breakfast for the first of the crew that arrived. "But if they didn't return their empty Pepsi bottles there was hell to pay. That was my only rule! Return the empties! Bottles are expensive! You haven't seen Joan Crawford yell until you've seen her hunting down a missing Pepsi bottle from some nook or cranny of a cluttered soundstage."

Bill said, "They liked you the last time you were in England. Maybe they were amused you were making a circus movie and you were running around in it dressed like that. But they might get bored and turn on you this picture. The British press is fickle. It's still the press."

"I've given them so many interviews and so much free Pepsi they adore me. It's a shame I can't break Pepsi into the British market more. They're all so damn loyal to Coca-Cola because the American government shipped so much here during the war for everybody to drink for free. France too. Now they're damn loyal and it's hard to undo that. War really makes an impression on people. So I went and blazed new soft drink trails in Spain, Africa and South America where everybody else had ignored them. I won't cry about being left out, I'll just make new friends. Damn they're not drinking Pepsi in China and Russia. I hate communism so much! When Castro took all my Pepsi sugarcane fields I thought I'd blow a gasket." She stopped talking. She didn't mean to open that painful memory in 1963. She was in Dallas with her husband crying about that to Nixon, plotting about how they'd bring down Castro entirely so she could get her sugarcane fields back. Her dear friend John F Kennedy was in town that day, too. Just after she'd mocked all his security, to his face, bragging that she went all over the place without any security at all, only thinking about jewel thieves at the time, his brains were blown out all over his sweet wife in the backseat of an open convertible. Those were horrible times. Then she realized Bill was talking to her.

He said, "You worry and plot too much for them. Forget them. Pepsi has gone flat on you and dumped you down the sink. I wouldn't worry about them so much, still. Just do what you usually do and get yourself humped by the current costar. Trog does have something on him for you to flirt with, I hope. Or is Bette Davis playing the part so they won't need a mask."

Joan laughed. Then she said, "Wait a dog-gone minute. Don't be so crabby and crude. When this movie puts me back on top then Pepsi will be begging me to do a whole new slew of commercials, and maybe I'll finally get London and Paris to drink my stuff over that old tar pit shit, Coke."

"Dream on."

"Bill! You aren't too old to dream! Never be too old to dream! You're my Peter Pan. I'm your Cinderella! We must always dream!"

"Dream? I can't believe you ever dreamed they'd drink Pepsi in Zululand and Nairobi. They have grass skirts. They have no coins. They have no vending machines."

"You terrible snob. You don't need a bra to drink. And where we went north of the largest cities of South Africa I handed out baby goats. Goats are their own vending machines. You haven't been to Zululand so don't have that snotty tone with me. There are lovely people everywhere. They sang for me and it was very moving! You don't need a vending machine to get a song when you have friends! It's a small world after all…it's a small small world! And I bought such intriguing art in Africa and it's all on display in my apartment, shelves of it. Gorgeous woodcarving. It's marvelous how primitive art in that design contrasts so beautifully with modern architecture. It's very appealing. You could learn from that. And such lovely memories they hold of Al and I on our adventures together."

Al Steele was her last husband. They met at a party in 1950. Al Steele worked for Coca-Cola but quit when he saw Pepsi going under. He bought Pepsi cheap, married Hollywood's top movie star, and they toured the world for Pepsi to take it from being the shoddy "kitchen cola" in old beer bottles to being Coca-Cola's glamorous main rival. He died from a heart attack in April 1959. After riding so high she was left with spells of depression and loneliness.

Joan continued to Bill, "And no I didn't pick up a voodoo fetish doll to stick pins in, to put Bette Davis in her place. She's already fallen off her shelf all by herself. She's alone and through now, from her own bad manners!"

He hung up.

"Hello?" Joan thought about Bette Davis playing Trog without a mask. She thought about a Bette Davis voodoo doll looking just like a trog, and she laughed again. Then she grew concerned about how crabby Bill was. She decided she should redecorate her apartment when she got back to New York. That would give him some work and would cheer him up again. She decided that her apartment needed a new look for the 1970s and only Bill was clever enough to know what that would be. She decided she should do more promotions for William Haines Designs.

Joan dialed up Gloria Swanson and asked her, "How is Bill Haines? How's his adorable husband Jimmy? How's the happiest married couple in Hollywood? Billy seems so crabby and cantankerous these days. Are they doing okay? Is he that crabby to you, too? Is his business doing okay? We should mention it whenever we can, to the press, to help them get more press. Bill needs cheered up."

Gloria Swanson asked, "Is that you Joan?"

"Of course it's me."

"You must have a terrible cold. You sound like a frog. I wouldn't have even guessed it was you but who else calls me and starts talking about old gay men?"

"I have a nice thermos of throat tea I sip before I do any lines. Cinnamon, honey, lemon. It clears the pipes. Is Billy and Jimmy okay?"

Gloria said, "They're fine. Why do you ask? What happened? Why worry about that at this hour? Do you realize the hour? What have you been taking for that cold? Only natural cures I hope. I hope you have a cup of White Oak tea with you right now."

"My throat tea is all natural. And I don't know what White Oak is and don't tell me, I don't want to talk about all that right now. Bill seems so cantankerous when I call. He keeps trying to get me to doubt the quality of the movie I'm in. That isn't like him."

"Is it cheap?"

"It's an economical movie. I was never in the epics. They always gave me the movies that didn't cost too much money but they made all the money. More profit margin that way. Bill used to be my biggest cheerleader about that. And I was his biggest cheerleader for everything he was doing. And you too. You helped him so much too. He trusts you as much as he does me. Is anything wrong?"

Gloria's tone darkened. "He probably just doesn't like that you usually call him up with no regard to your time zone. Do you know what time it is right now in New York—in Hollywood?"

"Oh he's like a big kid, huh. Mess up their nap and they get so crabby. I can't tell what time it is anyway, I'm always doing something. The only time I have for knitting anymore is when I finally get to bed or when I make my morning calls. And then it's hard to knit when I'm always blowing my nose. This damn cold!"

"Joan, why did you call?"

"Why are we friends? I forget. Is it because we were at different studios and didn't compete for roles so we could actually chat nice at parties? I suppose Hollywood had a lot of parties. So I suppose in the 1930s we chatted a lot more than we realized."

"We both played Sadie Thompson and rattled the bluenoses. But we did it different. They were very different productions."

"Yeah, you had a monkey and I didn't. I should have done it with Tallulah Bankhead's kinkajou...but that would have made the movie obscene and the conservatives hated it enough as it was. It kept shitting down my back. Oh the many gowns that were ruined." Joan was really thinking about how the role didn't get her the respect in Hollywood that she'd hoped. *Rain* had been such a prestigious play but movies were controlled by the Moral Code. Also, at that time, her fans expected stylish romantic fluff out of her not the defamation of a spiritual leader by a prostitute in Pago Pago.

Gloria chuckled. "And we both have the same best friend, Bill Haines. We always need to compare notes. Bill and Jimmy have been like kids to the both of us, haven't they. We always run to them when there's a crises, or we need a recipe, or anytime. Luckily nothing so horrible has ever happened again as when the KKK came and dragged them out of their home and beat them up until they were almost dead. Oh, how you and I tried to get them to press charges with the police. We all know it was their neighbor's fault. But they wouldn't dare go to the police they were so afraid."

"Yes, I've adopted them, too. I adopt a lot, huh. When you get that close to people it's a risk. Sometimes it just breaks your heart when things don't turn out perfectly with all the people in life you've adopted. When you care that much for someone you want everything to always be perfect with them."

Gloria Swanson said, "But I had much better luck with my kids. Luck, I guess. But then you also spoiled yours so much."

Joan nodded ardently as if that could be heard over a phone. "I didn't mean to spoil them like that, I tried to hold back. I made sure I had rules. I also wanted them to have what I didn't ever have, growing up."

"Mother to mother, I can tell you that I've been lucky. My children are all angels but I've seen so many children around me go crazy and end up in jail or worse. There seems to be no rhyme or reason. Hollywood was the worse place for children. Too many things. It was a world of treats and toys. Too many adult parties. Such an unreal decadent world. We thought we'd all be kids forever."

Joan remembered the morning after the pool parties there were usually swimsuits laying abandoned on the bottom of the pool, and cocktail glasses were often down there too. "I adore children. I get to work with a little girl in this movie. Chloe. Trog steals her away and I rescue her. Carrying her away from the cave is my favorite part of the movie and we've figured out how to do it so I don't put my back out or knock her head on the side. We're good friends now, Chloe and me. We hit it right off. I always get along with children. Especially now that I'm always handing out bottles of Pepsi. Children love treats. Joan Crawford is treats. I'm going to call Bill back now and try to cheer him up. He needs treats. I worry about him. He's so crabby these days. I don't think he'd even be impressed if I was working with Stanley Kubrick."

Gloria gasped. "Kubrick? He doesn't know how to tell a story. I went to see his space movie and when I kept waking up all I heard was snoring and Strauss. I don't know why people keep talking about Kubrick Kubrick Kubrick, the *greeeat director*, other than that he knows how to spend a lot of money and likes classical music."

Joan said in a low tone. "Kubrick actually owns our Trog mask, for real. It's from that space movie. Our Trog was one of those ape-men from the beginning of that movie. Does that make this movie a sequel to his movie? I hope he stays away until we're done shooting with it. *Greeeat* directors can be so possessive and bossy."

"They haven't called you a ball-breaker for nothing. God forbid he should cross you."

Joan agreed.

Chapter three

Roderick Stuart Winklehorn, a handsome young man in his mid-twenties, drove Joan to the moors to finish location filming. They hadn't talked the first time he drove her because she'd been autographing a pile of pictures. This time she wanted to make a point to enjoy the view of the vast English country out the window. "I don't see this everyday."

He said, "Thank you for filming at my studio."

Joan assumed he was putting it that way because he lived in the village. So she grinned.

He was watching her in the rearview mirror. He blushed.

In the slice of reflection, Joan saw his cheeks turning red. "You're a sweet one. They don't blush in London anymore, I'm sure of it." Joan remembered how naughty stars were with their drivers in the good ole days, men and women stars, both, just to be very naughty. He suddenly looked terrified and she wondered what he could possibly be thinking. She asked, "Are you alright? Do I call you Roderick or Stuart? I'm so sorry I haven't asked sooner but I've had the cold and flu and have been so tired."

His face hardened. "Both. Just one and it sounds like I'm being scolded. It sounds like I'm being yelled at."

"Very well. *Roderick Stuart.*"

He flicked the front edge of the bill of his chauffeur hat as a salute.

Joan looked out the window again at the late summer scenery of the low course rust colored grasses and bracken as far as the eye could see. "Have you driven stars before?"

"You're my first, Miss Crawford."

She wished he'd said more. She loved the sound of his voice, his deep masculine tone and accent—the careful and proper sounding *Received Pronunciation* accent was first called *Public School Pronunciation*. Joan learned about it in 1929 when she learned how to not talk like Texan white trash anymore in her MGM speech classes, when she was learning how to be Joan Crawford for the sound era. She wondered how she could get him to say more. "Are you in school?"

He shook his head no.

"Are you working any place else?"

He shook his head no again.

"Are you from these parts?"

"Yes, Winklehorn is an important name here."

Joan sipped from her flask as she looked around at the inside of the car, confused. "Roderick Stuart? Is this a different car than we had yesterday?"

He suddenly looked nervous and shifty eyed. He finally said, "Yep."

"I was just wondering if I was imaging things." Joan sniffed her flask and realized it had smelled stronger in the car the day before. Then she realized it was the other car that had the chemical smell. It was like fingernail polish remover, not her booze. She became suspicious.

He gripped the wheel and started to drive tensely.

Joan grew nervous. "Please slow down. Roderick Stuart Winklehorn, please slow down." She put her hand out to the seat in front of her. "Slow down, damn you, or you'll bounce me right out of this car!"

"Just *Roderick Stuart* is fine." He snapped, then finally slowed down somewhat.

"You're about as friendly as a suction pump."

"A what?"

"It's a line from my 1955 classic *Female on the Beach*. I was almost killed."

"We're almost here!" He sped up again as he blurted, "Can you spot me two thousand quid?"

"What?"

"I need some money!"

"What?"

"Money! Money! Dough!"

Joan's eyes flashed harsh and fiery. "Most certainly not!"

"I'll pay you back, I promise!"

Joan became a little louder. "Most certainly not, and not another word about it!"

"You have to! My tarot cards told me you would!"

"Nonsense."

"But you're rich!"

"Neither a borrower nor a lender be! For loan oft loses both itself and friend!"

He frowned, kept his eyes on the road, pouting. "I've got gumption and I'm an aristocrat, you know, not just some nobody out of the booby hatch. My family is the oldest family in this whole shire. I know that was Shakespeare you just said. And I know Latin and have inherited psychic powers. Don't think I'm a nobody just because I'm a bloody driver right now. Don't think less of me just because I now have to work for a bloody living. Those days will soon be over. Soon I'll live as I'm supposed to. Soon I won't even need blooming money. I have the power to bring all the riches of the world to me. I have magic spells!"

"I never think less of anybody for having to work for a living. I've always had to work. I've worked and paid my own way since I was a child. And I still work hard so my children can have nice monthly allowances. And I work hard so I can give a lot of money to hospitals and charity. You *do* have the power to bring riches to yourself and then to share generously with others. Hard work. Do good. Play fair. Be kind. To thine own self be true."

"I'm not just broke...I need money!"

Joan chuckled. "Men your age usually do. And the ones who come from money usually need it the most. You've probably already made some lousy mistakes in your short life. We all did. We all still do. Gloria Swanson once told me not to carry our mistakes around but to put them under our feet and use them as stepping stones."

"You talk to Gloria Swanson?" He looked very impressed.

"Of course. We both have telephones. We both have the same best friend."

"I have a lot of things. I just need...money." He suddenly looked crestfallen.

"You'll find the most important thing to own is a good attitude."

He huffed up his chest. "I even own a mummy! A real mummy from Khemet... *the chosen*! That's what they called *their own* land—Khemet. We call it Egypt from a Greek word. I don't know why the Greeks just couldn't call it Khemet, too. I think that's rather rude of them to rename somebody else's country. We should all call it Khemet so they'll know we're all talking about *them*. The old ghosts can still hear us! Some of the ghosts don't know Greek."

"Oh really, I didn't know that. I bet that old dead thing must smell awful."

"No, she smells like a queen...like the desert rose. She still smells like roses from thousands of years ago."

Joan asked, "Can you sell the mummy? How much is a mummy worth?"

He nodded earnestly. "She'll rise and bring me riches! Not from selling her but from her magic! And just in time! My grandfather brought her back from a secret tomb in Egypt, himself, and floated her up the Thames! She was a great Khemetian queen, she was *the chosen*, waiting to rule again. And I can bring her back to life! I know the spells! I'll show you. We can make it into a great mummy movie, once we know what happens! It would be a great mummy movie! That would make money, too, on top of everything!"

Joan grinned, thinking he sounded sweet in his childish daydreams. "A mummy? Are you sure?"

He nodded again.

"Well I hope it's dead." Joan gave a theatrical grimace. "Sounds frightening."

Roderick Stuart said, "It's a mummy. It'll come back to life. Soon. The stars are aligned." He pulled up to her trailer in the camp. He opened the backdoor for her.

Before she got out, she asked him, "Where did you get a mummy?"

He put out a hand to help her up. She took it to touch his masculine hand. It made her shiver. He answered, "My grandfather was in Egypt for a while, to visit. Maybe he brought it back with him, then. Maybe he even nicked it from an old tomb. I don't know that part. I wasn't born yet. Everybody did that kind of thing, back then."

Joan stayed at the car to talk and enjoy him. "Are there many mummies in England?"

"Oh sure. Back when, mostly. I read about mummy unwrappings. They should have made a blooming movie about one of those."

"Mummy unwrappings?"

Roderick Stuart grinned. "A mummy unwrapping used to be a corker of a theme for a party. It was ghoulish and fascinating. Hosts hoped to unwrap treasure and secrets. Guests wanted to be there when it happened. But all those mummies might not be around anymore. I don't know what they did with them all after that."

Joan looked into his blue eyes. They seemed dreamy in a far away manner. "So it's not an old movie prop? The one that you have? You sure? You may just have something from an old mummy movie."

He nodded. "I'm quite sure."

Joan lowered her grand eyebrows. "Bray Studios is full of ghoulish movie props. Hammer Horror filmed there. A mummy movie was the last thing Hammer shot there, didn't they—before Hammer moved on to a bigger studio? I'm sure you know more about all that, than me."

He narrowed his eyes. "You'll see and you'll see it's real. And you'll see her great power. I'm going to bring her back! She'll rule the world again! She's *the chosen*."

Joan took a compact from her purse and looked at her mouth. She decided to add pale silver pink lipstick. "She can't look too good anymore. You know what Shakespeare said, 'Out, out, brief candle.'"

At that comment, Roderick Stuart looked angry and then insane.

Joan decided to ignore him. She grandly turned on her heel and went into her trailer.

* * * * *

The producer knocked on the door to Joan's trailer. "How's my Joanie? How do you feel?"

She called out, "Herman! Come in. I feel like I'll never shake this damn cold. Or plague. Is London all dead from this yet or is it just me who suffers?" As she talked, he stepped in to see Frenchy, her hair and makeup department, pinning a matching blonde hairpiece to the top of Joan's head. They greeted each other with a smile and nod. Joan continued, "I wish I was where there was sun and salt water. One year I had such a terrible flu and I was afraid it would ruin my whole winter and so I went down to Jamaica and after two days in the sun and saltwater I was healed. Cured. Ready for my next picture. It was a miracle of the tropics."

Herman Cohen gave a fake smile. "Maybe we can all go to Jamaica as soon as we're finished here."

"Oh dear, no. It's too hot this time of year and who knows what movie scripts are sitting at my apartment right now waiting for me. I must get back to New York and chose one. I'll be so busy. A movie star has to be several steps ahead. But the loss of Judy Garland was a blow. I swear I was getting better, with this damn cold, but after news of her passing I fell so ill all over again. I felt her tired soul suck the life out of mine. Her soul touched mine as she passed, I'm certain, like a drowning child reaching out. I felt worn out as she must have felt worn out. I couldn't give her any of my strength. MGM has gotten old and rotten. I'm glad I got the hell out of there when I could. I escaped. Judy never escaped."

He'd stopped smiling. "That was shocking about poor Judy."

"There's nothing we can do to help her now. Nobody can. Nobody has been able to for years. They say her liver was so diseased she was on borrowed time no matter what. All those damn pills. MGM had her hooked before she even did *The Wizard of Oz* to keep her starved and skinny and hyperactive and dancing the jitter bug all day long. She would walk around the lot stoned out of her mind screaming how she just wanted potato salad and MGM had goons trailing her no matter where she went just making sure she didn't get any. Once I smuggled some food to her at her own birthday party and the only reason I was able to pull it off was because I'm Joan Crawford. She hid in the bushes and ate some cake, a hotdog, and cowboy beans. Before the goons could find her and slap the paper plate out of her hands she was almost done. Victory! She had cowboy beans all down the front of her dress but she was so happy. I was so happy for her. We got the stains out before it was time for her to sing. It was her party and she was the entertainment. She kept changing the words to the songs so she was always singing about hot dogs and beans. She thought that was so funny. People complained that it was unprofessional but it was her own damn birthday party for chrissakes! How selfish of them to just think about themselves the whole time! Judy's birthday should be a day all about Judy! Now I'll just have to try and remember the good times…I remember a nice private sit down visit with her in 1953 just after *Torch Song* and we were in my kitchen before a party, just us two, laughing about old MGM stuff." Joan looked away and her eyes clouded over.

"How's your driver working out?" Herman asked.

Joan wiped her eyes. "Roderick Stuart Winklehorn? Why mention him? He's...oh...okay."

"You hesitated."

Joan looked mildly annoyed. "The young have to learn their place. Once they do they're fine. Don't tell me he has a record."

Herman nodded sadly. "Almost. As a juvenile he was caught sneaking into people's houses a few days before Halloween, one year. He climbed in through their windows and stole decorations and monster costumes. He didn't take any money but it sent him to an approved school for awhile—that's what we call a school for juvenile criminals here in this country."

Joan pooh-poohed it, waving her hand. "Boys. They can be such dreamers and rascals. It's a wonder all boys don't spend half their childhoods in jail for what they do at Halloween."

"Sorry we didn't get you any limousines. I know that's what you've come to expect and deserve, like our last film. You're the very best."

Joan smiled sadly. "That's okay. I'm in England now. Everything in proportion. And everything is just a little different these days, anymore, anyway. These days everything seems just a little broken down...a little worn out. A lot smaller."

Herman said, "We can get you a new driver if this one's too wonky for you."

"Oh no. I adore his voice. I could hear him talk about anything all day long, no matter what it is. He makes everything sound so smart. Funny how an accent and proper vocal placement in the mouth, alone, can do that. Maybe he really is an aristocrat. Otherwise, yes, he is a bit *wonky*, isn't he?"

Herman sloppily saluted. "Gotta go. Just checking up on everything. I have to see if the generators are working yet." On the way out the door, he hopped up a bit when he shouldn't have. He hit his head on the top of her trailer door, making a very loud bang. He staggered back inside against the wall.

Joan leapt up, left Frenchy, and grabbed ice from the Pepsi bucket. "Don't go anywhere! I'll take care of that right now!" She folded ice into a bright yellow cloth napkin. She sat on her bed and ordered him, "Put your head in my lap."

"I'll be fine."

"Nonsense. You'll faint. Just lay here for moment in my lap and let me tend to this. We can't let this swell." She gestured urgently for him to come to her.

He was tall so he didn't fit well but he reclined on her cot with his head in her lap and let her hold ice on his hair for a few minutes. He moaned.

Joan huffed, pretending to have no patience. "Close your eyes. This wallpaper will just make you dizzy. It does me, anyway."

He moaned again.

"When are you going to get married so a proper wife can take care of you?"

"You mean *I* take care of *her*? The man takes care of his wife!"

Joan grinned. "You always take such good care of me but I'll be your wife just this once and baby your poor noggin and take care of you." Joan looked off in thought. "Now that I'm thinking about it, maybe there should be a montage that includes Doctor Brocton giving Trog a bath."

"A what?" Herman gasped. "A bath? What are you talking about, Joan!"

Joan pushed him back down then petted his hair. "And the doctor needs to do other things. The doctor has to discover things. It can show what a busy and interested doctor I am...that *Doctor Brocton* is. The character would want to investigate Trog head to toe, and shampoo the hell out of him. It's supposed to be a clean lab...I hope."

"Discover things, eh?" Herman chuckled. "Well, those things will have to stay implied since the script can't be added to. We already have a tight schedule and we don't want this rated M."

In 1969 "M" meant "Suggested for Mature Audiences, Parental Discretion Advised." In 1970 "M" was renamed to "GP", for "General audiences, Parental guidance suggested" but then was changed in1972 to "PG".

Joan rearranged the ice on his head. "You're such a task master. I understand. I worked for MGM. Nobody cracked the whip at us like MGM in the thirties. They were slapping our faces if they weren't stabbing us in the back."

"I've never worked with anybody more professional."

Joan grinned.

"You're so good to me." Herman patted the ice pack on his head.

Joan leaned down and kissed his nose. "*You're* so good to me. We may not have time to go out on the town all the time, not this picture, this bubonic plague I caught has really taken me down a few pegs. But that's okay. I have such fond memories of the last time we were here in England. You were so marvelous to take me out to the opera and theatre almost every day after shooting so I wouldn't be lonely. You had so much to do but always made so much special time for me. You made me feel like a star in the glory days, again."

He was a knight in shining armor to keep Joan's flask for her so she could enjoy her drinks while they were out but the fans wouldn't see her drinking at the bar in the lobby.

He said, "Now you'll be going to bed very early, I hope."

"That…and knitting tea cozies for everybody. I've knitted everything but those by now in my life."

"Why do you knit like a crazy lady?"

"Like *a lady*. Ladies knit." Joan thought about how her fingers were always busy, even as a child. When she wasn't working to earn her keep she had a rosary in them. She would pray that she wouldn't starve to death.

With his head still in her lap, Joan quickly dabbed on more lipstick, looking down at him coyly, and then grabbed her knitting needles. She glanced about at her trailer. "I don't want to sound petty. I've done too many pictures and I know what's important, don't listen to what the press says about me and my movie star demands. Sure I expected a lot when I had my big comeback at MGM in the fifties, but that's MGM, dammit! They owe me! And I went overboard when traveling the world over for Pepsi but that was different. It was part of the Pepsi press—I always had reporters around and things had to look important. But I still would like just a few flowers in my dressing room. Is that too much to ask? I know that this movie is low budget but flowers are so lovely. It helps a star feel like a star before she has to go out and carry an entire picture on her shoulders all by herself. A star is always expected to move heaven and earth, and hearts. Flowers help."

"I did order them but I don't know what happened and I haven't had a spare minute to ask about it. But I did think about it just as I dozed off last night. And then I had nightmares all night long about it. The flowers were in a graveyard. I hate dumb dreams."

Joan patted his cheek. "Bless you for thinking about me so much."

There was a knock on the door. Freddie Frances, the director, entered and discussed a new problem with Herman. It was found that one of the generators didn't work and they wouldn't be able to use all their lights for "fill light" so shooting was to begin well before sunset to fit in all the required shots before it got too dark.

"Gremlins!" Freddie said.

Joan raised her arched eyebrows, aghast, and looked around as if one might show its little monster face in her trailer.

"Sod the art," Herman said. "Let's just get these shots in the can."

Joan forced a grin. "I'm sure it'll look magical no matter what, it's England."

Frenchy stepped forward and said to Herman, "Just give me five minutes to finish blending Joan's hair, the makeup is already done, and she'll be ready to shoot."

Freddie noticed Joan's cracked makeup mirror. "That needs fixed."

Joan waved it off. "It'll just break again on the ride back into town. Leave it. We aren't shooting out here on the moors for long."

The men left the women. Frenchy resumed fussing with Joan's hair, as she said to her, "This trailer could have come with a beauty shop chair. That would've been nice since you don't step foot in beauty parlors."

"Oh Frenchy, you know I'd love to visit a place like that and read all the magazines and gossip with all the ladies about the gossip of the day. But can you imagine what a ruckus that would make, a Joan Crawford in the room!" Joan thought about how she tried going to church a few times in New York but her presence was too disruptive, just by being Joan Crawford. And she heard that for many church services later everybody was still clucking about it, only interesting what she had been wearing. Joan assumed the same pandemonium would occur at a beauty parlor. "And I need my hair done every single day, anyway, sometimes twice a day unless I have a hat for the daytime. I can't go to the beauty parlor every single day, fun as that sounds. So we'll just have to pretend we're at one now. Tell me, what's the gossip of the day?"

Frenchy lowered her voice to a conspirator's tone. "You should hear what they say about your driver at the beauty parlor in town."

"Say it! Say it!"

"They say he's weird. Maybe because he came from blue blood. But none of them in his family are rich anymore. They say they all lost everything in horseracing or something like that. His father owned a barn of racehorses. But it all got lost."

"Where did you hear all that? All that in the beauty parlor?"

"You bet! That's the gossip. The women love to sit around and talk about men."

Joan asked which parlor.

"The one on Peascod Street in Windsor, Pes Croft. They just call it high street. That's what we call main street."

"Charming."

"I went there twice for a few supplies and both times I got an earful about everybody. But they mostly talk about him, Roderick Stuart, your driver. He interests them the most for some reason. He's young and sexy and still single…there's scandal…and an old family…and now he drives Joan Crawford!"

"He's blue blood? How interesting." Joan grandly puffed her cigarette as she put her nose in the air. "I came from the very opposite. I was born in a garbage pail and it went downhill from there until I escaped to Hollywood. He's nice. He's handsome. His voice with that accent is *very* handsome. And if he needs to make a buck driving Joanie around, I'll sure let him. The ladies at the beauty parlor are probably all clucking about him because the most eligible bachelor in town right now is all Joan Crawford's…all mine." She chuckled wickedly.

Frenchy put her hand to her mouth and smirked. "They call him a tosser."

"What's that?"

"I had to ask that, too. It's a man who masturbates."

"Oh really, now. What a bunch of hen-clucking nonsense from the beauty parlor. He's the most eligible bachelor, and now I have him…*in a way*. For these next few weeks he's *my boy*!" She chuckled again, this time quietly but pompously. "The beauty parlor can talk about *that*!" Joan suddenly wanted to bolt up, run out the door, and go to the beauty parlor to gossip about sexy young men in the village. It all sounded like so much fun. She pouted, feeling sorry that instead she had such responsibility and duty. She was sure she felt just like how the queen felt about people—kept from the world of commoners by status, circumstance and arrangements. She looked around for her stationary on the countertop. She decided she'd send the beauty parlor a nice thank you letter for selling supplies to her movie.

Frenchy was still talking about Roderick. "I think it's more than all that. He's suspicious, for sure. If he does anything weird don't be afraid to let Herman know right away. And tell me so I can tell the ladies at the beauty parlor in town. He needs reported on, I'm sure. People like that can snap, I bet... *blue bloods*!"

Joan squished out her cigarette in the ashtray. "Like what. What kind of weird? Inbred into insanity? Is he on drugs? You always have to watch it with the young people today. Most of them are on drugs."

"I don't know. They say he didn't like to talk much as a kid. He was very veeery quiet."

"Maybe he was just well behaved."

Frenchy said, "It was something to do with a death. Did you hear about the latest death in town? It's a small town so *everybody* is talking about it."

"No. Maybe that's why he was quiet. Maybe he was upset about the death."

"No it just happened. The police are keeping it all hush hush but what they know in the beauty shop is that a young woman died. Her name was Vanessa. They say she poisoned herself. They say she worked at the flower shop."

Joan shuddered. "What?" Joan put her face in her hands.

"Joan! What!"

"Vanessa!"

"You knew her?"

Joan looked up, squinting in unease. "Oooh! She was a fan! She was going to bring my flowers to me in person and then I could finally meet her. Poor Vanessa! Why would she kill herself? Why now? If she was a sad girl why choose now, now that things were so exciting for the whole village, having Joan Crawford at Bray Studios. She was a fan! She said she'd been a fan since Baby Jane! I have to realize the younger fans only know my latest pictures. They don't know the great woman's pictures." Joan put her face in her hands again and let out a horrible sounding moan. She felt always on the verge of tears these days anyway because of Judy Garland. It was a different shock from six years earlier when she lost her friend JFK. She'd been in Dallas talking to him in person just hours before he was shot. She hadn't seen Judy in a few years but they had a timeless bond from MGM. No matter where she ran into Judy they always instantly had too many silly things to chat about. They could always make each other laugh with just the smallest in-joke. Joan laughed as she wept just thinking about Judy's naughty wit. "I don't know who I just cried for. Vanessa, Judy, JFK, my husband…"

After Joan breathed heavily for a few minutes she collected herself. She turned to the mirror and took turns winking in it at herself with both teary eyes to make sure her eyelashes were still solidly on at the correct angle, and were in a slight arch higher than her own natural eyelash line to make her eyes look more wide open in photography. It looked subtly bizarre in real life. She pushed at the lines on her skin between her eyebrows, annoyed by them. She wished she could put a piece of stiff tape over it and keep it there. "They need to make better face tapes!"

Finally satisfied that her makeup was as good as it could get and she would look much better on film than she looked to herself now so close to her mirror, she took a big swig of vodka. After she refreshed her lipstick she walked out the door, repeating what the director had said, "Sod the art! Shots in can!" Joan grabbed her script and when she looked at it she stopped and came back in. "I think I need to wear the helmet for these shots. I'm on my way to the cave. Hand me the goddam helmet."

Frenchy gasped. "Your hair!"

Chapter four

Driving home after the days shooting, bumping along on a dirt road on the moors before they got to a paved road, Joan looked down at how her padded bra didn't bounce at all with the rest of her. She frowned then leaned forward in the car and asked her driver, "Roderick Stuart? When is the funeral for the woman in the flower shop who died? Vanessa."

"Why ask about her? What do you know about her? Why ask me?"

"Just tell me."

Roderick Stuart answered, "She was already put in the ground."

"That was fast."

"She was Jewish. They do that. I'm pretty sure blooming suicides put them away even faster, and that's what she did, she done herself in."

"Is the cemetery in the village?"

"Yes. Down St. Leonards Road. It's called Windsor Cemetery. Sometimes called Spital Cemetery. It's part of Winsor Castle and two army barracks in town. But everybody else has been put to rest there, too. It has sections for the Church of England, Non Conformist & Roman Catholic. And then there's a part for the others...like Jews."

"Is it far out of our way?"

"No, it's only ten minutes from Windsor Castle. Not too far."

"Drive me there if you don't mind. I want to pay my respects to the poor girl."

"At this ungodly hour?"

"It's not like it's midnight or anything. I'm not a witch. I'm not going to try and talk to her ghost in a cemetery, or anything ghoulish. I just want to see her grave on my way home from work. It's not *that* late. Not for Joan Crawford. I always work late. I'm not a lazy slob. Turn back. I want to get something from my trailer."

He looked annoyed.

"Turn back. I want to get the flowers that finally showed up there."

"Okidoke."

The car returned to Joan's trailer and he ran in and grabbed the flowers that had finally arrived. As they drove away again from the moors and finally sped down the long straight stretch of Imperial Road, Joan gently touched the petals. "Such lovely butterfly asters, daisy poms and carnations. So colorful and gay. Maybe too festive for the occasion. I'll get more appropriate flowers later as soon as I have time."

She spotted a note in them. It read, "Congrats on movie #81. And may there be many more." Joan ripped it away from the stem. The flowers would now go on the grave. While slowing as they turned onto St. Leonards Road, lightning flashed in the distance. There was a distant rumble.

The driver said, "I thought it felt like rain all day."

"Me too." Joan smiled. "It made a softer light when we filmed outside today. I was lucky to get that. Filming outside in LA is such a hard harsh light. It hardly ever rains."

"I thought film people hated the rain."

"It's hard to film when you have it raining on your hair, sure. But it's nice to have an even cloud cover to soften the sun. The whole air makes a huge filter overhead. When nature is working on your side and the whole sky is your diffusion filter it's hard to top that."

Roderick Stuart nodded. "England is always best. Best in everything."

"The best girls?"

"Sure."

"Do you have a best girl?" Joan gave him a crooked smile.

He frowned. "You're not British, but…can *you* count as one? I've wanted you to be my girlfriend ever since I saw *This Woman is Dangerous* on late night TV. Will you be my girlfriend for a week or two?"

"Well, I happen to *like* it unorthodox, arbitrary, and abrupt!" Joan winked.

"I bet!"

"Slow down. I'm just joking with you. That was a line from *Torch Song*. Bless you for harboring a flame for Joan Crawford, *but really*. Look at us."

He blushed. "That movie was exciting. *This Woman is Dangerous*. You were so interesting in that movie."

"Bless you."

"I suppose all the men say that to you—that they saw a movie of yours and fell in love."

Joan nodded. "Many do about one film of mine or another."

Roderick Stuart lowered his eyebrows. "You act so *blah* about it."

"No. I'm always grateful. I've just come to realize that that's what makes a star a star and not just an actress. People fall in love with a star. Love has been my career."

"*Movies* have been."

Joan explained, "Movies are just shadows, really. They show how the love is recorded. It's recorded love that can play back in movie theaters over and over again. It's really quite extraordinary when you think about it—love caught up in big rolls of celluloid, as if by a magic love spell, lit up by a projector. It's a machine with heart. You see it and feel it in your heart. You cry. You lust."

"Yeah, you'll never be my *real* girlfriend. You're a movie star. You aren't even really an English girl." He drove for awhile in silence and then recited, "When in disgrace with fortune and men's eyes, I all alone beweep my outcast state, and trouble deaf heaven with my bootless cries, and look upon myself, and curse my fate."

"You recite beautifully. You have a very nice voice. Shakespeare?"

"Yes! I'm impressed you know your Shakespeare."

"A lot of people think Hollywood stars are as dumb as a box of rocks. *I* would have been, I suppose, but I had many great teachers in my life. And none of them were in a school building."

Roderick Stuart added, "He's the greatest writer ever. Ever! England has the greatest and the best! Ever! But most people don't know his words at all."

Joan felt smart. "I recognized the words *fortune and men's eyes*."

Joan wouldn't call herself an expert. She studied Shakespeare mostly with her first husband Douglas Fairbanks Junior. They did plays together on the stage they built in their backyard. They performed many different things, just to do it, just because they wanted to learn, wanting many different acting experiences. They read the greats. Joan was often seen with a pile of books under her arm, there was always waiting time on the set to read them. Joan and Doug worked very hard back then—Joan even learned to sing opera.

Joan asked, "What play is that from?"

"It's a sonnet."

Joan gave a nod. She always thought she should have played Lady Macbeth. She had all of her in her, and not just the "out damn spot," but the ambition and drive and then remorse and despair. Joan had played all of those emotions by now. She could play layers of emotions and motivations at once. She was asked to be in *The Best of Everything* because she'd give the part of a bitch interesting depth. She was sad since her husband, Al, had just died, but she needed money at that time. She was flat broke. And they needed a good actress to give sympathy and importance to a small part about a mean boss, that was written rather shallow. Because Joan did it, she made the boss important and so people felt sorry for her. They saw that life had made her that way.

Joan said to her driver, "Just think how interesting I'd make Lady Macbeth since my acting always makes things seem more, anyway, and I add so much to the lines." She frowned. She realized she was now too old. She'd forgotten.

When the car stopped at the closed cemetery gate, Joan let go of the flowers in her lap long enough to pull a pair of glasses out of her purse, as she said of the gate, "Will it open?"

He shook his head. "It's chained for the night."

"Then we'll have to walk."

"What? It's a heap of bad luck to enter a graveyard with a chained gate."

Out the car window, Joan could see a walkway opening in the fence beside the gate. "Nonsense. Don't be scared. You're with Joan Crawford."

Her driver still seemed nervous. "It's so blooming dark. It's frigging bad luck to be in a cemetery after dark."

"Well then how are the hard working people ever to visit their loved ones?"

Roderick Stuart looked around. "But there's nobody else out here. It's a heap of bad luck to be the only ones in a graveyard."

"We're not all alone. You're with me and I'm with you. We need a flashlight. You *do* keep one in the car, don't you?"

He nodded. "Sure, I have a torch."

"I don't need to set the whole place on fire. I just need to see a little bit. A flashlight will do."

"No, that's what we call a flashlight here. A torch. The light doesn't need to flash. Not unless you want a flashing light."

"Oh. I suppose. I never thought of it that way."

With his torch in hand and switched on, he opened the back car door for her and helped her out as she held the flowers to her bosom. Then he pointed. "The Jewish graves are all in that back corner over the hill."

"Frederick! Take my arm. I don't want to twist my ankle. I can't see where I'm going too well. I don't want to fall on the flowers and crush them. Hold me tight. I don't break that easily. Oh, you're nice and strong. Tighter." They walked through the entire cemetery, down narrow paths and across grass, amongst stone crosses and roundtop headstones, pine trees and pine bushes.

"Blimey!"

"What happened."

He hopped on one foot a few times. "I just stubbed my toe on a low headstone."

"Yes," Joan said, "there's a lot of them here. A car wouldn't have gotten through all this anyway. This place was all started long before cars."

"I wonder how far we go. If we hit woods then we went too frigging far in the wrong direction."

Joan forced a brave chuckle. "If we get lost then you'll get your wish and we'll be in a heap of bad luck." They walked to where they finally spotted Star of David markers. The driver shone the torchlight on the names of all the markers as they walked along them. Joan said, "I don't see a tombstone with the name Vanessa on it, at all."

Frederick raked the beam of light across the grass just beyond the last marked grave. He said, "Oh wait. Here's a fresh grave. Very fresh. It has no marker on it. Nicked?"

"Maybe it's Vanessa's grave and they haven't finished making it yet. I bet it is." Joan put the flowers on the foot of the loose brown dirt rectangle of the new grave, took the torch from Roderick Stuart, lit up the flowers, and said a bit of Shakespeare from Hamlet, "And flights of angels sing thee to thy rest." Joan squinted at the grave. "Yes, those flowers are too merry. I'll go to the flower shop myself when I can slip way and get some that are more appropriate. Something elegant and serious. I hope the tombstone is up by then so I'm sure I'm putting them on the correct grave. And then it'll all look correct. It's a shame I couldn't give Vanessa a gift while she was still alive."

Joan turned away from the fresh grave and started to walk, her torch lighting up the ground at her feet. A cold mist blew over her face. She raised her light to see a billowing fog roll in around her. It felt as cold as ice. Joan shivered and thought she felt a finger on her shoulder. She turned. A woman in black was suddenly standing beside the grave as if she had stepped out of the fog. Joan couldn't see the woman's face. She tried to point her flashlight directly at it but she couldn't get it to show up. Joan called out, "Hello?"

The woman didn't say anything.

"Hello? Are you a friend of Vanessa?" Joan turned around and called out to her driver. "Where are you? We're not alone." A strong wind blew on Joan and the fog blew away. "Hurry! A terrible storm is coming!"

He stepped forward. "I'm right here. Who else is here? I'm glad we're not here alone. It's such blooming bad luck to be in a cemetery alone."

"Don't be so nervous! You're not alone. I'm here. And so is..." Joan didn't see the woman anywhere anymore. The fog was gone. She shone her light side to side and it only caught old tombstones and pine bushes in its narrow beam. "Hello?" Lightning flashed in the distance and illuminated the whole place. A rumble followed. "There was so much fog here. Where did it go?"

"It's just us. You must have seen a statue. Fog can come and go, with the river so close."

"No. The woman spoke to me." Joan shivered. "She said *murder*! No wait, she didn't speak. But I still heard *murder*. No, that was my imagination or the whistling wind saying *murder* but now it seems as if it was her voice. My mind insists on putting them together." Joan coughed. "I have the cold and flu...and Black Death also. I wouldn't doubt it. I suddenly feel just terrible...like I'll faint. I feel such a fever coming on...this night air..."

Roderick Stuart took her hand, and then her arm. "You're so cold."

Joan moaned. "I feel feverish again. And I feel so cold. So cold..."

He said in hesitation, "You feel..."

"Dead?" Joan glared at him.

He made himself chuckle. "I wasn't going to say that! What tosh."

She ribbed him. "Yes, you were." They hurried toward the car as wind howled through the pine trees. Standing at the inside of the gate, Joan paused to take one last look back into the cemetery as lightning lit it all up again. She said, "I couldn't see her face. I shown my flashlight, er, torch, directly at her face and didn't see a thing. Maybe she was wearing a wide brim hat and I was hitting that. That must be it."

"Maybe it was a ghost."

"Oh...it couldn't be that."

He asked. "Why not?"

"I've never seen a ghost before."

"First bloody time for everything."

Joan grumbled, "That's what they say."

They got in the car and when they were driving away it began to rain. Roderick Stuart turned on the noisy windshield wipers as he said, "That was frightening!"

"We're okay. We just missed a downpour. That's lucky. We didn't bring any umbrellas. I would have caught my death."

"That was frightening anyway!"

"We're okay! We're safe and dry. Don't worry about a thing." Joan coughed again and then said, "I can't wait to get back to my hotel. I have to get to bed early." She thought about how once she was in bed she'd pretend she was in a boat floating down the river as if in a Pre-Raphaelite painting, and in this painting the pretty lady is knitting tea cozies for everybody as she floats by. Everybody is getting one in a cheery lemon yellow. "I have a pile of yarn and I'm sure I can order more yarn from the village if I run short. You're getting a tea cozy too!"

"Oh, you aren't making a tea cozy for me. I'm just the blooming driver."

"The driver gets the first one. That's lucky for him and me, both. I've always given gifts to everybody in the crew. I have for every picture I've been in since the 1920s. Without the crew there is no Joan Crawford and she's grateful."

"Thank you Joan Crawford."

Joan shivered and hugged herself as she lay down on the seat. "I'll take care of everything. Don't worry about a thing." She closed her eyes and saw the inexplicable woman, again, in the cemetery. Joan's torch beam seemed to go right through her. She seemed to be made up entirely of the fog. Joan opened her eyes in apprehension. "That *was* a ghost!"

* * * * *

That night Joan sat up in her hotel bed, sipping vodka and knitting tea cozies, hearing thunder. She missed her doggies. They always made her feel plucky. She didn't bring hers since England would have quarantined them as they did all incoming dogs to keep out rabies.

Alone, she could only think about Vanessa now being a ghost and it unnerved her. Joan wished she had sleeping pills. She remembered back when she was younger she could take a long walk before bedtime and that soothed her nerves. But then she moved to

New York and those streets were now full of drug addicts that would mug anybody for cash to put toward their next high. She didn't dare walk in the dark English countryside outside her hotel right now, mostly because she was just scared of it. It seemed too much like Halloween right now. She remembered when she was in Paris she went to a doctor for sleeping pills and he told her to buy a big red apple instead. He told her to eat half of it at the Place de la Concorde and the other half at the Étoile. His prescription was a two-mile walk before bed. Since she wasn't taking a walk now she decided to imagine she was in a nice old-fashioned woman's picture, for her next picture, to calm her mind. Gloria Swanson would have to be in it so she could have a fun crazy-lady sidekick, and one who would cause a lot of ballyhoo for the press. Acting with Bette Davis was hopeless so maybe Gloria Swanson would work out better. Joan imagined different gowns they would wear.

Joan blew her nose too hard and gave herself a bloody nose. She stuffed many pink rose-scented tissues under her nose and reached for the phone. "Operator! It's a medical emergency! Get Gloria Swanson on the line, and pronto! No, only Gloria Swanson!" She instructed the operator how to do that and as the phone rang Joan told the operator all about her cold. When she got Gloria on the line, she asked, "How do I prevent nose bleeds? Didn't you once have a kid who always had nosebleeds?"

"That wasn't my kid, thank heavens. But I've heard you take some olive oil on a Q-tip and stick that up both sides of your nose morning noon and night. It helps keep it from drying out up in there. You're probably just too dry right now, Joan. And drink lots of White Oak bark tea for that cold! You sound awful!"

"I have to go. I'm going to sneeze!" She did. When her nose stopped bleeding she flushed all the red tissues away down the toilet, popped three cold medicine pills and went back to bed. She didn't feel any better so popped three more pills. "Being sick is sooo boring!" After Joan tipped back some vodka, she smiled wickedly. "I have an idea. I'll turn Bette into a troglodyte. I just thought about how it can be done. It can be done!" Joan wondered why she hadn't thought to do that to her before. She dialed the phone. "Yes operator. This is a long distance call. Gloria Swanson will accept the charges when she hears it's me. It's *Joan Crawford*." The phone dialed. "Gloria, you must do me a favor. Yes, I thought of something. Yes, it's about what to do about Bette Davis. No, this time I think I've got her goat, and good! She'll go ape bananas. For real." She listened to Gloria say something annoying. "No, I don't know if it's illegal."

Gloria Swanson laughed softly, then spoke again like a sweet girl, "Darling Joan, what have you thought of this time? And why don't you just let it go, anyway—just drop this feud you're having with her. It's bad for your karma."

Joan shook her head. "She would have completely ruined my experience of filming *Baby Jane* for me. Lucky for me, Bette couldn't ruin the whole movie for me because I had scenes with Maidie Norman. It was so nice to have her back. In fact I insisted on it and I was so relieved to find her available. She's the most sensible actress who's ever lived. She was so sensible that she rewrote all her lines to eliminate what she called, 'silly old slavery-time talk.' She wasn't going to be a silly black woman servant. There isn't a silly bone in her body. She was a nice antidote to Bette Davis. I first worked with Maidie in *Torch Song*. She was my sensible secretary."

Gloria stated, "I know who she is."

"It was so nice to work with her again. It's a shame she couldn't have played my lab assistant in *Trog*. She's so sensible you would have believed it, but they wanted a British girl for that. Not that you don't believe the one I have now. She isn't silly at all but she's so young. Maidie and I make such a great team. She plays off me very well. I really feel *myself* around her. Everything that is artificial just floats away. I know I'm in a serious drama."

Gloria said, "Think of the positive. Think of the nice actors you *have* worked with."

"I can't." Joan growled. "That Pepsi bottle full of pee left on the set of *Hush Hush* was the last straw. You just *know* who did that! You just *know* it! I'm going to get her good. I'm going to get that Bette Davis! Now listen. That Miss Davis will fall for it if it comes from you. Call your masseuse Slicky Stars and have him go up to her shack and knock on her door dressed in his gold swimsuit. Have him tell her that you sent him and she'll believe it. Have him do his full number on her. Just think where that all could lead!"

Gloria said in a low tone, "I don't think he'd want to touch her in that way."

Joan got louder. "No, not his romantic number! Have him do his full astro-project massage! The one with past lives regression therapy hypnosis things. That one. And the one where he stuffs tarot cards between your legs, that trick is just amazing. And make sure he adds plenty of primal screams and regression!"

Gloria moaned and softly whined, "But then we'll have to hear all about how she is really the Queen of Sheba."

"I thought Slicky Stars was *for real*. Not just a good rub-a-stud but a whatever else you call it."

"He is. He's a licensed hypnotic regression therapist and past life astrologer, and an acu-yoga masseuse with veda-chakras, and he speaks to 4-H clubs about soil erosion and other health food nut things. I supposed I could get him to drive up to Connecticut."

Joan said, "Bette is only spitting distance north of you, so of course he can get there. What a snob of her to live in Connecticut. She always thought she was better than everybody else. Well I'm in the Royal Borough of Windsor and Maidenhead, now, near Peascod Street. We drove down that when they first took me through town. You could see the castle tower from the street. So charming. They said it's the oldest street in town. And we're at Water Oakley, I think, too! That's it! Is that the same as Hertfordshire near Dunstable? That's where I'm at, too, they said. I'm at Bray Studios, named after the nearby town of Bray. But I'm sure they said that the studio was in Windsor at Berkshire. And I'm at Charring Cross and the River Thames, too, I think. I'm at all those places at once somehow! Hell I don't know. We're also filming on the lawn of an estate that looks like a grand castle called Oakley Court where they say the French Resistance operated out of in World War Two. And there's a place here called New Lodge at Winklehorn. So damn her and her pretentious address. Look at where I am now! You just can't beat all that! Didn't that all just sound unbeatably fancy? She can't beat all that!"

"I'll have to see if he's in New York, now, anyway."

Joan asked, "You don't just know?"

"I live in New Jersey two miles north of the George Washington Bridge. He shacks up with somebody in New York in Hotel Chelsea and so I can't just look out my kitchen window to see if his light is on at home. He goes all over. He said there's something astrologically important happening soon. He could be in Hollywood right now for that, for all I know."

"That's so far away. I want him to do Bette Davis up good, *now*."

"When he was last in Hollywood he exorcised the ghost of Mae West from Rock Hudson's home."

Joan gasped. "She's dead? She is not! When did she die?"

"She didn't die but she did some of her own soul migration and got lost for awhile inside of his couch, from what I heard. It took awhile to find her but then it was so unusual—but then look at her. Does anybody ever expect anything normal from Mae West? Slicky Stars went too far with her. He's really very intense. Mae thought that it was just his huge muscles that made him that way. She told me he made her have wandering Ka. Her Ka wandered and she got lost in Rock Hudson's couch. It sounds comical but not if you understand the grounding nature of Rock Hudson, what Rock has done on his couch, and the nature of all couches."

"He did something to her caca? Her shit got stuck in his couch? What? Gloria! Please do try to make sense." Joan grabbed the vodka bottle again and poured more in a glass.

Gloria explained, "No, just her Ka. It's an ancient Egyptian word. Slicky Stars likes those a lot. Ka means *the soul*, the way they first talked about it in the pure ages, before the idea of the soul got so ruined by all our tacky modern holidays and shopping. The Ka is the astral being that accompanies the mortal body and doesn't think about shopping at all. Mae always complains of Ka problems and it wanders a lot now ever since she decided to never go out again and she gave up on all shopping. It's complicated. I'm not saying it quite right. But anyway hers now does it on its own because you just know the astral beings aren't helping her out any with that one...she's not really dead yet so she's on her own. She told me she had an out of body experience and saw the top of her refrigerator. I told her *so what*. She reminded me how very short she was, as tiny as you and I are, and she would have never seen such a thing any other way."

"Astral beings? That made no sense. I agree that I don't think you said it quite right."

"Astral beings...they're like guardian angels. They're the dead who have gone before us and they wait to help us in our time of transition. They intercede for us and guide us into eternity. The Egyptians wrote about it. I didn't just make it up."

Joan said, "That sounds a lot like what they told me when I was raised a Catholic."

"It's all the same, really," Gloria said. "Except when Slicky Stars pushes his luck and gets things happening in this earthly realm that really don't need to happen yet. But it's such fun. He's always going too far with the movie stars and the occult. It's all very exciting. I'm hoping things go too far also this weekend. I'm going to a séance he's hosting this weekend and I'm hoping I can get Rudolph Valentino to do a strip tease just for me. The stars are aligned so very special right now!"

Joan darkened. "The dead would do that? I don't know about that."

"Rudy promised! When he was still alive he promised me he would when we were filming *Beyond the Rocks*! He almost dropped his pants in the stagecoach, we were laughing so hard. That was May 1922. I can't believe we only made one picture together. It was so popular. He should fulfill all his earthly promises before he goes on to the great beyond! His soul is still weighed down. Osiris demands cosmic order."

Joan asked, "Do you think Bette Davis even has a soul? After what she did to me on the set of *Hush Hush Sweet Charlotte*!"

"Everybody has a soul. Of course. You're just being silly now. And you never know about her past lives and what that could all involve. Bette got all that fame and spitfire from somewhere. And I don't think she had time to get that much all in just this one lifetime. She's got past lives full of spitfire too, for sure. I think she's constipated."

"She's a backlog, for sure. I want Slicky Stars to take her back to before caveman times. I want to see how far back we can take her…and then leave her there with all the trogs and lizards."

"I don't know if that's ever been done before." Gloria laughed girlishly.

Joan guffawed bawdily. "Don't you think it's worth a try? Send him to her. Tell her it's all your idea. She thinks you're harmless. It can't hurt her too much. I'll pay you back when I'm back in the States. Don't make me think about exchange rates right now."

"Oh now let's not be small. I'm rich. I've got oil wells pumping pumping pumping right now out in Pasadena or wherever they are anymore. I'm richer than you'll ever be so let's not talk money," Gloria said to have fun with her *Sunset Boulevard* dialogue, then added, "Have you tried chrysanthemum tea yet? It brings back youth."

Joan took a gulp of her vodka. "Come again?"

In an excited feminine voice, Gloria explained, "It clears the eyes and all the veins. Sex is much wetter and better then. It wets everything up inside you as if you're a dewy girl again. I sip it all day long. It comes from China all dried so you make it like a tea. It's naturally sweet but you can add honey if you insist. It's full of so many minerals that I think of it like drinking sweet mineral water, not tea. I still want my other tea. I suppose you're getting your tea in England. And proper! With scones!"

"Chrysanthemum? The flowers? You can drink flowers?"

"Yes. I'll send you a box. It comes in dried sheets. Just pull off a bit the size of your thumb and put it in your press-pot. Leave it in there at least fifteen minutes. It'll break apart and expand and you'll have a press-pot full of floating white ghostly flowers. It's fascinating. I like to stare at it floating around when I do my special astro facial yoga, too, to help balance my auras. It's peaceful, anyway. I want my spirit to be as pretty as those flowers. You *did* bring your press-pot! I have six or seven near me at all times."

"No don't go to all that trouble of sending me any. Bless you, but I'm closer to China right now than you are. I'll have some sent to me from London. If London doesn't have it then I'll know you're just making things up, to try and get me to eat the lawn and drink twigs and pine trees and whatever else you're always trying to get me to do to be organic like Euell Gibbons. I'll read his *Stalking the Wild Asparagus* I promise."

Gloria gave out a big tired sigh. "Joanie, this long distance phone call must be costing you a fortune. I know I'm not paying for it. So I suppose I should let you go now."

"No wait. I forgot why I really wanted to call you. But now I remember. The flowers. I think I saw a ghost. Do you believe me that I saw a ghost? I'm sure of it."

"Sure. I believe. What did it say?"

"Nothing. But I think it was the ghost of a girl who sold flowers. They say she poisoned herself…but I don't know. Something makes me think that's not true."

"A girl who sold flowers? What a pretty ghost."

"I couldn't really see what she looked like. I have to go now. I have to figure out what happened and then I'll tell you all about it. I think she was murdered but I have not a scrap of evidence yet. How do you get clues like Miss Marple, I wonder? I'll get back to you when I have all sorts of clues and you can tell me what it all means.

In the meantime, let's get Bette, and good! When we talk about her again I want to hear that's she's regressed to a trog, which is what she's always been anyway…just savage and unfit for polite society!"

Chapter five

When Joan awoke she sat up in bed as she enjoyed her room service coffee and crumpets. She thought about how busy she'd been lately in her life. She thought about her latest TV shoot, the premiere episode of *Night Gallery*. At first she was bummed out when she found out that a nobody kid was going to direct her, somebody who'd never professionally directed before, let alone a movie star. When Steven and Joan first met she was soon most impressed. She found out he wasn't the spoiled brat kid of some Universal Studios executive. He was a clever nobody who got in from his own talent and perseverance. A Joan Crawford story! So she instantly took him under her wing and moved heaven and earth to make sure he got a fair shake. He got Joan Crawford and all her influence. While shooting the show she taught him everything she knew about moviemaking. She even helped Steven while he was shooting scenes that she wasn't even in. Joan knew movie shots! Joan knew what works and how to cut the crap and get to what works quickly. She decided that it'll be the best TV episode of the year and Steven Spielberg will be the hot new director in Hollywood. He has drive and talent and has Joan Crawford watching his backside as he learns the ropes.

She lit another cigarette, popped three cold pills, did some isometrics with her hands pressing against each other, put on her padded bra and dialed up Bill Haines again.

He groaned. "Cranberry! Do you know what hour it is? Are you on drugs?"

"I miss my doggies. They always get me going. It's foggy so it looks cloudy but it's no time to dally. I thought I heard Vincent Price laughing in the night but I know that can't be possible. But it sounded so real it turned my blood to ice. It gave me terrible dreams that he was going to chain me up in the basement. The rain and thunder has finally gone. I have so much to do today! I'm such a busy movie star. Do you know how much I've done this year? And

I've missed seeing you so I can at least call you on the phone to chat since you're my best friend in the whole wide world. Gloria Swanson always insists she's your best friend. Do say it's really me!"

"There's a time change."

Joan lifted each leg. "Yes, you need coffee now? I just had three cups because I just couldn't get started and now I feel like I'm about to shoot out of a cannon."

Bill Haines repeated, *"There's a time change!"*

"Oh...damn...that's right."

"Joan, damn you! And why are you talking so fast?"

Joan rattled her cold pill bottle and wondered why it was almost empty already. "Do I sound nervous? You know how I get when I feel like things are piling up against me. Sorry. Sorry. Everything is different here and I'm all wound up. You know how I am, you know how things are! And I'm in a different country! You just never know what kind of odd thing will be different to make you feel stupid in a different country, and one that speaks English so I can talk and think I know what I'm saying but I'm not saying what they're hearing! Yes I know the difference between biscuits and cookies but I can't believe how I keep forgetting that when I say I'm on the second floor of the hotel it's really the first floor for them because in England their first floor is really what they call their ground floor and they don't call it the first floor like we do. So here I am up in the air and they expect me to call it the first floor, just because they do. Some things I'll never get used to here."

"I'm sure it's a very nice hotel. I suppose you're hogging all the budget so this movie is going to look as parsimonious as they come."

"Parsimonious? Oh what a big expensive word for *cheap*. Nonsense. With the money I'm making you'd think I was starting over in this business. And if it wasn't for the promise of my name and face on the movie poster the movie wouldn't have sold to the banks for a penny. The reason the movie has any money at all is because of the name Joan Crawford stuck to it. Do you think Ida Lupino's name would have sold this movie? She's great in bit parts but I have to carry this whole movie all on my shoulders and mine alone. Me and Trog!"

"What lousy scene are you filming today?"

"Bill! You grumpy man! Stop saying that! It's not lousy. It's a nice movie! This has been the year of Joan Crawford and I'm on top again. I've done so much lately! And did I tell you that when I was at the American Cancer Society fundraiser I had a nice chat with Colonel Sanders and I made a lovely deal with him to serve Pepsi with his Kentucky fried chicken? Jack Benny was there, too, and he was so funny." Joan chuckled at the memory.

"I saw the script, Joanie."

"To *Trog*? Well you didn't see how it looks. It all will look so nice."

Bill asked, "When Trog has his dream how are you going to show all the dinosaurs from his past? Dime store hand puppets? I don't trust this producer to be able to pull too much out of a hat."

Joan explained, "Herman Cohen has bought excellent footage from Irwin Allen's film *Animal World*. Nobody went to see it, it was a documentary in 1956, so it will all seem like new footage. Willis O'Brien who did *King Kong* and Ray Harryhausen who did *Jason and the Argonauts* worked on the moving dinosaur models—top talent in that field of work. And when I said it would look good I was talking about all the young people. They have such nice haircuts. You wouldn't think it was 1969 in this movie. They're all so polite and kind. They all look so clean and nice. You can sure tell we're not filming in LA!"

Bill said, "The story. Really, Joan. You and a trog creature with scenes like that? The story is boneheaded—why are you having to defend the existence of a trog? The modern world would be ecstatic to have a trog. Yet you're having to defend him to keep him around for study, scene after scene, as if he was the latest version of neighborhood crime."

"This movie is going to be so good. I recently realized that when talking to Gloria the other day that it's going to be the child of *2001: A Space Odyssey*. A sequel, sort of, practically. It'll be about what happens next and everybody will be interested in that. At least everybody interested in the science fiction genre, and there are many of those. Just think of all the *2001* fans that will now come to this picture to see what happens next! Think of all the tickets sold! Joan Crawford movies always sell tickets."

"Have you lost your mind?"

"Of course not, it's a movie and *will sell tickets*." Joan repeated a line from her 1950 noir crime thriller *The Damned Don't Cry*, "The only thing that counts is that stuff you take to the bank, that filthy buck that everybody sneers at, but slugs to get."

"No. Have you lost your mind to think to mention your movie and that movie in the same sentence? *Trog* and *2001*."

"Don't be a snob. Mine will be more entertaining. And I was told all about it by the man in charge of props, a most sensible man, and I'm so excited. He said that when *2001* was finished filming here that Kubrick ordered all the props and sets burned afterwards so that they couldn't be used by anybody else ever again. Well we know how that works…we know how things turn up anyway. One of the ape-man masks was snuck out and it went on the black market, and now it's Trog! Kubrick is just furious that we have it now. I hear he lives close by and I bet he'll stop by our film shoot just to yell and cry. And he'll want to meet Joan Crawford. If he loves movies like he says he does he'll want to meet the star who paid for MGM. There'd be no *2001* if it wasn't for me. There'd be no MGM! Me and Judy and Gable paid for it all!"

"How do you know what Stanley Kubrick thinks?"

"I also heard on the grapevine that he was fascinated by *Straight-Jacket* and now he wants to make his own axe killer drama. So I bet after he visits our film set to yell and cry, he'll ask for my autograph and chat with Joan Crawford. I'm sure. It's a shame I don't have that same axe with me to give him, the one I took on all my publicity tours. He would have gotten a thrill out of that as a gift. I wonder what I'll give him as a gift! And I'll make sure I knit him a tea cozy, too! "

"At least he'll be able to tell the difference between the two of you."

Joan asked, "Two of who?"

"You and Trog!"

"Bill! What? What the hell? Bill! What's gotten into you! Of course I don't look like an ape-man!"

"No, anymore you look more like a hippopotamus with a cow pie on her head, like you looked in your circus movie."

"Bill! You can't talk to me like that!"

"I'm your best friend. I'm your mirror. I can too. And I say just look in the mirror. Look in the mirror, the reality one… *before* all the face tapes."

Joan hung up. She poured a drink. It worried her that her best friend since 1925 had become so crabby and curt. She sucked furiously on her cigarette. Finally, she decided that when she got back to New York she'd go and visit him and his husband Jimmy and they'd play cards and talk about old times. They'd talk about how nothing was any good anymore until they were all happy again.

She slid out of bed, went to the tall cheval floor mirror, clamped her cigarette between her lips, and pulled her slacking cheeks back tight with her hands. "Damn him! I want more face tapes! I'll show him!" She thought about how when one ages their face slides forward until it seems the only original thing left is the tip of the nose. She looked toward her pile of cosmetics. "More eyes! More lips! I'll show him how good I can look in a Joan Crawford picture!"

* * * * *

Early the next morning in the old large pantry that was now a wallpapered dressing room in Down Place, the manor house at the heart of Bray Studios, Frenchy worked on Joan's hair.

Joan grumbled, "I'm glad we're done filming on the moors. I was starting to fear the crowd would turn into a mob scene for real. All that Pepsi wasn't enough, they got hungry, too. You would have thought they already had heard about my deal with Kentucky Fried Chicken and they were sniffing around for some of that too."

Frenchy nodded. "You would think they would just be happy being immortalized for all time on film in a Joan Crawford picture."

Joan regarded a heart shaped candy box full of steak cubes in the compartments meant for chocolates. "I think I don't need to worry about my diet for the next few days." She grabbed her belly and then the front of her padded bra. "I'm picture weight and I'm staying that way for now. I think we should toss that out to the dogs."

Frenchy guessed what Joan would want instead, "Shoe string potatoes?"

Joan gave a nod. "I've been thinking about them all night. I love how they cooked them up for me fresh at Chasens. Now it'll have to be tinned. It's still better than nothing."

"I'll get you a can of them and you'll only eat three of them, feel guilty, and throw the rest of them away."

"*You'll* finish them all if I do that. So I won't feel guilty for wasting food, either."

Frenchy laughed because it was true.

A young woman entered holding a stack of boxes, topped with some newspapers. Joan and Frenchy glared at her intensely until she said, "I'm so sorry, I couldn't knock...my hands are so full. Here's your bits and bobs."

Joan kicked her leg up. "You could still kick the door. Bits and what? Bits of what?"

"Yes, I could have. I didn't think of that. So sorry. Bits and bobs. You know, your various things from the beauty shop."

Joan started to kick both legs up, slowly, deciding it would be her exercise of the moment. Frenchy grabbed the boxes from the young woman, as she said to Joan, "These are extra things from the local beauty parlor that I ordered. Just in case."

Joan told Frenchy that was good thinking and then asked the young woman, "Bits and bobs? Is that beauty parlor talk?"

"No. Just an expression, I guess, for any sort of various things. It doesn't have to just be from the beauty shop."

Joan asked the young woman, "And what's your name?"

"Tilling Applecheeks."

"Because of your...cheeks?"

"That's my name."

Joan stopped kicking and said to the young woman, because she was just standing there looking awkward, "Miss Applecheeks, don't think I am paying you for them."

"No, no. I'm sorry I was staring, so. It's just that you're Joan Crawford! And please just call me Tilling."

Joan smiled. "Bless you. I didn't mean to bite your head off. It's just that it's going to be a long haul getting me made up to look like Joan Crawford and the clock is ticking."

The young woman said, "You look so beautiful as you are."

"Bless you, but I can't very well go before the cameras looking like this. As I've always said, 'If you want the girl next door, go next door.'"

"I want to be a Hollywood makeup artist someday. Any advice?"

Joan grinned. "That's nice that so many women these days want to cross the garden gate and go to work. Mostly because people today want more things. It was first two chickens in every pot and then two cars in every garage. Now families want two homes, one for summer at the lake and they want boats and planes. And college is so expensive and kids had better get an education if they're going to be anything in tomorrow's world. And there's all the dresses a modern working woman has to have—so many for work, entertaining and play. Yes, if you want to live the modern life of the 1970s you need your own job. Of course the main reason for your own job is for your identity. A woman who depends on shopping and bridge clubs for a life has only half a personality." Joan winked at her. "You work at your mother's beauty shop? That's nice you're planning your future already. So many children just think of toys at your age."

"I'm twenty-three."

"Oh my. You're such a tiny elf. And I thought *I* was a tiny elf. You look thirteen to me. Tell, me because I'm so fascinated, your shops on Peascod Street are so charming. The street is so charming. I was driven down it when I first came to town. I was told it was the oldest street in the whole area and had been turned into a one way in 1963. So we only went that one way but I can't imagine it ever being a two-way, it's so tiny and narrow. I felt like I was on a film set. Tell me about your beauty parlor there. I don't remember seeing one. Is it tucked away and hidden? Has it been there long? Did they have beauty parlors in the middle ages? I could just imagine horses and carriages going by."

"And maybe Roman chariots."

Joan looked at the young woman in surprise. Her expression was fierce.

Tilling quickly explained, "Rome was once here. Maybe the street is as old as back then."

"Oh, perhaps." Joan gestured around herself. "They say this movie studio started as a country house built in 1750. I wonder what type of wallpaper was here first. How often do you all wallpaper around here? What's your beauty parlor called again? I presume it's been well wallpapered too."

Tilling Applecheeks suddenly got haughty. "Pes Croft. That's the original Middle Ages name that the street had. This whole shire started as a vast pea field to feed London, after London grew from what it had just started as, a Roman trading post. Peas were a staple in medieval times. To call it *peez cod* is incorrect, then, because the medieval pronunciation would have been *pess cot*. We at the beauty parlor always say the name of the street correctly. It's the oldest street in Windsor, heading directly towards the main entrance to Windsor Castle. Our beauty shop is just up from Darvilled Grocery Store at 92 Peascod Street. It's hard to see from the street. You walk down a hallway next to the china shop. It keeps it exclusive that way. Upstairs from that we have a beauty supply store for smaller salons in the area that are on this side of London."

"You want beauty advice?" Joan looked stern. "I'll tell you what I've been thinking lately. Wouldn't it be nourishing and moisturizing to coat your face and hair in peanut butter?"

Frenchy took a large step back as she gasped. "Oh good lord!"

The young woman looked puzzled.

Joan said, "I have so many masques I'd love to try but I'm really too busy. But don't you think peanut butter has the protein and oils?"

Frenchy made a disapproving face. "And salt!"

"Oh. Oh…then you must always make your own, from scratch, at home. Make it without salt."

Frenchy asked Joan, "And how would you wash that out when you're done?"

"Peanut butter and bacon! Well…if it's a masque then just use the bacon drippings."

Frenchy swore at Joan.

Joan snapped back, "Well that always reminds me of my last husband. He loved peanut butter and bacon so much."

"That doesn't mean it'd make a good masque. Unless you want to be licked."

Joan told Tilling, "I'm going to put together another autobiography as soon as I'm done here and I want to tell people the secrets of the stars. *This* star, anyway. I need to tell them about beauty masques. I have to be most original and clever. Otherwise just read something Milton Berle would write."

Frenchy said, "Just be honest and tell your real secrets. You damn well know you've never covered your own head and hair in peanut butter and bacon before! And you never will!"

Joan pouted. "Milton Berle will probably write a book all about how rude he is."

Frenchy asked, "Why are you suddenly so mad at him? What has he done?"

"Wasn't it you that told me he was on *Hollywood Squares* and made some comment about how I trim my eyebrows with a hedge clippers?"

"No, that was Paul Lynde."

"Oh." Joan calmed and rubbed her lips in thought, then rubbed her fingertips across her cheeks in circles. "I wonder if mayonnaise would work better. It's a bit lighter and might wash out better, afterwards. And it's still protein and oil." Joan nodded to the young woman. "Here's some advice for life, from me to you. A beautiful woman is beautiful because she stands beautifully. She doesn't jitter and sway and fuss with her own fingers. She doesn't constantly use her hands to help her say every word, or to try and make up words when she has none in the first place. She doesn't pull on her belt and tug at her dress as if it's all the wrong size. Either keep your hands off of it and throw it away when you get home, or learn to sew."

Tilling looked down at herself. "Was I doing all that?"

Joan nodded. "And more. And I don't know what you look like. Your hair is in your face. Your ears are not hangers for your hair. Constantly tucking your hair behind your ears is distracting. Learn ballet. Have you noticed how ballet dancers walk down the street? They always move with grace and beauty. And moisturize. Even your elbows. You never realize how many people can see your elbows. And I don't care how skinny you are—if you don't have strong muscles you'll have a big floppy gut. Sit-ups! Sit-ups! Sit-ups! Don't be lazy!"

"Thank you Miss Crawford. It was an honor meeting you. Today's my birthday. It made my day!"

Joan grabbed the nearest bottle. It was Balmain's Jolie Madame perfume. She held it out to her. "Here! Happy birthday!"

"I could never take that!"

"Of course you can! It's your birthday! Happy birthday! Now you can brag to everyone that you have Joan Crawford's own personal perfume!"

"Then they'll just think I pinched it."

Joan wagged her finger at her. "If your reputation was good then you wouldn't even think to worry about that." Joan grabbed paper and a pen and wrote on it that she gave Tilling a bottle of her own perfume. "There. It's documented, now. Now everybody will know this is an authentic Joan Crawford perfume bottle. And here's ten dollars. Your friends will also believe you better when you're telling them while buying them all a nice refreshing Pepsi and pizza!"

Tilling thanked Joan profusely as she backed out of the room.

"Bless you! Have a beautiful birthday!" Joan reached for a pile of newspapers that were brought in with the beauty supplies and opened the tabloid *The Daily Mirror*. "I hope they mentioned my

Pepsi charity I did in London, the one for the Aged Poor Society at Joseph's House."

"I doubt it."

"Damn it. Charities need lots of publicity. That's why I do them all the time. Joan Crawford means publicity. A charity is nothing without press. It should be on the front page."

Frenchy pointed out, "It was for a Catholic charity. You know how they don't report on religious things too much."

She flipped the pages impatiently. "But I'm the quintessential Hollywood movie star. Quintessential. That means I'm the model, the ideal, the ultimate. My first husband called me that. At that time some others called me the quintessential poseur. They just mocked me because I always tried to improve myself. Some people didn't want me to get too good…nor smart. I didn't listen to them and I got damn good and smart!"

Joan paused at an advertisement for low cost wigs. "I hope my next movie is a role where I can wear a big round wig on my head that looks just like a *big* round wig on my head. Have you noticed that's the fashion, now, to wear wigs that look just like you're wearing a wig? Even the young people are wearing wigs so they can wear bobs and not cut their hair, so they can change their hair in a second. Or have instant curls. I've heard that even Kmart and the dime stores sell them now so everybody can afford them. It's so nice to see people interested in fashion and grooming. It's nice to know that schoolteachers and waitresses and secretaries can wear wigs at work to help feel pretty and lovely all day. You never have a bad hair day in a wig. What confidence the working women of today have! I want that look, too. I'm always an icon of the times!"

Frenchy made a pinched expression. "Dime store wigs all look tacky and vain. Usually you're pointing out what is tacky and *off the rack*, to me, as something bad. What's gotten into you?"

Joan held the newspaper up and shook it in a sudden burst of anger. "Damn, Frenchy, where am I? I'm supposed to have an interview in here! I've given so many lately I should have six! Where the hell am I?"

"Open your eyes. Right there." Frenchy pointed. "Between 'Vicar Has Bake Sale With Irish Nuns', and 'Queen Stores Her Cheerios In Tupperware Containers."

"That's Faye Dunaway, not me."

Frenchy pointed again. "I guess they used her picture because you're talking about her. Look. 'Joan Crawford back in London to film *TROG*.' You're right. That is odd they use her picture."

Under the picture of Faye Dunaway it read, 'Joan Crawford does not think all new stars are dirty slobs.' Joan read the article and then commented, "Yes, I have complimented Faye. She is one of the few new ones out there who knows how to look like a star and has the guts to push it as far is it needs to go to get anywhere. Look at her in *The Thomas Crown Affair*. The hats, hair, dresses, makeup and attitude. Every inch a star in that movie. She didn't just wear the latest fashion. She pushed the fashion. She made sure you know she isn't the girl next door, off the rack." Joan loudly tapped her fingernail on the page. "Look, *me*. And Faye! Look who isn't here anywhere. Bette Davis is nowhere. Bette is not talked about at all. She is through! What's she done lately? I just replaced my kid on that soap opera to save her spot while she recovered from emergency surgery. I moved heaven and earth to get her that spot on that show and I wasn't going to let a brush with death take that away from her. My kid wants to be famous and I'm going to make sure she gets famous one way or another! And what did Bette Davis do that whole year? What has she done this year? I just did a Blackglama ad wearing their best black mink coat. It'll be a full-page ad in all the top fashion magazines around the world! I just filmed the pilot for *Night Gallery* and made new friends with brand new talent! I went to the biggest charities this year where I even made piles of money for the Cancer Society and at the very same time I made new deals for Pepsi because I know how to juggle! Bette just sat at home on the floor… drinking herself dizzy making drunk phone calls talking on the phone only with herself because she has no friends."

As Frenchy blended Joan's hairpiece with her real hair on the front and sides, Frenchy said, "Bette is on the phone badmouthing you all over right now. She's so jealous of you, of course."

Joan raised her great eyebrows in alarm. Then scowled. "Of course. *I* have a movie."

Joan thought about when Bela Lugosi once told her, "Without movie parts I was reduced to freak status. I just couldn't stand it." Joan feared the same. She feared not working at all far worse than she feared the possibility of being in a movie that did poorly at the box office. If you were working then you were still in the game. If you were still in the game then there was always that next chance at another movie that might finally be the big hit to put you back on top.

"What does Miss Davis have?" Joan continued to Frenchy. "Wrinkles. Sour grapes. She walks to an empty mailbox in housedresses. I bet every time I'm on the Merv Griffin show or the Mike Douglass show she just screams and screams like a drunk idiot until she can crawl far enough to the TV to turn the channel. Now don't hold back on the gossip, what is Bette Davis saying these days about me to the press? I can take it. I didn't get this far in this business without having nerves of steel. So just say it the way she says it."

"She says your movies are getting worse and worse and it shows you've lost it, playing these bad movies like you're going for your next Academy Award. She says you would have taken the job of the ape-man if you could have, just to have a part. She says that's sad and pathetic."

"Is that all?" Joan sneered.

Frenchy gasped. "Is that all!"

Joan waved it off. "She's *aaalways* trying to ruin my parts. She has only really done that once so far in my life, for real, really ruin my part. And I'll get her back someday for that. But so far she's never actually stolen one of my parts for herself like she has so many other people…and she never will steal a part from me! Not over my dead body!"

"She *did* also say you should kill yourself now."

"Bette is so stupid anyway," Joan scoffed. "I should have taken the job of the ape-man, she says? It's not an ape-man. It's a troglodyte. That's why we call him Trog. Trog is not a name like Biff or Scott. It's because he *is* a trog. She's so impossibly stupid. And I have not lost it. I'll play every role as if it's worthy of the Oscars because I'm a professional and I know what a job is. A job is hard work. I don't decide ahead of time that a film is bad and so then I act in it like a buffoon, as if I want the audience to think that I know that I'm really too good for it all. That's garbage. I don't get to decide it's camp so that I think I can play it camp from the get-go. I play it like a professional and if the kids think it's camp, later, well so be it. Everybody has opinions. I'm on to my next picture by then."

Frenchy said, "Bette Davis is just teasing you because she knows she can."

"She's rude and is just planting nasty thoughts in people's heads. Nobody would question my doing a movie with a trog in it but now they will because she told them to. Now my fans will only see me with a rather unkempt caveman. That'd be fine if the first thing they saw was my giving him a good bath. That little fur skirt of his hasn't been shampooed since the ice age, you can be sure. His furry things need shampooed."

"I don't think that's what anybody will be thinking about when watching the movie."

"Well it's what *I'm* thinking about! But I suppose science movies aren't about a good bath, although I really don't know why not. Science should be sanitary. Nobody will know about all the things there really are for a nice lady scientist like me to think about." Joan took a deep drag on her cigarette as she frowned. "Nobody will know what Joan Crawford really thinks about. Nobody will be thinking about poor Judy and Vanessa. I will. For some reason Vanessa's death deeply disturbs me. I suppose death is harder when young people die. Poor Vanessa, to give up on life. People have no idea what stars really worry about while making their movies. There are so many things to think about and be afraid of."

Frenchy sadly shook her head. "If only people knew what you went through behind the scenes of your movies."

Joan took another look at the picture of Faye Dunaway. "Pull my hair up a little higher right in the front. I am a star! And don't let anybody forget it! A star! Damn it!"

Chapter six

After filming the fight scene with Trog and the German Sheppard on the lawn at Oakley Court adjacent to Bray Studios, a fight that would have to be cleverly edited to keep the dog from looking so happy and playful, Trog joined Joan where she was already sitting off to the side. Chairs were set up facing each other in the shade of a majestic tree.

Trog pulled his entire headpiece off and rubbed his sore nose where the mask was smashing it. Then he slouched and sunk wearily in his chair. Joan said, "It's time for Trog to have a bath. I mean *break*." She winked at him and took a long swig of her spiked Pepsi.

He asked, "What were you filming while I was filming?"

Joan said, as she put her empty thermos of her special throat tea away in a bag. "I'm sorry did it disturb you? I almost killed once when that was done to me. I was filming a close up for *Sudden Fear* and Gloria Grahame was sucking on a sucker right next to me the entire time. That made me so furious. How dare she. Before the director yelled *cut* I turned and ripped into her, she smacked me right back, and I tried to punch her through the wall until seven stagehands had to pull us off each other. How dare she! I was the star of that Joan Crawford picture, how dare she! And Norma Shearer never liked my loud knitting needles, but don't get me started on her. I should have lodged those into her tiny little weepy eyes. But don't get me started on her."

Trog said, "No, no. You didn't disturb anything I was just doing. I was just wondering what you were up to. A Pepsi Commercial? A promo for exhibitors?"

"That one was for Muscular Dystrophy to show at the next Jerry Lewis marathon. I figured since I was all made up these next two weeks, so much, I might as well film charity spots for television between some of my shots for the movie. I can't be there in person, I'll be in Brazil for Pepsi. Now I'll be in the show anyway. They had a camera here so why not do it when in full makeup. And look what a hypocrite I was when talking first to that man from the newspaper. I gave beauty advice and I said to avoid sitting in soft chairs, which spread the hips. Look at this chair. At least I added that a lady should walk around the house with toes pointed inward…for crucial extra leg toning."

"Good idea. You don't waste time. Get your money's worth from the makeup."

Joan pushed on a gauze face tape at her cheek. "Yes, even the newspaper people came with a camera."

"Nobody asks to interview me in my Trog mask. But that was funny that we got that shot of Trog drinking Pepsi. You really know how to get Pepsi in there too."

"I'm hoping to film nine charity spots for TV while I'm made up like this. I think it's a nice look on me and I want to get my money's worth. And when I do charity I want to have different looks. I don't want people to get tired of seeing me on TV all the time asking them to give to The March of Dimes, heart disease and lung cancer always looking the same. It's gruesome stuff, disease, so you have to make sure you look nice in a variety of hairstyles. Especially Joan Crawford. Look great or people turn you off, or turn on you."

"Oh yes, Miss Crawford. You look aces."

Joan opened a Pepsi bottle and gave it to him. As he tipped it back she bent to the side to lower her view until she saw a bit of his jockstrap under his fur skirt. She asked him, "Are you circumcised?"

He sat up straight and put his knees together. "No, I wasn't, why would you ask me a thing like that?"

"If Doctor Brockton is going to get a sperm sample to freeze and she finds out Trog is circumcised then wouldn't that complicate her theories about the ice age?"

He rubbed his sore nose again. "A what?"

"If Doctor Brockton is going to freeze his sperm she first needs to warm things up. Joan Crawford knows about biology."

"I don't know if I like talking dirty with Joan Crawford."

"Twenty years ago my costars insisted on it. Don't be so shocked. It's 1969. I thought that's all you young people did was talk about sex."

"No. Not really."

Joan grandly lit a cigarette as she thought about how dirty Judy Garland and Tallulah Bankhead used to talk around her, and it used to have her feeling as if she was laughing her eyeballs out. "Oh? Well then I'll talk motherly. Trog, when is the last time you had a shampoo?"

He laughed while glancing at his mask with the wild black wig on it, then took another gulp from his Pepsi bottle.

Joan made herself chuckle. "I'm just enjoying myself this picture. That's nice I can do that, for once. It isn't as if I have to worry that you'll stab me in the back and steal some of my lines. I don't worry about anybody in the cast trying to pull the rug out from under me. For once I'm doing a movie where I don't have co-stars fighting with me to steal my limelight, trying to take the whole picture away from me, trying to make it a movie all about them instead of just giving in to the fact that it's a Joan Crawford picture."

He held up his Pepsi bottle in a grand salute. "I'm honored to be in a Joan Crawford movie."

"Bless you."

The director Freddie Frances walked up to them. "Okay Joan, we have the camera ready for the reverse shot. In this scene you see the dog attacking Trog so you order the tranquilizer gun. Where's your hair and makeup?"

He wasn't talking about what was on her head and face, but Frenchy, the hair and makeup department. Joan pointed at the 1857 castellated and turreted gothic mansion behind her, with her thumb. "She's inside. I sent her in when I was filming a spot for Jerry Lewis. It's so warm today and she looked faint. I ordered her to lie down. She's not indefatigable anymore, poor girl." Joan winked at Trog. "When I can pronounce *indefatigable* I know I haven't had too much sippy. Try saying it after a few too many and it comes out utterly shattered, like a Bette Davis impersonation. In-de-fa-tig-a-ble. Try it!" She chuckled as she glanced at her empty throat tea thermos. "Frenchy couldn't say *anything,* let alone *that*—she just got pale. One of these pictures I should let her retire. But I hate to let her go. She has such artistry in her hands. Look at how great I look and it'll hold. I can do summersaults and her hairstyles would all hold. I'm already all gussied up and can manage from here. Don't bother her now. Let her rest. I'll just freshen it up again." Joan pulled a rose paper from a tiny dispenser packet and pressed it on her nose to take the shine off, redid her lipstick, and grabbed a Chinese fan. She jumped up. "I love how Joan Crawford looks in the movies when she has a gun!" She furiously fanned her face as she traipsed off to where reflector mirrors were set up to bounce the sun around and give her flattering fill light.

As she filmed, a police car pulled up to where Trog was waiting. There was quarreling and then the car left. When she finished her shots she walked across the vast lawn to where the crew was now hysterical.

"Bullshit!" Joan yelled. "I'm trying to film and you're all going ape bananas right next to me! Gloria Grahame did that to me once and I punched her in the pie hole!"

Freddie looked like he would faint. "Joan. The film is ruined. What'll we do? How can we go on? How can I direct a monster movie anymore without a monster? They came and took the Trog mask. The coppers took it away!"

"Who? Bullshit! They have no right!"

Trog said, "Stanley Kubrick was in the back seat of that police car. He wanted his Trog mask back. He wants all props from *2001* burned."

Joan yelled at him. "And you just let them take it?"

He looked down. "*Awww man*, I did put up a fight. But they were the coppers."

Freddie looked at his shoes. "The movie is ruined. We can't go on without that mask. The backup mask looks horrible."

"This is bullshit!" Joan clenched her fists. "Nobody sabotages a Joan Crawford movie like that and gets away with it. Never go down without a fight! Where does Kubrick live?" She looked around.

Freddie pointed north. "Close by. He rents a house just outside of Slough. Between Slough and Heathrow Airport. Just up that way, I think."

"You sure?"

Freddie nodded. "Yeah, he had a nice little get-together last year for English directors in his backyard. Somebody brought him an expensive bottle of something and he passed out on the couch while we ate him out of house and home. He's a lightweight."

"This is war!" Joan raised a fist. "I need my weapons! All my weapons of war! What do I need?" She pointed to her driver. "Roderick Stuart, I want a bucket of ice and two Pepsis! Put them in the back of the car! Make it four Pepsis!" He ran off.

She pointed to another crewmember. "Get me that other stupid looking ape mask, the one for backup. That crappy thing might come in handy!" He ran off.

She pointed to another crewmember. "I might need a can of spray paint. Red. Put it in the back of the car!"

She pointed to the dog. "You get in the car and wait." She pointed to Trog. "Give me your skirt."

"But...I'm not wearing anything under here but a..."

"Off with it now!"

"I'd be nearly starkers!"

"Nonsense."

"My bum!"

"You're wearing more down there than most modern dancers."

Roderick Stuart returned and enthusiastically offered, "I can break into his house and get the mask. I'm good at that."

Joan shook her head, not able to take her eyes off Trog's jockstrap. "No, if you get caught at your age with your past that'd put you in the slammer for a long time. I'll have to leave you out of this."

"But I'm your driver."

Joan ignored him, turning to the director. "Freddie, you drive me to Kubrick's. You seem to know where it is. We're going to war. War!"

"With a bucket of Pepsi?" Freddie looked puzzled.

Joan snapped her fingers. "Oh that's right…what was I thinking…I'm not nearly well armed enough…and bring me the axe!"

Freddie raised his eyebrows.

"Any axe will do. Don't worry, Joan Crawford will take care of everything! Let's hurry before he gets a chance to burn our Trog mask!"

Joan collected her things in the car then Freddie drove her toward Kubrick's house. Bumping down the road, Joan griped, "Kubrick Kubrick Kubrick, the *greeeat director.* It's directors like him that are spending money like it has nothing to do with anything, that are ruining Hollywood. It's just common sense that you can't spend more on a movie than you hope to bring in, in ticket prices. Don't these spoiled new directors understand shopping? Business? Paychecks? Don't they know what a ticket is and why it's there at all? All of Hollywood has gone down the drain because it can't figure that out! Look at *Camelot, Dr. Dolittle* and *Chitty Chitty Bang Bang*! You can't spend that much and expect to sell enough tickets to get that back! And those aren't family films…nobody can sit through something that long! Now Hollywood is left desperately riding on the success of *Paint Your Wagon* and *Hello Dolly* to make it some money and keep it from going totally bankrupt. Those two movies spent more money than all those others put together, and will probably be three-hour long bladder busters, too. Hell at the movies! I saw a most charming live production of *Hello Dolly* once at a small dinner theatre. It was in a sweet little riverboat on the Mississippi River at Saint Louis. There was even a real staircase coming down the back of the room and we diners were all suddenly extras in the story since the climax of the musical takes place at a restaurant. Our waiters all started singing and it was so delightful. If they could have put that night on film they would have a hit, and all the ticket money would be profit! *Trog* will save the movie industry! *Trog* will teach Hollywood that you can spend a little bit of money by being clever and frugal and you find that most the ticket prices will come back to you in profits so you can afford to make a next picture, and then a next picture. And when big bloated movies like Kubrick's space one are ever made by accident then it's only right that some of the props made for it should be reused again and again to help make more sensible movies like this one! Damn it!"

Freddie said, "Save some of your energy for Kubrick."

* * * * *

The car parked. Joan stomped up to the house and rang Stanley Kubrick's front doorbell with her elbow, her hands full. He answered the door out of breath and then slammed it in her face. She rang it again. He finally came to the door again, still out of breath. She pushed her bucket of ice and Pepsis into his arms. He took it. With her other hand she handed him the axe.

He finally asked, "Joan Crawford, what are you up to? You aren't getting the Trog mask if that's what you're thinking. It's mine."

Joan waved off the car, yelling at Freddie and the dog. "Go and leave me with the *greeeat director*!" Freddie backed the car away while the dog barked nervously out the backseat window.

Joan gave Kubrick a movie star smile and then walked into his house, sniffing. She didn't smell burnt rubber so she smiled, relieved. She patted his cheek. "Don't pull such a long face with me. We're practically old friends being in the movie business and all. We're going to have a Pepsi and chat about Joan Crawford. Open some Pepsis! I was just being told you loved my film *Straight-Jacket*. You want to make an axe drama, too."

He stared at her, wide eyed, amazed at her dynamic animated force. "Not *loved*...but I did find it fascinating in a B movie sort of way. What if that could be done as a giant multi-million dollar epic. A horror epic! Why shouldn't horror ever be done as a big A picture, as a big epic? You're not here for the Trog mask? Of course you are. You can't have it. I'm going to burn it."

Joan winked at him and sat down on the couch. "We'll talk about whatever you want. We have all day. Pour Pepsi for us and add a little vodka, please. Do you think they'll ever get those men on the moon? You know I've become so fascinated with science now that I'm making a science fiction movie. I always absorb my movies when I make them and become them. Now I can't stop thinking about science. Do you think they'll really be able to land on the moon...and then we can only pray come back again in one piece?"

"I show how it's done in my movie."

"But you just had models on strings. But in real life they have to *really* do it. I don't know how they can. It sounds so exciting but I'm a realist. I remember when the Hindenburg blew up. Just because you build it and put people in it doesn't mean it doesn't blow up. That blew up because it was stupid. It might just be a stupid thing to think we should be walking around up there on a place like that, like the moon of all places. People are people and we grew up on Earth for a reason. But we go to the bottom of the ocean, and we aren't fish. So what do I know about how clever people can get."

He nodded and mumbled something to be agreeable while Joan took a swig of her drink.

She winked at her bottle, and then said to him, "You'll notice Pepsi is much better than Coca-Cola. Pepsi doesn't have as much sugar and that's a good thing. Coca-Cola has enough sugar in it to throw you into shock. Who wants that! Pepsi is more sensible. We didn't do it to be cheap, don't think that. We did it to make a beverage that's more refreshing. I call it a diet drink since it has less sugar. Too much is just too much. And add some booze to yours. You're not Shirley Temple." She looked around, taking in the whole room. "Nice wallpaper. They could take a color photo of us in here and we wouldn't clash with it."

"A photo?"

"I always plan for that." Joan poured.

"It's too early in the day to drink."

"Nonsense. If I can do it you can do it. You're a big man. You can handle it. And it isn't every day that you, the great director, gets a fun visit from the greatest Hollywood movie star. I made Hollywood. If it wasn't for me who knows what kind of film industry you'd even have to work in today. You couldn't have made your movies if I didn't first pave a path for you. And it was damn hard work! Paths don't make themselves. There was a lot of dead weight. There was a lot of folks throwing shit in the way! But I made it through, working like a mule, and my movies brought in all the money for MGM. My movies paid for everybody else's. Now you're making films for MGM, too."

"*Fun* visit?"

"Yes this is! Oh most definitely. Fun! Not as much fun, of course, as Judy Garland and Tallulah Bankhead were when they were rolling out the barrel. They're a barrel of naughty monkeys.

May they now both rest in peace." Tallulah had died the year before from emphysema.

"Yes, they were great stars. The greatest."

"I'm only human. But I *am* Hollywood! You should be thrilled, being the great director!" Joan smiled big, then glared angrily at his drink. "More vodka than that, please. You too. Here let me pour, you pour like a little girl. Cheers. I bet it's nice living so close to the airport." She scooted close to him on the couch. She thought he smelled sweaty.

Kubrick scooted away from her a little. "I hate flying." He stared in fascination at her face tapes buried under thick pancake makeup. "You were filming."

"I'm always filming. When I'm not filming scenes for *Trog* I'm filming spots for charity so I don't waste the makeup—it takes so long to get it up this far. I love flying. It takes me all over. I hate flying too but I have to deal with it like an adult. I have so much work to do the world over. And yes, I was filming a lovely charity spot for Jerry Lewis just now. Is there anybody who does as much charity as me?"

"Jerry Lewis?"

"But I help him out with his and he doesn't help me out with mine. If I'm not helping out with a charity somewhere it's because my schedule is already filled and I can't be two places at once, unless we start sending out drag queens in my name. With my movies, game shows, fan mail, charities, kids, and Pepsi I'm always doing many things. I was one of the judges for the first Miss America telecast in color. I organized USO A-GO-GO at Madison Square Garden. At Chauveron restaurant I presented a check to the Negro Fund and then the Mental Health Association at the Palmer House. That's both in New York. Oh, and I was just in a parade with Leonard Nimoy. We were both Grand Marshalls for the Seattle Seafair parade. That was a gas!"

"That's a lot."

Joan nodded proudly. "I could go on and on. Hollywood gave me so much so I always want to give back. I'm grateful. Drink up and let's have a Joan Crawford party right now. You've got the real Joan Crawford on your casting couch! I mean…couch. A special party just for you because you're the great director! Let's have a party worth writing about in our next biographies."

Kubrick gave a crooked smiled. "I'll never fly again. I don't have to anymore. I'll just sit back and make everything come to me, now. And you were filming a movie with my stolen mask. How could you be in a movie so pathetic as that?"

"I beg your pardon?" Joan batted her many eyelashes at him.

He stared back and forth between her two eyelash lines, the fake eyelashes at more of a perky arch than the real ones, so they slightly diverged.

Being stared at as if she was looking bizarre, Joan talked faster. She put her hand on his knee and rubbed. "Darling, I was afraid to fly and was used to getting my way about things, being Joan Crawford. I finally got to where things came to me, too. But my last husband, Al, would have none of that. I was always accustomed to being in competition with men but he taught me how to be a companion again. He taught me to be part of a team. He said we'd both go farther that way, that people do better in teams of two. And if we were going to be a powerful couple then I'd have to be willing to be as outlandish as he was. I always thought I was outlandish enough but he told me I needed to fly if I was going to really make my mark on the modern world of movies and business. I told him I was afraid and swore off flying. I said movie stars as big as me didn't have to do things they hated anymore. But he said I'd never be afraid of flying ever again *because he said so*! And he said the Pepsi jet was waiting. I asked what the hell it was waiting for and he said it was taking me to Las Vegas to get married with him. That was 1955. We were going to be a team, for real! I was going to get neck deep in business for real! He was going to start off my new life, a whole new chapter, for real! We flew right then and there. He wouldn't even let me pack or make any phone calls to my kids and friends. I told him I had to tell somebody I was getting married and he told me they'd all find out on the news, and if I had that advantage over everybody else then I should use it. He always told me to use my advantages. And he was right. I wasn't scared on that plane. I was thrilled because I knew my life had changed and there was no going back. I've been all over the world in that Pepsi jet ever since. We made Pepsi international. We had no borders or limits. My first year with Pepsi I flew over 98,000 miles for them. I haven't counted since."

He stood up so her hand wouldn't be on his knee anymore. "Why did you give me an axe?"

Joan slapped his ass as she fibbed, "Oh that's not just *any* ole axe. Don't you recognize it? That's the axe I used in *Straight-Jacket*. And I know how you want to make a movie with an axe. So I thought it would be the perfect gift for the man who has everything."

He turned and looked down on her. "You sure?"

Joan batted her eyelashes and grinned big. Then she looked away, shyly, but really it was just to make sure he couldn't inspect her eye makeup tricks anymore. "Sure, I'm sure." She took it from the coffee table.

"Really? You brought it with you to England?"

"You should have seen my luggage." While Joan autographed the handle, she said, "Bette says I keep it under my skirt at all times. Cheers to that, huh? Cheers, I say!" Joan made sure he saw her arrange her skirt. "I heard through the grapevine that you loved that movie. So it's a gift. I thought I'd switch prop for prop and get Trog's mask back."

"No way."

"I realize that now. I can't always have my way. When everything is always coming your way then you're in the wrong lane. So just take the damn axe, nothing in return. It's famous. You're famous. You'll love each other. I want you to have it anyway. I'm so thrilled you loved my axe movie."

"I found it *fascinating*," Stanley said. "Whenever I see a horror movie I think about how I should do one, just to do one that's a lot bigger and better with a proper epic budget and good actors. They're always so badly done and cheap looking."

"I don't do horror flicks. I am a serious actress, of course. My dramas sometimes have moments of suspense." Joan lit a cigarette and waved it grandly before him like a magic wand to hypnotize him.

"I think horror is a perfectly fine genre, if done nicely."

Joan gave an uncertain shrug. "If you want to throw your respectable career away. Well I hope your *horror movie* has an axe in it."

Stanley gave a reluctant nod. "Yes…I *would* like it to have an axe. I want somebody to have to chop through a bathroom door to kill somebody hiding inside—they thought they were hiding and now they're screaming and screaming bloody murder. Chopping, screaming, anticipation…very exciting."

"Brilliant!" Joan kicked out of her high-heals and put her feet up on the coffee table. She rubbed her legs. "Make sure you're careful. If your actor isn't used to swinging an axe he can take his own foot off. It took awhile for me to get so I could swing it and it not fly out of my hands. I'd never handled an axe since my early movie days. So when I first swung that axe the handle kept flying out of my hands. I'm so lucky I didn't hurt myself or anybody else. It's true, axes really are very heavy at one end. If you're not used to that kind of thing at all then it's really very unwieldy."

He sipped and nodded, watching her lovely long legs.

She wiggled her toes. "I finally got so good at swinging an axe that I took it with me on my publicity tour. Bette Davis was jealous and said I kept my axe up my skirt." She pulled her skirt up. "Now where would I put that?"

Stanley saw the flash of her panties. "That…I mean…I…I read that you stole the part. Naughty naughty."

"That's it." She winked at him. "Loosen up and ask Joanie anything. We're friends, now…old movie pros, and we can talk shop. Fix us both another drink and I'll tell you the story of how I did not steal anything. Here, let me pour. I'm not pouring for a church mouse. I'm pouring for a man. I know how to pour for men. I know men. They like to pour. Yeah I wasn't the one first intended for *Straight-Jacket*. Everybody is saying I stole the part from Blondell. They say I'll steal a part from anybody. That's Bette Davis who's always stealing, not me. She hasn't stolen a part from me, yet. I'd fight her too much to ever let that happen. But she's *ruined* my part once before, and she did it when I was too sick to fight back. She ruined my part in *Hush Hush Sweet Charlotte*. I'll get her back for that. It might be too late for that, though—she has no career left to ruin."

"What did Bette Davis ever steal?"

"She stole *Little Foxes* from poor Tallulah Bankhead. Tallulah was so much better in that role on Broadway. Bette was just rude mannerisms. She's the rude selfish one! I don't steal! I didn't steal the *Straight-Jacket* part from Blondell. Don't listen to the gossip."

"What happened, then?" Stanley asked. "I heard you stole it from her like a dirty rat."

"I don't steal!" Joan insisted. "Poor Joan Blondell. She's my dear friend! I wouldn't ever dream of doing anything to upset her. I didn't steal her part, I saved her career by taking over her part for her."

"That's a tall tale."

"It really happened. She had a terrible accident and I took over for her. She begged me to cover for her, and we had to keep it all hush hush. She'd been drinking and she walked through a glass table or door or wall, she's not sure what she did. But it cut her up very bad. She had such a bad cut on the inside of one leg she couldn't even walk for a long time. I can't mention that to the press or else the insurance industry will never cover her for another movie again, she's already notorious for being a clumsy drunk and so she's already expensive to insure. She's done so many films and still wants to do many more. I didn't steal a movie from her, I saved her so she could go on to make another! I saved her career! She begged me to, to cover for her! I didn't need a movie at that time, I was up to my eyeballs in Pepsi and TV. But I did it as a favor to her."

"Wow, I didn't know that."

"You have the hiccups now and it's all my fault. Let me pour you some water." Behind his back, at the sink, she made sure the glass of water was half vodka. "Hold your nose and drink fast. Throw it all down at once. I don't mind that the press is saying I stole the part. Not really. As long as they're talking, that's all that matters. Bad press, good press, it's all the same. It's press. It's when they stop talking about you at all then you're Bette Davis. In-deee-faaah-tig-a-ble press!"

As Joan entertained Stanley with more Tinseltown stories, she drank him under the table. After he collapsed on the couch, she grabbed her shoes and ran barefoot out to the street. "Were'd yah all go?"

Freddie stepped of the waiting car. "Here, Joan. Over here!"

"Where? I don't see anything!"

"Over here!" He waved wildly. The dog barked.

She finally spotted the car in plain sight, beside a tall bush to hide it from the house, and ran to it. She fell in the bush, swore at it, then turned and asked, "How's my lipstick?"

"You okay?" Freddie asked.

"Who cares about the damn bushes."

Freddie said, "That didn't take as long as I thought it would."

Joan pushed at the front of her padded bra as if it might have gone askew, causing her to fall in the grass. While she was down there she looked for her heels where she had dropped them when falling into the bush. Then she threw her heels in the car and winked at Freddie. "I love your English accent. You're so cute. Cummie waggidy doggie! Cummie! Cummie on to mumsie boo! Smell the Trog skirt. It's full of Trog smells. Trog butt and bits. Bits and bobs! Balls!" She convulsed into fits of wild husky laughter at why his mask would also smell anything like that. When she caught her breath, she resumed, "Now come on, cummie pretty baby honey sweetie pie wagsy and find the stinky Trog mask!"

She grabbed the replacement ape mask, swore at the bush again, and then took the dog into the house. The dog soon sniffed out the Trog mask stashed in a rolled up throw rug stuffed under the hallway china cabinet just off the dining room. Fifteen minutes later, Joan ran back to the car with the Trog mask held high, and the axe in her other hand, victorious. "Burn some rubber, baby, I just burned some rubber, baby. We're making a goddam get-away! Bonnie and Clyde!"

"You switched masks?" Freddie asked. "He'll know that. He's not blind. We'll come right back!"

"Balls! He ain't gonna bother you ever again!" In the back seat, she slammed the door and then she hugged and kissed the dog. "No, I'm not so stupid. I took the lousy replacement one out to his backyard and burned it. It made a nice black burnt pile for him to see. I burned it! It was a cheap piece of crap but the rubber was just thick enough to leave a mess. I burned it! And I ruined some of his grass. I burned it, baby! And then I wrote a note for him and left it on his table. It said, 'You lousy bastard, you vandal of art and culture, burning that nice Trog mask has ruined it for all time. And I decided that I'm giving the axe to Freddie, he's a much better director. Cheerio."

"Thank you."

Joan chortled. "Bless *you*! When he wakes up he won't remember that he didn't really burn the Trog mask himself. He'll just see that it's done and figure he did it. He won't recognize what's in his backyard as a fake. It's burned beyond recognition. He'll think he won. Let him think he won until the movie premiere. Now he'll stay away and out of our hair. Let him stay in his house and gloat. That's how I win!"

Freddie asked, "What was the red spray paint for?"

She kicked at it with her foot since it was on the floor. "I ended up not needing it. I just wanted stuff. When you go to war you don't really know all that you're going to need so you just need lots of stuff. I think I had enough stuff and a can of spray paint left over. I won. Let's go make a Trog movie!"

As Freddie looked in the read view mirror, he noticed that Joan had a piece of the bush sticking out of her hairpiece. "I should take you to your hotel. You need to rest. You're three sheets to the wind."

"Nonsense!" Joan yelled. "I wanna film a Trog movie now! We have the mask and nothing can stop us—we're infatig-be-table! I wanna feed Trog shnakes and wizards…shnakes…*snakes* and lizards! I can do it! Let's make a goddam movie! Goddam it's hot in here. Drive fast so I get a nice breeze through the window!" She started to hiccup. "I need a drink!"

Chapter seven

The next day, Freddie Francis knocked on Joan's dressing room at Bray Studios.

Joan glanced in the mirror, pushed up at the front of her bra, grabbed a tube of lipstick, and called out, "Come in." She dabbed pale pink wax on her lips.

"You really put fire into that last scene. You give the dialog such emotion and conviction. I'm surprised you're not under the weather after yesterday."

"Hair of the dog." Joan picked up a Chinese fan and waved it at her face as she sipped at her vodka in her Pepsi glass. "And now I'm knackered…or as we say in Hollywood, *pooped*. But…for just a moment. I always get a second wind." She got up and handed him a Pepsi from her bucket of ice. She wiped her hands on the sides of her dress to dry them and lit a cigarette.

He thanked her and gave a playful little bow. "How refreshing. I'm glad I finally get to work with you. To see you work is fascinating. You have such intense concentration. You give every second all your energy. You're always full of detail…and emotion. I've always wanted to work with you my whole life. It's a blooming thrill."

She grandly sat back down. "I'm glad you think that. I find everything about England a *blooming thrill*." She winked at him.

"You're the most fascinating star. It seems you've almost made England your second home and it is an honor."

Joan gave a nod. "A most welcoming home. When I was here in 1960 the prime minister had me for tea at 10 Downing Street. That was a wonderful time, and such an honor!"

"And you've even met the queen when you've been here before. I've never met the queen. Wow, to chat with the queen! Please tell me about that!"

Joan grinned proudly and fiercely blew cigarette smoke off to the side. "In the fall of '56 I flew here to film *The Story of Esther Costello*. And that was when I had the most thrilling experience of being introduced to Queen Elizabeth. I'll never forget a single moment of it. I felt like we connected for a timeless moment as we had a nice chat. We're two completely different women but I just felt a special connection. We seemed to share souls. Women's souls. It was the Royal Command Film Performance. Marilyn Monroe was there. Damn her bullshit. She was in England that year filming *The Prince and the Showgirl*. It should have been called *The Prince and the Slob*. Marilyn was still getting her hair done in the line while the queen was walking in. And she didn't know how to curtsy. These actresses today act like tramps and tarts. Marilyn didn't even show up for the rehearsals the day before and it showed. She was lost. She looked like she'd just fallen out of the back of a pickup truck. I was with my husband so I didn't bother to help her this time. I used to help her all the time when she first came to Hollywood. But I stayed at my husband's side. She was lost. She was stubborn. She stayed lost."

"That must have been exciting. I saw the newsreel. They played it at all the movie theaters for months. It was such a popular newsreel. We all wanted to see it again and again."

"Bless you."

"What did you think of the movie they showed? *The Battle of the River Plate*."

Joan rolled her grand eyes. "War movies are one thing but this one was just awful. I couldn't follow it at all. The script really was *utterly* undisciplined. When it was over I remember turning to my husband and asking him what was that about, and why were the Nazi men portrayed with such sympathy and nobility in a British war movie? He just shrugged. He might have fallen asleep."

Freddie chuckled. "Yes…it was done rather badly, for being so big."

"*The Story of Esther Costello* was a much better picture. Because I did it, people believed it. The critics said that it wasn't everybody's cup of tea but it was great. The New York Herald Tribune said that it isn't a Joan Crawford picture without plenty of anguish and so my fans would have their usual good time. They called me queen of the art form…of the *woman's picture*. I learned sign language for it." She held up both her hands and gave him an energetic example of sign language. Her cigarette did not go flying out from between her fingers although it seemed like it should have. "I just said that I have the warmest respect for you."

Freddie thanked her.

Joan thanked him back in sign language. It looked like she was blowing a kiss from her chin. "I love learning new skills for new characters for new movies…like how for this one I talk about science. That's new for me, too. I never thought I'd ever be in a movie talking about sperm and it's all completely wholesome and educational. Not that I'd ever talk like that in any other kind of movie." She became flustered. "The filth they make nowadays and pass it off as entertainment! And now the kids run off on their own to watch what they want and there's no parents and no standards. Of course kids are curious about sex but that doesn't mean they should have it so easily displayed like that. It'll certainly turn them all into sexual slobs. Who knows how they'll start behaving now because they can see the stuff they can see and it shows it the way it shows it. This whole new generation of moviegoers will be ruined and will expect such new shocks in all their movies. Their imaginations will no longer be required. Love stories will no longer be lovely. They'll be tacky filth! Emotion will only be expressed with clothes coming off and everybody seeing everybody's naked butts. Drive-ins have just become pornographic parking lots. Filth! And when will the crowds have had enough—when will the audience start demanding to see all of our internal organs, too?"

"I hope you don't think monster movies are filth."

Joan laughed away her tension. "Oh no, certainly not!" She touched his arm. "They're great! They attract the young away from the lousy sex filth and into good old-fashioned Sunday school lessons. Sunday school but at a drive-in on a Saturday night. That's what they really are. The monster movies are age-old morality plays." Joan thought about how safe she felt when she spent a few happy years in a convent school and the nuns told her fantastic stories. She felt like a rosary was in her hand. To stop her thumb from wanting to count beads and pray, she rubbed her hands together. "They're the classics but modernized with the gizmos of science—lab equipment and car chases. Oh. This movie doesn't have a car chase. That's a shame. I look great behind the wheel with a grim expression on my face, ready to screech around a corner. But of course you *can* have a modern morality play without a car."

Freddie interrupted, "I do try to make mine moral lessons, to some extent. Bully for me. Thank you for noticing."

Joan redid her lipstick as she stood up. "You're a master of filmmaking, show me the back lot. I need some air. I need to walk. I can't breathe. What a warm day again. This dressing room is stuffy when I'm out of air." She grabbed her flask, lit another cigarette, and then asked, "What door do we use? This studio is so eccentric. So many fascinating nooks and crannies and so many doors off to who knows all where."

"Yes, let's pop out for a bit, shall we?" He went to a door on the other side of the room and held it open. "Yes, it was built piecemeal from Down Place, this manor house. Who knows how many secret passageways this place has. I was shown a few. There are walls within walls from the attic to cellar. They say the cellar even has a cellar and from that room there's an underground tunnel to the river. But I was told that caved in many years ago so it doesn't go far. I should try to find it someday. Watch your step."

Joan stepped up where the floor rose three inches and entered a narrow hallway. "Maybe we'll find treasure behind a panel or bookcase before we're done. Or a skeleton a hundred years old. How exciting! I feel like I'm at a Halloween party every minute that I'm here at Bray Studio."

Freddie said, "Once I heard organ music but I couldn't tell where it was coming from. I don't scare easily but that was very creepy."

"Maybe it was just a radio somewhere."

"That might have been all it was."

Joan admitted, "I heard Vincent Price laughing in the darkness the other night. Maybe all of England is haunted!" She shivered at the memory.

He gestured forward. "I wonder if we might have a look back here." They walked up a hallway as Freddie explained, "The back lot is just a bit of yard on the other side but it's been many places in many time periods." He opened the door.

At the end of the hallway Joan stepped outside and squinted. "Maybe there's a nice breeze back here."

They walked along the wall of a newer building where their trog cave set was within, then walked alongside scaffolding that was holding up the backsides of facades, until they came to the open yard. Freddie raised his Pepsi bottle to it in salute, and said, "When we had to go outside for exterior shots of Baskerville Hall, inns on dirt streets, old London for *The Phantom of the Opera*, Dracula's castle, Cornish hamlets, we put them all right here."

Joan walked down a slender curving lane and stepped up to a narrow bridge. She could see where the creek below it stopped a short distance at each side. "You even dug a creek. It makes it all so clever for such a small area."

Freddie walked across the narrow bridge made up to look like stone. He turned to look back at the tattered village set. Joan followed. He said, "We first dug this trench six years ago to be the moat in front of Dracula's castle. That's long gone now. Christopher Lee fell through the movie ice and was imprisoned down there until the sequel, so we really did have to build something to film some action on, and not just paint the whole castle in on glass."

Joan scowled. "I've read how much he didn't like to play Dracula. It's a part dammit. He got his name over the title for four minutes of film time. I've worked so hard all these years to keep my name over the title. He didn't know how lucky he had it to have a part like that. He shouldn't have complained. He should have been grateful!"

Freddy shook his head sadly at Joan. "I'm sure he was just afraid of being typecast. He thinks of himself as a serious actor. He probably doesn't want to end up like Bela Lugosi."

"Bless his heart. I didn't think of that. It's a shame how quickly actors are kicked into a corner."

Freddy pointed. "The roof of that house looked a lot better when we filmed. It was thatched but that's all blown away since then. This was a village for *Frankenstein Created Woman*. The story was about soul transference, for a change, instead of just body parts."

Joan asked, "How does that work? How is the soul moved about? There seems to be so much interest in those aspects of life these days."

Freddie shrugged at Joan, and said as he chuckled, "I saw that film and still can't tell you. It looked good though!"

"Gloria Swanson knows all about that. Just ask her what happened. Even if she didn't see the movie she knows about that topic."

He pointed at the hollow buildings. "It's just a small slice of the village anyway. Hammer always made you think you saw more than you did. Bernard Robinson designed all these sets and he was so clever to make it all this cramped, to fit so much in, but on film you couldn't really tell that it was that way, other than it was all so interesting to look at. It set such a mood for the period."

Joan frowned as she sucked on her cigarette. "It all looks so abandoned. It looks like nobody has filmed back here for years."

"Nope. 1967 was the last time a camera turned back here. Hammer now films at Elstree Studios. For some reason Hammer has decided they've used Bray Studios all up, or something, for they have this studio up for sale. A Hammer film hasn't set foot in here for a few years now. Sad. There's no reason the imagination couldn't have continued here. People will miss this back lot and not even realize it. They won't see Dracula's moat again."

Joan pointed off to a white sagging wall with a large dogtooth-patterned window screen in it. "What was that? That doesn't go with the rest of this village."

"At the same year *The Mummy's Shroud* was also filmed. You can say that's also Hammer's last film at Bray, done at the same time. That's part of a small stretch of backstreet Cairo in 1920. It had a balcony overlooking it. It was Hammer's third mummy movie. For being so low budget it still was able to make a museum set that had real Egyptian artifacts. England is full of them so they were able to get their hands on them. Hammer always makes things look just right."

Joan rubbed her chin. "The film had a mummy. Right?"

"Oh sure."

"Are there still some movie mummies laying around here? Are they all just chicken wire and papier-mâché, but look real? You all make things look so ghoulish and real."

"No, all the mummies were men in costumes. They looked all wrapped to high heaven but it was all sewn together so it went right on lickity-split with a zipper up the side. On the far side, away from the camera. Of course."

"Of course." Joan winked.

Freddie said, "They're now talking about doing Bram Stoker's *The Jewel of the Seven Stars*. Hammer can't call it that of course. That title has no horror genre draw. Maybe it needs to be called *Night of the Mummy's Tomb*. Or *Death from the Mummy's Tomb*. I hope I get to direct it, no matter what it's called."

"*Sex and Drugs in the Mummy's Tomb* will get the kids of today." Joan remembered a dream she had in New York. Vanessa the flower girl was murdered horribly somehow and then Joan was Miss Marple but had no cue cards so she couldn't solve anything until a mummy came out of a box and strangled her until she woke up in a cold sweat.

Freddie thought Joan looked faint and asked her if she was okay. "Shall we go back in out of the sun? It is indeed a warm sunny day and we don't have straw hats."

Joan shook the odd memory of the dream away and walked across the bridge toward the studio. "What's that? What's that over there!" Joan walked to a waist high wall that was artfully fashioned of plaster and paint to seem like stacked stones. *Monster* was freshly spray painted across it in red. "Who did this?"

"I have no idea. Probably some kid."

Joan shivered. "It's a clue. Of something. I'm sure it is."

"I wonder what it means."

"I just know it's a clue. We saw this sort of thing on the front of my trailer when we were filming on the moors. I wonder what it means. I wonder why it's there. I wonder if the same person did both. Or is it a cult? A gang? Why?"

"There you are!" A stagehand waved at them. "We have the rocks put back up and we're ready for another take."

Joan asked Freddie about the scene they were about to return to, "You don't think those boulders are bouncing too much when they fall?"

"I'm sure they'll cut the shot once the bouncing starts. Just to make sure, I'll tell the editor your concerns."

"He'll cut. I'm sure," Joan said. "I wouldn't want him to think I'm telling him his job as if he doesn't already know it. I won't butt in. Of course this movie won't allow bouncing rocks."

He praised her about how smart she was about moviemaking.

"You have such a nice voice." She took his arm. "I adore the British accent!"

He said, in cockney, "That's enough buggering about." They walked back to the cave set and dropped the fake bouncing boulders again as Joan yelled at Trog to put the little girl down.

* * * * *

When Joan was finished with her shots in the cave set, she hugged her director. "You're marvelous. I feel in good hands with you as my director on this sort of material."

She wasn't just saying that to be nice. Freddie Francis had an impressive career. He started in movies as a clapper boy. Then when he was in the Army he became a cameraman director and editor to the Army Kinematograph Unit at Wembley to make many training films. After the Army he spent the 1950s as a cameraman to many feature films. After an Academy Award for his camera work he began the sixties as director of horror classics with Hammer Films.

Joan walked back to her dressing room holding her thermos of throat tea. Vincent Price was sitting there with Frenchy. He wore a full brown beard but he was still instantly recognizable. Frenchy said, "Joan! Look who's here! Vincent Price! *Vincent Price*! He says he's been in your pool!" Joan opened her arms. They kissed each other's cheeks.

Vincent asked, "Joanie, darling, you look gorgeous!"

She put her hand over her mouth to laugh. She said to Vincent while she glanced naughtily at Frenchy, "It's been years since I had you in my pool!"

"Decades," he said.

Joan's eyes misted up as memory came back to her. "What a surprise. A surprise from good ole Hollywood."

Frenchy asked them both, "When did you meet?"

"I will never forget," Vincent said. "It seems like yesterday."

Joan snapped her fingers. "Like it was yesterday. Oh, damn. If only it could have been yesterday. It must have been 1939 and Helen Hayes wrote a lovely letter of introduction for you to me. You and I wrote back and forth a few times. And then you were finally in Hollywood and well dressed for it—a swimsuit at my pool party. I swam with you until I wore you out." She laughed again.

He pouted comically. "You said it would be a potluck. In Missouri that just meant whatever was leftovers. At your house it was a feast for twenty? Thirty? Fifty? How many were there that night?"

Joan shook her head. "I think it was closer to twenty. But I don't really remember that part."

"I'll never forget. You made me feel like I was number one. You were so kind. I don't think I've met a kinder star in all Hollywood. I was an outsider but you made me feel so welcome. I dared to dream that I could someday be a star of your stature."

"You didn't do so shabby. You certainly made a name for yourself."

He looked off in thought. "Nobody was as welcoming as Joan Crawford."

Joan gave a sad smile. "I'm an outsider. They hate outsiders. Oh, they're polite enough—that's how they are. You don't know the things they've made me do trying to protect myself. And how ashamed I've been sometimes because of them. You don't know how they are. But you'll find out, as I have how they whisper, small talk, laugh! As if you have to be from the South to be any good! Oh, they're so smug, and namby-pamby! I wish I could get rid of them as easy as this trash!"

Vincent pretended he had been following that but then gave up. "What?"

Frenchy said to him, "Joan's been under such strain."

Joan chuckled. "That was some of my dialog from *Queen Bee*."

"Oh." He chuckled with her. "I thought you'd lost your mind. Yes that was a great movie. I sat through it twice. Oh your movies are so dazzling. Didn't we watch Joan Crawford movies at that first party? After we swam and ate? I remember movies after it all."

"We watched two Spencer Tracy movies, none of them with me. These days I'd be showing yours. You've had such a marvelous career. It's a shame we didn't star in anything together. Can you imagine how much fun that'd be?" Joan squeezed his arm. "I hope we can do that soon!"

Vincent pouted out his lower lip, this time looking serious. "*You* with me? That would be an honor. You flatter. My career as a schlock star is over if I do anymore movies like the one I'm in now. It's beyond schlock. The script makes no sense and I'm barely in it, not if I'm to be a star of any sort." He took her hand. "You're still a top-shelf star."

"Bless you." Joan spotted her Chinese fan, grabbed it, and furiously fanned her face. "You're in London to make a movie?"

"Of course. Otherwise I'd be on Hollywood Squares right now."

"Oh how fun that we're here right now making movies at the same time. I'm a scientist trying to give Trog a bath but the script won't let me. I could give you a shave, too. Are you playing a wild pirate? My what a beard! What is your movie?"

"My movie is *Scream and Scream Again* and I'm supposed to be the lead but I really don't have too much screen time. I'm a Doctor Frankenstein type. I have a big vat of acid. That pretty much sums up the whole thing up. Schlock with little shock."

Joan hoped he didn't run around too much in the picture—literally *run*. She thought he'd looked like a complete ninny when he was required to run near the end of *The Last Man on Earth*, ruining the serious tone of not only his character but also the whole movie.

She gave a hopeful grin and said instead, "As long as your name is big on the poster. Look how I helped out William Castle with *I Saw What You Did*. I was dead before they had a chance to change the reels but I starred on the marquee and poster and looked every inch a star."

Vincent rolled his eyes. "Indeed I'll be the star of the movie poster. It'll be one of those movie posters designed to let everybody down. I'm sure."

"I'm sure *Trog* will just have me screaming on the cover. We took a bunch of photos for that already. I don't think that sets the tone for this movie. I'm a very serious thoughtful pleasant scientist." Joan lit a cigarette. "But, yeah, movie posters."

"A little birdie told me you don't have anymore scenes to shoot for the next few hours. Let's go play!"

Joan nodded in the direction of the cave set. "I just yelled at Trog, good. Now dozens of men in army uniforms are going to spend the next few hours filming all that army stuff…shooting up everything with guns. In the end they get Trog, of course, with lots of red paint, I'm sure. It's just the way these sorts of pictures end. I don't need to be there while they shoot all that. The director is very experienced."

Vincent said, "What a clever idea to make a movie about a trog."

"It's because we got the mask from Stanley Kubrick's space movie. And it's a beauty." She winked.

Vincent rolled his eyes wilder. "I'm sure your movie will be better than his."

"His cost a fortune."

"Have you seen it? Have you actually sat in a movie theater through the whole thing?"

"I admit I haven't." Joan smirked.

Vincent closed his eyes. "Such a snooze. It goes on and on with the audience having no idea what it's really all about. *Trog* will be a much better movie because Stanley isn't directing it so people will always know what's happening."

"I hope so."

Vincent explained, "A friend told me the novel of *2001: A Space Odyssey* is all very clear. There really is a story going on there. I should call Mr. Kubrick and tell him perhaps he could improve his picture by having somebody with a marvelous voice narrate from the novel, from time to time throughout the movie, to help the audience out."

Joan nodded. "And you'd be wonderful as that narrator!"

"You, too, Joan. Nobody says it has to be man."

"Yes, bless you. Now that I've done *Trog* I'll be thought of for more science fiction material and I'll make many more movies. I have expanded my range. I'm always growing as an artist. Maybe now they'll think of Joan Crawford when they want science shows narrated for documentaries. They always want a voice of authority."

"Let's go play." Vincent Price put his hand out to hers. "Let's look around together. I want to see this marvelous old place. I've always heard about Bray Studios. I'm so intrigued by the idea of making so many different movies in one old country house." He took out his pocket watch from his sea green jacket and checked the time. "I won't take up too much of your time. I promise."

Joan said, "Take me! I mean, take all my time. I'd love to kill time with Vincent Price! As long as you talk to me the whole time. I adore your wicked voice. Narrate our tour through Bray Studios!"

He put his watch away. "First, I'll race you across the Thames. You still swim, I hope."

Thinking about how dirty that water must be, Joan said, "Darling, some other time but now I have to keep my hairdo nice. I have other things today and I'm sure they'll also want me to scream some more, for some more publicity photos, before the day is over. I need hair for that!"

He pulled on the front of his beard. "You still the strongest swimmer in all the world, I bet."

Joan nodded, faking a smile as she thought about how she almost drowned to death a few years ago in Atlantic City when she got caught in a bad undertow that would have killed most people. Nobody on the beach noticed her going too far out and it took her many hours to fight her way back. She kept her ocean laps parallel to the shore after that. Joan shook the memory and said, "Later I have a high tea for a March of Dimes promo. Lots of photos, of course." She grabbed his hand and pulled. "We have a few hours. Let me show you around the studio. It's so small, for a studio, but there's so much to see. There isn't another like it. It is so unlike the studios in Hollywood."

Vincent looked around the old room with affection. "Yes, filming in old British country houses. How splendid."

Joan looked around her dressing room, with him. "It looks so dirty but it isn't really. It's just old. It's impossible to get old things to really look clean."

Joan remembered when Katherine Hepburn told Howard Hughes, "Everything is dirty—we just do the best we can." Later Tallulah Bankhead told her the same thing while sitting on the toilet after a queue of drunk men had just used it. She was naked and had cookie sprinkles in her pubes. Joan was pretty sure Tallulah was shouting the Hepburn line but the party was very loud. Between Tallulah and Hughes it helped Joan put her own compulsions of cleanliness into perspective.

Joan continued to Vincent, "I just wish there was air conditioning here. My makeup always feels so dirty on my face without it. Does your studio have air? It's such a warm summer."

"No." He chuckled. "Of course I was joking about swimming out there. It is a warm enough day for it though. My movie is just shooting a few minutes downstream right now in Chertsey, in Surrey." He pointed in a few directions, not sure offhand where he was orientated. "We really could swim there if we could swim anymore. I'm not in any of those scenes they're shooting today, though. So I'll try to get into some of yours. You won't mind me standing around in some of your shots, would you? I promise I won't say a word." He looked coy.

Joan chuckled. "That might be funny. But this picture isn't supposed to be funny in that way. The trog mask looks very serious. It was expertly done. It's a serious movie about science and its social ramifications in the community. Everybody worries. People don't like change. I'm surprised the movie doesn't have the villagers out with torches and pitchforks." Joan grinned at the idea that the angry mob at the cave was kept calm by a Pepsi concessions stand, that made it into some of the shots. "I play a doctor full of understanding and wisdom, so of course it's me against the world, me against a frightened town."

"I wonder what the rooms look like upstairs. I wonder what's in them now. I'd love to find an old wardrobe where we step inside and find ourselves in a winter wonderland…air conditioning!"

She fanned her face faster. "I'm sure it's even warmer upstairs. You want to really tour an old country house? Let's find a secret passageway down in the basement where it's cool. Let's find a hidden treasure or whatever else smugglers might have been hiding. I'm sure all those things are down where it's cool. Let's find the secret of Bray Studios!"

"Why do you think there were smugglers here once?"

Joan pointed at the floor. "There's a hidden tunnel from a basement room to the river. Why else would they have that?"

Vincent looked off in thought. "Maybe…for unloading after a day of shopping in London, by boat? I don't know."

Joan grinned big. "Maybe we can find that—the old piles of things from days of shopping gone by. Maybe we'll find a box of old drugstore purchases from the last century. It would be fascinating to see such old cans and bottles." She turned to Frenchy. "I won't be gone long. How long can one be away to see one old house's basement."

Frenchy said, "It's a pretty big place. Don't get lost down there."

Joan grabbed a scarf and tied it around her hair like a turban to keep spider webs out of it. She shuddered. "Maybe there's bats down there, too. It might be just like a Vincent Price movie."

"Should we bring umbrellas?" Vincent asked. "Not to open but just to have to poke and swing at things, like a Peter Cushing movie?"

"I won't worry. You're taller. They'll be flying to you and miss me. Bats!" Joan looked in the mirror and decided the bright orange scarf would look best in a color photo, but a floral one would look best in black and white. If someone took a shot of her as she came back up and it was ever printed it would probably be printed in black and white. She changed scarves. She pinned a broach to the front of it.

Joan and Vincent lit candles and went down basement stairs that were just beneath the wider main stairs that headed to the upper floors. Once they were at the bottom, they joined arms. Joan marveled in a hushed tone, "Feel it? So nice and cool. I could live down here."

"And that smell. What is that smell?"

Joan breathed in deep. "The smell of...*old*?"

Vincent stepped forward as he held his candle close to discarded movie equipment from just a few decades before. "Look at all this old stuff. This certainly ages quickly, doesn't it. They're always making better machines."

Joan moved her candle back and forth to see to both sides of her. She illuminated a tall stack of wooden folding chairs. "Now they just need to write better scripts."

"Look at that tea cart. I love that chair over there. Some of this furniture could be hundreds of years old. *That* never goes out of style. To sit is to sit—and it's nice to do it on something gorgeous."

Joan asked, "Which way do we go? To the left or to the right?"

Vincent pulled Joan to the left, whispering. "I want to find a secret room."

"I'm sure they're all around us. If we enter one we might end up in London, or the attic, or that winter wonderland through the wardrobe. Who knows." She shivered and took his arm. "Take your time. It's so nice and cool down here. Are you sure you aren't just planning on bricking me up in the wall, or burying me alive, or whatever it is you do all the time?"

He chortled. "And you never know when I revert to thinking I'm in the Tower of London again and I'm about to feed you to the rats or stuff you in a vat of wine like when I was Richard III."

"See, you did Shakespeare. There is no finer honor for a serious actor."

"It was rewritten in plain English, they added ghosts, and sold it as horror. I'm afraid it wasn't all that."

"Still, it sounds delicious. I know about your movies. I've heard stories."

He asked, "You didn't *see* them?"

She started to go left again but he pulled her the other way, as she said, "I've seen you running around in them when they've been on TV. I've been too afraid to see most the Roger Corman ones. They say they're spectacular." Joan shivered again.

"Spook-tacular" He chuckled.

"And I'm not going to be tingled while sitting in my theater seat. William Castle is always pulling something. We've both worked for him, we know how he'll do anything for attention, bless him. It's a shame we didn't work *together* for him."

Vincent softly said, "When William Castle made his movies with you, you were what he was pulling. You were the gimmick."

Joan nudged him. "Now I'm a gimmick. I don't know if that means I made it or I'm through."

"Maybe it just means that you're so unparalleled that the name *Joan Crawford*, alone, means something big and special like the latest spook vision and butt tingles."

"Bless you."

They walked around for awhile looking at antiques, holding tightly onto each other and holding their candles out at arm's length, to see. Vincent finally said, "What's behind this door? Or should we go behind that door on the other side of the room? So many doors!"

"What's behind this wallpaper? More wallpaper? Can wallpaper patterns put you under a spell? I fear I'm becoming obsessed with wallpaper in this country."

He chuckled. "You should see my dressing room. It's amazing."

"In England the wallpaper seems to cover something more than just walls. It seems to cover a secret. It seems like if you rip it away you'll see something older, and fascinating. The pages of an old scroll, maybe, hidden behind the wallpaper and maybe lost forever! Maybe lost books of the King James Bible are hidden behind the wallpaper of England."

Vincent agreed. "In my dressing room I think I'm surrounded by thousands of tiny pirate ship steering wheels! It's all a plot to drive me mad!"

"You should have seen my trailer out on the moors. Cartoon flowers in manic rows in unspeakable colors. It was all designed by a maniac." Joan pulled him toward a red door. "This way. What's over here? More fascinating antiques, I hope. I'd love to see an old spinning wheel."

Vincent chortled. "Until it begins to spin by itself."

"Then I will scream. Why are we whispering?"

He bent over to put his lips to her ear. "Because we're waiting for a ghost to moan? Or, so the monsters can't hear us and pounce us?"

Joan jolted. "Don't say that! When *you* say that it sounds so very frightening!"

He put his candle to his face and smiled to her in mock chagrin.

Joan said, "You have the most frightening way of saying things. I hope I don't see any rats. I will scream."

He asked, "If you're so afraid why did you come down here?"

"I forgot about rats and if I'd thought about them I would have worn boots. Then I wouldn't be afraid. Let's go back and find me some boots." She turned around.

He pulled her back. "We're down here now let's look around. If you want to scare the wildlife away then we can be loud."

"Hush!" Joan insisted. "You'll just advertize our presence to all the monsters." She looked behind herself again and whispered, "Thank god they aren't sneaking up on us yet."

He whispered back, "We must be careful!"

Inside the next room, they had two other doors on opposite walls to choose from. They chose one and inside saw a large wood table. Joan quietly said. "That would be nice for a party. How many do you think that would seat?" She walked around it holding her candle out to it. Ornate carving was around the edge. The legs ended in lion's feet. "Twenty-two? My dining room table in Hollywood sat eighteen and this looks even bigger. How did they even get it down here?"

Vincent said, "Noel Coward always told everyone that Joan Crawford not only knew how to give the best parties but also knew how to go to her own parties. I couldn't agree more. You still have such marvelous parties these days?"

Joan chucked. "Nothing as marvelous as the one you first went to. Not because it was my best party ever. But…"

He nodded and continued for her. "…It was my *first* party in Hollywood. It was my first anything in Hollywood. I'll never forget it. It was a beautiful night. It had been too hot all day long. I was so wide-eyed and in awe at your party. I was in awe of you. You dazzled. You literally dazzled. Were those real diamonds on that wrap you put over your swimsuit? Boy they shimmered in the dark. I felt like I was in a fairytale that night."

"Just pretend diamonds. And I'll never forget meeting you. You were so strapping and manly in that swimsuit of yours. I flirted with you all night. Couldn't you tell?"

He shook his head. "I would have never dreamed you were just flirting with *me*. I thought you were flirting with all the stars of the night sky. I thought you were just that way."

She laughed. "I am that way, aren't I. Do you have a cigarette?"

He took a pack out of his jacket pocket and lit her up from his candle. He said, "I never saw a woman look so glamorous in all my life, and yet seem so casual about it. You were so at ease. You were like a happy cat that night. I will never forget that night."

"I was happy in those days. 1939 was a great year. Compare that to a party I had in 1953 where all of Hollywood's biggest stars showed up. Lucky my backyard could hold many hundreds. Where were you? Did you have a movie out that year?"

He nodded. "*House of Wax.*"

"You should have been there. It was the place to be. I was so nervous that night that Bill Haines had to hold me up half the time."

"You? Nervous at a party. You were famous for being the one who had the most fun."

"By then I was nervous about everything. I was silly and vain and felt old at forty-nine. I felt like I had to prove I was on top in Hollywood all over again. I felt like I had staked my reputation and life on that party. I even had flowers tied to all the tree branches. Tables were everywhere. All the stars were there. Where were you? Don't tell me you found a better party that night."

He smiled at her until she stopped looking angry. "I heard all about that party. They say it was the biggest party Hollywood had seen in years. Judy Garland even sang. But I was out of town. I was in New York filming something for TV…for the Phillip Morris Playhouse. Do you still entertain now that you live in New York?"

"Yes, but I now don't have a lawn that fits several hundred movie stars. I live very high in the sky. So I try to keep it at ten these days. That's my favorite number to mix. That's the most important part of giving a dinner party…knowing that you *should* mix people. People shouldn't just stay with who they came with….just as long as they *leave* with who they came with. I try to make sure my parties are a mix of politicians, journalists, new actors, artist and poets, and old friends. And I mix them all up together. Young people are welcome too as long as they're not hippies. I don't want my guests getting fleas or social diseases, and no arguing about the war. If I want a larger crowd I just rent two rooms at a restaurant, one room for drinks and then the other for sitting down to eat. Then I don't have to hire all that extra staff just for one evening. A restaurant already has them. 21 is my favorite for that. They have ten private banquet rooms so they're always ready for me. Bill Haines told me once never to have people move from place to place for one party, just room to room at the same place. That was one time when I wanted drinks at my house and then dinner at Chasen's. He stopped that idea. I'll have to have you over the next time you're in New York."

"I'd love it!"

"When you come over, if it's spur of the moment, I'll just have you and me at the card table like I just did when Ivan Rebroff popped over when he was in New York last. He's the greatest Russian baritone."

"Yes, I've heard his wonderful singing."

Joan continued, "I'll have my maid fix us peanut butter and bacon sandwiches."

"You can't fix your own sandwiches?"

"My hands will be too busy. We'll also be playing backgammon. If you don't play I'll teach you."

"I bet there are no crusts."

"She takes a cookie cutter to the bread slices. So yes, the crusts are gone. If your timing is good you can stop by for one of my family dinners when I have the kids over and it's my famous

Mildred Pierce meatloaf. And maybe there will be a Joan Crawford movie on TV. I'll make popcorn and we can watch that. If it's one of your movies on I'll have to sit in your lap. I'm sure it'll be terrifying. Have you seen *The Story of Esther Costello* yet? I learned sign language for that one. I bet you haven't had that requirement yet for any of your pictures. I bet I have one on you with that one. I would sign something for you now but it might be too dark to see it all properly. They say sign language can so easily be misinterpreted as looking naughty. That's so embarrassing when that happens. It seems if you do it wrong, or it's seen wrong, it doesn't become gibberish but usually becomes something else entirely. A fan once wrote me and told me they thought I had said something naughty in *The Story of Esther Costello*. You know how that bothers me. I can't stand mistakes."

Vincent sniffed. "What's that smell?"

"What smell. A dead body? Oh no."

"No. Not anything scary. I don't think."

Joan shook her head. "I just smell *old basement*. And cigarette."

They both sniffed. Vincent finally said, "It's oil of…North African Wild Rose."

"I wonder why you'd smell that now. I don't smell anything." Joan sniffed loudly then took a drag of her cigarette. "Are you sure? Maybe you just smell my perfume all of a sudden."

"No. It's something else. Something odd."

Joan sniffed at her wrist. "Maybe it's my rose papers. They have powder on them. I press them on my nose before we shoot. It keeps the shine off."

"I should try that. I'm sure my nose gets shiny too. I never thought to worry about that. I wonder if I have a shiny nose in all my old films."

Joan chuckled and playfully nudged him. "Now you're mocking me. Did you hear about the All Monster Film Festival they had in London? I heard it was all old Universal monster movies. Maybe next time it'll be all Vincent Price movies. They can do all Joan Crawford movies although I don't strictly do the horror genre. I'm a serious movie star. But *Trog* is a monster movie, too, I suppose, if you open your mind enough to think about it that way. It's really a dramatic film about science and I play a serious scientist, of course. It will have wide interest and great box office. I'm sure it will open brand new doors for me. Maybe the film festival will start showing horror films that are really actually dramas, with serious actors, because of their moments of suspense. I suppose my last several films fit that description."

"Yes I heard about that film festival." He shuddered. "I'm so glad I was very far away. I heard that the kids who were putting it on were so stoned on drugs that they couldn't even focus the projector. Nobody could figure out how to keep the reels in order, or even knew when a movie was over at all—everybody there was so out of it."

"Oh dear. I'm glad you didn't have anything to do with it, then. I'm glad you warned me about it. You never know when they want you to show up to meet the fans and they're all stoned out of their minds. That's how things are these days. The sixties have become crazy. I have no idea how anything gets done at all with everybody so stoned. How did you hear about it being such pandemonium?"

"Peter Cushing called me on the phone the next day, so upset. He said he went to sign autographs and couldn't stay three minutes, it was such pandemonium, for sure, such a travesty. *Dracula* was playing and somebody in the theater was playing an electric guitar so that you couldn't hear the movie at all."

"That's awful. I hate the smell of pot. I would have been sick. Too many kids are just lost on it these days. I believe that the reason most of the kids are on pot and other junk is because they don't have enough love and discipline at home."

"Peter only mentioned the smell of burnt popcorn, if I recall."

"Burnt popcorn? That's awful! I must ask you Vincent and don't think I'm crazy…I'm afraid to even bring it up because I'll sound crazy…but…the other night I heard you laughing in the night."

"What?"

Joan chuckled nervously. "I told you I'd sound crazy. It really did sound terrifying."

"Where were you?"

"In bed in my hotel. Hornfield Court. Shivering under my covers! It gave me terrible dreams that you were going to chain me up in the basement!"

Vincent laughed. "Hornfield Court! Yes, I was there! That must have been the night I was at the hotel bar with a few friends. You must have heard me on the way to the car. We had a lot of laughs."

"Well don't do that anymore! It sounds terrifying! Who knows how many people you terrified! You sounded like Vincent Price! It was diabolical!"

He tried to suppress a laugh. "Well I suppose I do." Vincent put his hand up. "Quiet. What's that sound?"

"What sound? The sound of what?"

He whispered even softer, "A heartbeat?"

Joan listened then whispered back, "Yeah, right. The tale tell heart?"

"I hope not. Do you hear it?"

Joan shook her head again and insisted she didn't.

"It sounds just like a heartbeat."

She tugged angrily at the side of his jacket. "Vincent. Really now. You're just pulling my leg trying to scare me."

"You don't hear it?"

"That isn't the pipes?"

Vincent nodded. "Maybe it's just the pipes."

Joan asked, "Why would pipes sound like a heartbeat?"

Vincent shrugged. "It sounds angry."

"I was just going to say that. It's a jealous heart!" Joan whimpered, "It hates us!"

"You hear it now?"

Joan softly whimpered. "I think so!"

Vincent turned and screamed.

Joan turned and screamed. Then after she caught her breath, she said, "Frenchy, where did you come from?"

Frenchy smiled. "Here, Joan, I thought you would want your flask as you explored. Neat old house, huh?"

Joan looked surprised. "Were we that loud? I thought we were being very quiet and sneaky so the monsters wouldn't hear us and pounce on us. How did you find us all the way back here?"

Frenchy looked confused. "Because I just followed you. I was behind you the whole time."

Vincent Price suddenly looked confused also. "I didn't see you standing there this whole time."

"Whole time?" Frenchy shook her head.

Joan said, "Yes, Vincent and I have been down here for a long time now, just visiting. Ten minutes maybe?"

Frenchy shook her head. "Nooooo."

Joan nodded. "We've had quite the chat."

Vincent said, "Oh we have been down here longer than ten minutes." He took his watch out and looked at it. He jolted. "Joan! My watch says we've only been down here one minute!" He showed it to her.

"That's impossible." Joan looked at her cigarette. It was still long. "My cigarette hasn't burned down at all. Vincent. Vincent! What does this mean?"

Frenchy nodded. "Yeah, you were only down here for a minute because you weren't far ahead of me before I decided you might want to take your flask with you. So I just followed you until you stopped long enough for me to hand it to you. It didn't even take a minute."

Joan's wide eyes widened in fright. "That's not possible!"

Frenchy asked, "What isn't possible?"

Joan looked around the dark room in fright. "This basement is under some spell!"

Vincent also looked horrified. "Time has stopped!"

Joan grabbed both of their arms. "Let's go back upstairs...in case that's true. I hope I don't look a hundred years old when I hit the top of the stairs."

Vincent said, "The way it has worked so far they will have aged more than us. They might be the ones who look a hundred and they will wonder why we don't too."

Joan paused. "Really? Then maybe I should sleep down here at night. And do all my knitting and letter writing down here, if time has stopped. Wait a minute. Are you sure that's how it works?"

Vincent shuddered. "Of course I don't know! Joan! You're shaking like a leaf!"

Joan nodded. "If feel as if a ghost were near. I felt a ghost hand touch my neck. I felt something angry and jealous...but I don't know. That's not possible. My imagination." She nervously laughed.

Frenchy asked, "What are you two going on about? Is this a game?"

Joan repeated to Frenchy, "You were *not* just behind us the whole time...w-we were talking *for a long time* just by ourselves before you found us. We didn't see you with us for a very long time. At least that's how it seemed to us."

"But I was just behind you the whole time, I swear. I was right on your heels. Not even a minute passed." Frenchy crossed her heart. "Otherwise how would I know you were in this room way back here? I walked here with you." Joan looked at her cigarette and it still hadn't burnt down yet.

When they returned to her dressing room, Vincent took his watch out again. The glass face on it was cracked side to side. "Broke! Look! How did that happen?" He looked pale.

Joan took it to see it. She put it to her ear and didn't hear ticking. "Dead! It's all *my* fault. I took you on the most frightening adventure. Blame me. Don't be upset. Vincent, I'll get you a nice new gold watch with something romantic added to it from Joan Crawford. You need a Joan Crawford watch. And you get a tea cozy, too. I'm knitting everybody in the production a tea cozy. Your production is so close to mine that you get one too."

Frenchy asked Joan, "Why do you have tears in your eyes?"

"I'm sure I'm overreacting." Joan grabbed a tissue and dabbed at her face. Then she selected a lipstick and opened her compact. She gasped. "My mirror! Broke!"

Vincent recited, "Out flew the web and floated wide—the mirror crack'd from side to side, 'The curse is come upon me,' cried the Lady of Shalott."

Joan threw the compact away, reluctantly shrugging. "I'm sure it's nothing." She made herself smile. "I haven't thought about that poem in years. My first husband said we should make it into a movie. He'd play Lancelot, of course. He told me that since I looked just like a Pre-Raphaelite painting anyway, my grand chin, that I'd be perfect as the Lady of Shalott." Joan looked down into the garbage can, baffled. She started to shake again as she thought. Vincent finally walked to her and put his arm on her shoulder. In a frightened little voice she said, "Your watch broke. My mirror broke. What does this mean? What curse has come upon me? Or…maybe this has nothing to do with me at all."

Vincent said. "Maybe sometimes things just break by chance." He didn't look convinced.

"And you smelled rose oil. And heard a heartbeat."

He hugged her tighter.

Chapter eight

It was almost dark when her driver, Roderick Stuart Winklehorn, drove Joan away from Bray Studios. "I could have filmed six more hours today. Why do they all have to give up so early." Joan knew all about union rules but she was just still too full of energy to go back to the hotel and knit. "I wonder if the beauty parlor is open. Drive me to the beauty parlor. I want to see it, if I can."

"Where is it?"

"They said on Peascod street. Pronounced *peez cod* or *pess cot*. It's near a grocery store. And it's a hallway next to a china shop. And the name of the beauty shop means the name of the street the way they first said it in the Middle Ages when it was all about peas. Do you know the one?"

Roderick Stuart nodded. "Darvilles Grocery Store is next to the china shop. We'll see what's there when we get there."

"And watch how you drive there. It's a one-way street these days. I went down it when I first toured Windsor, when I was first driven to the studio from the airport. It's such a lovely area. I enjoyed seeing what I did, very much. I imagined horses and carriages. I imagined chariots from Roman times, if the street is that old. Rome used to be here."

He nodded again. "Peascod street is tricky and old. Maybe as old as all that."

As they drove down it, Joan griped, "I can't tell how the numbers go. I remember now it's near 92nd street. The grocery store is there."

"Yes, it starts at number 4 at the east side of High Street and goes to 72 at the Criterion Public House and then picks up again at the other side of the street and keeps going from there to 143 at the west end of High Street. But it doesn't have odd numbers on one side and even on the other, so you can't look for it that way."

"My you know your streets. What a professional driver."

He shrugged. "I grew up here. It isn't like having to know the streets of London. Now that's a wonky maze."

Joan turned to look out the other window. "Now I'm completely baffled. As long as you know where you're going." She rolled her window down and poked her head out. She smelled a slight waft of baking bread. "It looks just like a movie set in this light. I feel like I'm in a Charles Dickens movie." She quickly leaned back inside and rolled up the window. "Or Jack the Ripper!"

"This isn't scary. I think New York would be scary."

"Yes, I never go out at night in New York. Too many people hooked on drugs who are in trouble and are desperate and would kill you for a nickel."

Roderick Stuart asked, "Is the rumor true that you were in some scenes in *Rosemary's Baby* but they cut it? What was the scene? Why did they cut it? New York looks so scary."

"Oh *pfff*. That's only a rumor. I visited the set with my dear friends Van Johnson and William Castle. But it was only a visit. They considered a shot for the movie of Van and I walking through a lobby so Rosemary's husband could see us and get all jealous that we're famous and he wasn't. I could have told him right then and there that before you go so far as sell your soul to the devil, for fame, try the casting couch. They fuck you anyway and it's so much better than the cold hard floor. But that would have led to a different movie." She gave a husky chuckle.

In the rearview mirror Joan could see his eyes go wide with thought.

Joan continued, "Mia Farrow was a dear and was a lovely hostess, keeping us company. She's so pretty and sweet."

"You didn't film a scene at all? I wonder why some say you did."

"No, dear. The lobby scene wasn't filmed, probably because Van didn't know who Roman Polanski was and asked who the tiny Pinocchio was. Made him mad. The fans probably started the gossip anyway because I looked so good on their set, and everybody else thought I was made up and costumed for shooting. But I always go out dressed like a movie star. That must be it. That must be what started that rumor that we'd already shot something."

Roderick Stuart asked, "Is it true the devil turned the lights out on you all when you visited?"

"They blew a fuse. It happens all the time shooting on location."

"Is it true Mia Farrow collapsed on the set a couple of times, the evil was so intense for her?"

Joan looked puzzled. "Why would she do that?"

"They say the evil was so thick on the set that you could smell it. It smelled like death. It smelled like devils. It made her ill. She couldn't sleep and was as pale as a ghost and could only film a few hours a day before she'd faint."

"Don't be silly. It was only a movie based off a book. Mia was a doll and was only acting a part. She wore pale makeup. She's so kind, warm and charming that evil wouldn't even know what to do with her if it found her. If you felt frightened while watching the movie then that's only because the director and actors did their job and did it very well. Just like *Trog* will make you believe in science and…trogs!"

"Groovy. I sure wish I could have spent time with Mia Farrow! Man-oh-man!"

"I bet you do."

Roderick Stuart blushed and drove in silence for a while. Then he stopped the car and pointed across the street.

Joan looked out her window, now doubting. "Maybe I should just go home. It could be stupid." She shrugged. "Oh well, I'll just have to take my chances." He opened the door for her.

Joan got out and walked towards the row of shops. A sheet of newspaper blew down the street at her. It clung to her leg. She pulled it off and tossed it into the wind. She came to a door that had a plaque on it that read, Pes Croft. Joan pulled on the door. It was locked. She spotted a buzzer and was about to press it when she saw a woman walking down the hall. Joan backed away. As the woman walked out the door, before it closed behind her, Joan slipped through it. She walked down the long narrow hall. "Hello?" She repeated louder in a phony heavy cockney accent, "*Ahllo*!"

She heard radio music and a voice that sounded like Tilling Applecheeks. "Back here. Who's that?"

Joan entered a backroom and saw Tilling standing behind a grand old-fashioned beauty chair. She was snipping the split ends off a young woman with long blonde hair. Tilling paused at the sight of a top movie star in her shop. "Joan Crawford! It's Joan Crawford! Joan Crawford! I had such a nice birthday thanks to you!"

The young woman with long blonde hair gasped. When she finally composed her expression, she rose from her chair and held out her hand. "What an honor! My name is September."

After Joan shook her hand she went to a box of tissues on a counter and blew her nose then went to a turnstile full of lipsticks to find a new color.

Tilling looked confused. "I'm just gobsmacked a movie star stopped by this little ole shop. You come in because we missed something we were supposed to supply your movie with?"

"No, just dropping in to say hello."

Tilling smiled. "Oh! For a bit of a chinwag!"

Joan touched her chin.

Tilling clarified, "A bit of a chat!"

A new Beatles song came on the radio, "*all we are saying is give peace a chance.*" Tilling turned it up until Joan's annoyed expression caused her finally to turn it back down.

Tilling said, "The Beatles. The greatest band. England has the greatest band. The world's greatest music is British."

Joan said to Tilling, "I hope you don't mind that I just dropped by but I finished with filming for the day. The crew has families and meals to attend to. So before I wander off to my hotel room I thought I'd stop by a few places in England—just to see England. An ancient beauty parlor seemed a fascinating place to see since I'd heard about it from you. It indeed looks full of history."

Tilling waved her arms around at the intricate tan wallpaper of art-deco lattice, swirls and waves. "This shop goes back to the 1920s. That's not old for around here. But I wouldn't buy any of those lipsticks if I were you. Some of those are probably a couple of years old by now."

Joan blew on the turnstile. "You keep it dusted. That's nice. As long as makeup stays sealed it'll last forever. And it almost lasts forever once you open it. That's because they put so much mercury in it all. It has to last. Mine doesn't last because I use it up so fast but not everybody is in my line of work. But it's nice to know it's always sanitary no matter what. Not that I share my makeup with anybody. That's just untidy. Why would I share my lipstick with some slut so she can rub it on her syphilis—that's most the younger actresses these days. But you can go ahead and share a color with a girlfriend. That doesn't sound too awful, especially if you're having a slumber party and playing makeup. It's a good way to learn skills from each other. But if you drop a lipstick in the toilet it gets thrown away no matter what. I don't care if there's enough mercury in it to kill an elephant. It's just sickening!"

Tilling said, "I wonder if there's any makeup still around in people's drawers from 1920 that could still be used. Sure, it should be in a museum, but I just wonder."

Joan shook her head. "I don't know when they started using preservatives in makeup so I don't know. I'm pretty sure by the 1920s, though."

September puckered. "I hear they once used lead!"

Joan replied, "I think that was for color. Makeup used to be so unhealthy. But now it's modern and sanitary. Lipstick still has lead in it, don't let them kid you, but only in small quantities. I have friends who are industry insiders. I know all about cosmetics. But then cosmetics are the uniform of my job. My armor. My mask. My Joan Crawford." She looked around and took in all the various things, large and small, of a beauty shop. She half-hoped it had a bar. "1920. Do you still have some old boxes of products from back then?"

Tilling shook her head. "Oh no, our lipstick isn't that old. Nothing is. If anything is still around anywhere that's that old it has to be forgotten in people's trunks, in basements."

"Shame. Back then everything was so much better. They had beauty cream back then that promised to erase all wrinkles, made your hair grow in thick, and made your teeth white as snow. Creams really did take away muscle aches and freckles, pep ills gave you pep, and stomachaches were cured fast with real peppermint, not the fake flavors they use today. Maybe I should visit the backrooms of an old British drugstore and see if there are a few old forgotten trunks a hundred years old. I used to marvel at the things they had on the shelves when I was a kid. Nothing works like that anymore. Do you still carry Queen Helen's Miracle Mud? I think that was a British brand. It was green and soothing and firming; it made your face feel like a pillow mint, and so nice. They did ban arsenic wafers. Thank god. Those were to improve your complexion. Not everything is a good idea, it seems. People would get greedy for better and better skin and eat more than the recommended dose. And then there was Lash Lure. It was an aniline eyelash dye that caused many cases of blindness. And even some deaths! And there was Koremlu, a depilatory cream that contained high doses of rat poison. Do you still have Miracle Mud? I'm sure they stopped making the version with radium. That shouldn't be sold, of course. They used to put radium in bath salts, too. Those were the days."

Tilling frowned. "Oh, no. We don't have old products that old."

Joan didn't see any lipstick colors that interested her, she had a much bigger selection in her turnstile at home, so she walked across the room and sat in one of the tan boxy Nagahyde chairs lining a wall. "Pity nobody thought to save stuff from back when it was all good. They don't make mud now like they used to. They didn't save anything in Hollywood, either. Hollywood was good for throwing old stuff away as fast as it could. The 1920s were the dawn of time in Hollywood. I'd just started in movies, then. Most those old films don't exist anymore. They threw them away as soon as they thought nobody wanted to see them anymore, and the old movies were in the way of whatever was new new new. Clear the shelves. Movies aren't made for the *art* of it, sadly. Not primarily. They're only made for one thing and that's to sell tickets. When the sound systems were installed in movie theaters, in the early thirties, suddenly nobody had any use for most of the silent movies anymore. Very few had music added to them and so then they survived, like the Jesus movie Cecil B. DeMille made. But that was an exception. Poor Gloria Swanson had so many of her films fall off the face of the earth right away. They were probably all just thrown away the day movie theaters installed speakers. Some of my silent films are lost for all time, too. Nobody thought of putting films in a library, for the ages, at that time. They only thought about how they couldn't sell tickets for them anymore."

Tilling nodded. "Fascinating."

"But enough about all that. What do ladies *really* talk about in a beauty parlor? Do you talk about me? Oh, I suppose there's all sorts of things to talk about. Have you all seen *The Women*? The movie opens with hundreds of women in a beauty spa getting their hair and nails done as they gossip enough to start a whole movie plot! Do you really all sit around and talk about men?"

"Sure." Tilling grinned.

Joan grinned. "Who? Anybody I know?"

September grinned. "The only one you would know is your driver."

Joan blurted in a naughty tone, "They say he's a wanker!"

September disdainfully rolled her eyes. "Oh he was my squeeze for awhile so I know all about that. He doesn't give you too much to squeeze."

Tilling asked, "Tiny?"

September shrugged. "If he could get in the mood I'm sure he'd be big enough. No, he's too soft and squishy down there. I tried to make him hard. He don't get hard."

Joan raised an eyebrow. "How would you know that?"

September insisted, "If I can't make a proper cucumber in his pants than nobody can. We were dating for a short while in London. His idea of dating. And *at our age*." September looked exasperated. "You'd have thought we were still in primary school. We would keep all our clothes on and just snog. I'd rub at his dobber and he'd just stay soft and squishy. I tried to make him the luckiest man alive and he just wouldn't go there."

Joan smirked. "I've always said that love is like a fire. It either warms the hearth or burns down the house. How was it with you?"

September thought a few moments and then answered, "It was not a fire at all. In fact now that I think about it, he grew distant and mad…insane. I never thought about it before because I was always only thinking about myself at the time, of course. But it seemed he would get touchy. I don't mean he would touch me, but he would act as if it suddenly upset him that I would touch him. Of course I could touch him anywhere I wanted—I was his girl. But he would go into one of his mad trances and stand there and holler about how, 'The monster is on the loose and the villagers are screaming in the streets with pitchforks and torches and angry faces and angry minds! Everybody is killed and stomped on and smashed away for all time! Everything burns down! The windmill burns down! The dam breaks! The monsters are washed away in a great deluge. You can't look at me, then! You can't touch me, then! You can't diddle me and diddle me and diddle me! And the studio will stay mine and I will sell it and make the money I need! I will make my money! My money!' That's what he would go on about…so odd." She laughed. "He must have done that performance a dozen times."

Joan didn't laugh with her. "He sounds rather distant. Disturbed. Troubled. Not able to get too close to anybody."

Tilling sadly shook her head. "I just read a book, *My Self Esteem, My Road to Happiness*, and it says that when a person doesn't have any closeness with others then they have no self esteem, then they can have trouble shagging."

September scowled. "Your opinion is always based on whatever the last self-help book you read was."

Tilling glanced over at a stack of paperback self-help books on a corner table. "Well then what do you think is making him wonky?"

"Wonky droopy sad?" September answered, "Drugs. I think he's doing dobber killing drugs. Heroin will do that. Maybe he's on heroin."

After Joan told them that the kids of today were all going to pot, doing so much pot, she decided she needed a drink. So after telling them how charming the beauty parlor was, she excused herself and ran back out to the car. She sat in the backseat and silently sipped. Finally, Roderick Stuart looked at her in the rearview mirror, narrowing his eyes suspiciously. "What."

Joan raised an eyebrow. "What *what*?"

He said in an accusing monotone, "The way you're looking at me."

"I didn't realize I was looking at you in any sort of way. But since you're telepathic...a young girl by the name of September was in there. Let me guess when her birthday was."

"No, her grandmother was born in September and she named her. And she raised her. She was like her mum. Her mum was a hippie before they were called that. One of those free thinkers from the olden days. Her grandmother was like that, too, but not as bonkers. Not running around in togas and turbans trying to be Gandhi or Isadora Duncan, so much."

"Did you date long?"

"Her. She has kooties. I know it. We just snogged a little."

"She has what?"

"Kooties. I saw a little bug in her hair once. I bet she has little bugs all over her."

"Roderick Stuart! Are you sure that's fair?"

"I don't know. I don't know enough about kooties and little bugs and how much they can get all over your body. I just know I saw little bugs on her and I really got the creeps. If she told you that she saw little bugs on me then she's all wrong. They came from her. They jumped from her onto me. As many as could try. I tried to stay away from her, or at least shook my clothes out when we were done kissing—that's all I dared with her, and afterwards I gave her a breath mint. What did she say about me? How did she try to drag me down to her level?"

"Nothing." Joan lit a cigarette. "That's enough about her. I am *really* wondering about another young lady." She leaned forward in her back seat. "Is Vanessa from the flower shop your sister or something? You have the same last name."

"No. We just have the same blooming name. But we aren't related…that I know of. Why. Did you hear more gossip about it? It has nothing to do with me. Don't accuse me."

"I was reading about it in the paper. The paper even finds its way to the dressing rooms of film shoots. We try to stay informed even when shooting out on location."

"Sure."

Joan blew smoke off to the side. "What did you know of Vanessa? I'm very disturbed and am curious. I hope you don't mind my asking about her."

Roderick Stuart said, "It's a small enough village. We all know who everybody else is, for the most part. Especially people like Vanessa. You always knew where to find her…in the frigging flower shop."

"How long did she work there?"

"I don't know."

Joan raised an eyebrow. "Was she pretty?"

"Sure."

"Did she have a boyfriend?"

Roderick Stuart stiffened, and blurted, "I don't know anything about that. Diddle! Diddle! Why? *Why?*"

Joan Crawford slowly narrowed her eyes as she blew a thick lingering puff.

"You look suspicious! I didn't do anything! Don't look at me like that!"

"I didn't accuse you of anything so don't act so guilty." Joan became even more suspicious.

He grumbled under his breath, "You can't diddle me and diddle me and diddle me!"

"What was that?"

"You can't diddle me and diddle me and diddle me! And the studio will stay mine and I will sell it and make the money I need! I will make my money! My money! I will make my money! My money!"

Joan asked, "What is that all about?"

"It's my studio but you wouldn't understand. Never mind. But I really do need to borrow some money!"

Joan raised her voice. "Not another word!"

* * * * *

That evening in her hotel room, Joan looked out her tall window and saw the full moon. She changed padded bras, dressed into pink pajamas, posed in front of the dressing mirror for a moment to approve of her shapely figure, and then crawled under the bed's thick cozy floral duvet that almost matched the bold floral wallpaper. She wished her doggies were climbing all over her as she put her script over her lap. She grabbed a pencil. She looked close at it. It seemed yellow no. 2 pencils were a thing of the past, they all now had swirly psychedelic paint over them all. She opened her script to the front cast page and looked at the name of her costar, Michael Gough. She said to it, "It sounds like *Gawf*. I must remember that. I'm sure that when I said his name yesterday it sounded like *Goof* and I'm sure I was very rude. I must remember *Gawf*." She turned the pages until she was at the scene she would shoot in the morning. She put on her reading glasses. As she read aloud, she started knitting.

"In my orange dress with the two-tone candy-stripe collar, I say, 'Trog has been frozen all during the ice age, and has now come to life to teach us about the past, if we will study and learn. We know that under certain conditions life can survive many years while frozen. Sperm has been frozen for many years'…Then the good doctor walks away from the filing cabinet in Joan Crawford come-fuck-me pumps. I talk about sperm. How shocking. It really is going to be shocking no matter what. Well, sure, it's 1969, and it's in the context of science, anyway. The film will come out in 1970 and that date sounds so terribly modern. How scientific of Doctor Brockton to want to preserve some of Trog's sperm. If I preserve Trog's sperm then he can be studied by science many years after Michael Goof has killed him off. If I preserve his sperm we can have sequels. I must insist to Herman Cohen that Doctor Brockton be allowed to have sperm to study! I must think modern about all this! I must think sequels. All the exciting movies do that these days. A sequel started by sperm will be quite a gimmick to get the kid's attention."

Joan thought about that awhile with a grin on her face, and then continued reading her lines. "Trog can help us piece together the history of human behavior. In Trog's mind are secrets. Secrets of the origins of all animal development…and man's development. Secrets that can take us back millions of years. However difficult and however great the risks, we must try to unlock the secrets of this prehistoric mind.' And then Michael Goof says, because he's such a meanie, 'That is the opinion of a godless heathen!' And then I want to slap a good sound shaming Joan Crawford slap, but I respectfully say to him, 'What I say is the consensus of all educated belief. Nearly everyone accepts Darwinian theory that man evolved from lower animals like Trog. Give me a chance to study Trog and unlock the secrets in his mind. It is important to science.' And then Michael Goof says, although he is really Michael Goon, 'You shall also have murder on your hands and the mockery of the world! You will be to blame when Trog becomes uncontrollable for you. That horrible creature must be destroyed! Destroy it now before one of us is destroyed by it. It is wild and dangerous! The whole town is in peril! Your reckless research will be the end of all of us!"

The lights went out in the hotel room and it was pitch black. Joan put her knitting on her script and then held up her hand and couldn't see it. "Am I blind? Have I gone blind?" Lightning flashed outside and she could then tell that she hadn't suddenly gone blind.

She heard wind whistling through the windows and it sounded to her like it was saying, "*Murderrrr.*"

"Who's there?"

She thought she heard a woman crying.

There was a knock on the door. "Miss Crawford?"

"Come in and I hope you have a candle."

A hotel manager entered with a candle.

"Bless you."

He set it on the nightstand next to her.

"And please draw the drapes. The windows are whistling like something frightful. They're almost talking to me and saying all sorts of frightful things for a dark and stormy night."

"They don't leak air at all. They're all new windows. London Pane. They were put in six years ago."

"Nonsense. They're like sieves. It sounds like I'm in a haunted house. It sounds like they're saying *murder*. It sounds as if a ghost is crying for justice! *Murderrr*! It's horrifying!"

He tried not to glance at her as if she was crazy as he closed the curtains and left. The candle sputtered and almost went out. Joan held her hand out. She didn't feel any draft. She heard the windows shriek even louder but the gossamer curtains didn't budge.

She started to feel cold. She blew out the candle and slipped deep beneath the duvet and decided it was time to sleep. As she finally drifted off, the whistling wind turned into a woman's soft voice, repeating the word, "Murder." She wished her doggies were with her. Though tiny, they still made her feel safe from all the bumps in the night.

*****

In her dressing room, Joan threw six wire hangers onto the floor as she said to Frenchy, "How did these get in here?" She only traveled with canvas covered wooden hangers. She always had extra on hand. "These things should stay far away from actual clothes. These wire hangers will ruin the shoulder line in minutes and I can't afford that. My clothes are my uniform. Everybody's are. Don't people care what their shoulders look like? Everybody should."

Frenchy gave them dirty looks as they lay on the floor. "Look how long it took you to train your dry cleaners to never send you anything back on wire hangers. I don't think England has been so well trained by Joan Crawford."

Joan huffed, picked them back up and put them in the garbage. "They ruin the shoulder line. Everybody should know that. So, yeah, it's amazing how much work it took to keep them out of my house all those years." She sent all her clothes to the dry cleaners on her own wooden hangers and expected them to come back that way. "Is it asking the cleaners too much to take care of clothes? It isn't like they had to buy the wooden hangers. I supplied them all, for myself. Remember when I once had all those cards printed up that read 'no wire hangers' and I pinned them to everything I sent out. Finally I just had to call them up on the phone and yell at them in my finest crazy lady movie star voice '*no wire hangers, ever*' and that fixed things right away!" She chuckled. "Boy did I scare the kids that day."

"Nothing replaces powerful acting. When you played it nuts in *Straight Jacket* I guess all you had to do was think of the dry cleaners and there it came out of you."

"I thought about my mother and how much she only liked my brother. Sure she liked my money. She spent all that she could. I wouldn't even give it to her, she'd just tell the department stores that she was Joan Crawford's mother and to send me the bill. But the whole while she only liked him and she bought things for him too, with my money." Joan made fists. "That's what I thought about! My damn mother!"

"Then let's not think about it if it makes you so mad."

Joan took a deep breath and forced a smile. "I suppose I'll have to buy Bray Studios a whole set of wooden hangers to keep their costumes nice. It'll make a nice gift for the studio. I give gifts to all the people I work with but wouldn't it also be nice to give a gift to a studio, especially such a small impoverished one as this. Just because they're small and poor doesn't mean they *want* to look shoddy. They'll appreciate wooden hangers to keep their clothes nice. Hangers always get carried off, naturally. I wonder if a set of 300 will last long around here." Joan went to the phone book. "Where does one order a set of nice wooden hangers in this part of the world? I wonder how I can have 'a gift from Joan Crawford' stamped on each and every one."

Frenchy looked distressed. "Oh no. Don't do that to them. Then everybody would want one and they wouldn't last in the studio for a minute."

"You're right. It should be stamped on them 'Property of Bray Studios.'"

Chapter nine

A crown gathered in a large room in Down Place for a court scene. Before filming began Joan Crawford redid her lipstick and then walked around and greeted everybody and signed autographs. The manor house was not air conditioned so Joan had a Chinese fan always fluttering to try and keep her makeup fresh.

A woman asked, "How do you keep so fit and trim? You always look so healthy!"

"Bless you. I must put all that down in my next autobiography. I have many tips I would love to share with other women. I must try and explain my way of life. It's an extraordinary life but I think I have tips anyone can relate to." She wondered if she could just admit that the bottom line of any diet was to be deathly afraid of not always looking like a hard working movie star. If she even gained a little too much then Bette Davis would cackle about it, she just knew it, saying Joan didn't look like a movie star anymore. Joan would never give Bette a chance to gloat. That was her real diet secret: fear of ridicule from her enemies, fear of letting down her fans, fear of not being Joan Crawford anymore. "Bless you."

The last man she came to, to greet, was a constable standing against the wall. Joan patted him on the chest as she said, "Your uniform fits you so well. You look like a real police officer."

He smiled. "I am. I'm playing the constable and *I am* the constable. They asked me to do the part because I already had the clothes for it."

Joan rubbed the back of her hand against his badge. "That's sensible. That's charming that a lot of people from this village have parts in this movie. I think they asked you because you were the most handsome of all the police officers, er…constables. What's that say on your badge?" She squinted. She didn't have her glasses on.

"They just call me Bobby the Copper around here, for a chuckle."

"Bobby is a very nice name and nothing to laugh at. Bobby, tell me, I know you know so don't keep it to yourself, but do you really think Vanessa from the flower shop really actually committed suicide? Really?"

"That's all what it looks like. I shouldn't be talking about that, though. That's a private matter."

"But I'm Joan Crawford."

"Yes, ma'am. You are. And so all I can say is that there was the bottle of poison right there and it said it was poison so it isn't like she did it by accident. And…and right there on the very same table was a very incriminating letter as to why she would want to do herself in like that. It was shameful. So shameful for her."

Joan wrinkled her grand eyebrows together. "Shameful? What could be so shameful?" Joan raised her eyebrows. "Why? Was she a lesbian?"

He looked shocked. "How did you know? You psychic?"

She grinned proudly. "Some people think I am, Bobby, when it concerns my fans. But I also have been around the rodeo too many times. I know about things. And I know what lesbians are… otherwise known as Tallulah Bankhead. I always went to her parties. Everybody made sure they did. They were always the place to be, if you were anybody. Once I showed up with gold glitter in my hair. An hour later Tallulah popped out onto the balcony stark naked and she had gold glitter in her pubic hair and she yelled like only she can yell, '*Joan Crawford just went down on me!*' Everybody laughed so hard they almost died. I had to laugh because she was always such a card and she would do anything for a laugh. But Tallulah wouldn't do as well in a small town. I assume people in small towns keep things like that a secret."

He had red cheeks. "Our village isn't used to blooming parties like that. It was shocking to find out we had even one lesbian. Sure we know about them in London. But not in a quiet place like this."

Joan winked at him. "Lesbians are everywhere."

"I supposed I could have thought she was one. She wasn't married. The girls usually have their husbands picked out by their senior year in high school around here."

"Women are getting married later and later these modern times."

He suddenly looked panicked and went pale. "I forgot myself. I shouldn't have told this to anybody. Now the gossip will get out and they'll blame me and I'll lose my job. Loose lips sink ships! Please don't tell anybody she was a lesbian. A village like this needs its secrets. It's none of the village's business anyway. A constable should be professional and not blab about things like that anyway. I forgot myself. A film shoot is so exciting. It's so exciting to be chatting with Joan Crawford on the film set that I forgot myself!"

"Bobby, I won't tell your secrets if you promise to keep telling them to me. Don't worry about my spreading gossip like that in your lovely village. I don't think I'll be back to the beauty parlor. I'm a movie star. I don't even know anybody in the village. Well, I know you now but you're the constable." She rubbed the back of her hand across his badge again.

"Thank you, ma'am. You sure are cheery for having to wait so long for them to shoot the scene. You'd think they'd have the lights up before we even showed up."

Joan absently gesture at the lights. "It's easy to light an empty room. It's hard to light a room full of people. I find the conditions in England primitive compared to Hollywood but the film crews here are very hard working and professional. And so charming. I have no worry that I'll look great under the lighting here. British lighting is always gorgeous. Something I think they light things too bright in Hollywood. Nobody else in the world can equal how the British dress their sets, too. British set decoration is unrivaled. The attention to detail is most impressive! You should have seen my doctor's office. It looked like I had worked and lived in there for decades but it didn't look messy at all. It didn't seem like a set at all. British films always have such a marvelous look because of that attention to detail. British sets always look so smart."

He smiled proudly.

The director Freddie Frances walked up to them. "Would you take your place Miss Crawford so we can make sure your light is perfect?"

Joan grabbed Freddie's arm and kissed his cheek. "Bless you." She sat in her place and looked at the lights on their tall stands, understanding the effect they would have on her face. She drank a cup of her special throat tea, then stood and yelled, "Poppycock!" The director ran over and Joan said to him, "I'm not an ingénue!" With the back of her hand she slapped her neck just under her chin. "It's too hot under here!" She sat again and sternly sucked on a cigarette as the workmen scrambled to raise the lights to give her more of a shadow on her neck. When they finished she carefully pressed a powdery rose paper all over her nose to make sure it would have no shine.

When Freddie finally called order, she redid her lipstick. He called "*action*."

Joan Crawford recited her lines to defend the likes of Trog. "Trog can help us piece together the history of human behavior. In Trog's mind are secrets. Secrets of the origins of all animal development…and man's development. Secrets that can take us back millions of years. However difficult and however great the risks we must try to unlock the secrets of this prehistoric mind."

Costar Michael Gough carped, "That is the opinion of a godless heathen!"

Freddie yelled, "Cut!"

Joan complimented Michael on his forceful delivery, making sure she included that she was really God fearing and not heathen at all, that she loved England, the Queen, and that she was still considered a young actress. The crew changed the camera angle.

* * * * *

When they finished filming all the shots needed for the court scene, Joan grabbed the constable's sleeve. "Bobby! Do you have time to come to my dressing room? Or do you have to hurry out to write parking tickets? I bet you make so much money on the tourists to Windsor Castle."

"I have the whole day off."

"Come to my dressing room! I insist!" She grabbed him by his sleeve. He follower her in and after she gave him an ice cold Pepsi, she lit a cigarette and stood in front of an electric fan. She asked, "Tell me what that suicide letter said, I need to know."

He sat and sipped. "I can't tell you that."

"Bobby, I'm Joan Crawford and if I don't know then I'll not be able to sleep at night, wondering about what happened to that poor fan of mine, I mean, that poor girl."

"It has another woman's name in it. I can't tell you her name."

"Of course you will because I'll go visit her and comfort her and tell her I understand and tell her all about Tallulah Bankhead. What did the letter say?"

"All it said was, 'Miss Hill, I'm sorry that we can not get married and live happily ever after with our great lezbian love."

"That's all? Who's Miss Hill?"

"We don't know. There could be a hundred Miss Hills in England. And she might live in France. The odd thing was she spelled lesbian with a z. *Lezzzbian*. I would think she would know how to spell that."

Joan asked, "Are you sure it was her handwriting?"

"It was typed."

"It wasn't signed?"

"No."

"So how do you know she wrote it at all?"

"How many lesbians do you think this town has?"

Joan asked, "Do you really think a love letter would be to Miss Hill? Why wasn't her first name put down? Or a pet name? Why so formal? Are you all so formal? I thought everybody these days was informal."

He shook his head and looked blank.

"Has my driver, Roderick Stuart Winklehorn, ever been in trouble for drugs?"

"Why, has he been driving you off the road?"

"There's something shady about him. But I can't put my finger on it. What can you tell me about him?"

"He's never been charged with anything but they say the All Monster Film Festival he was involved with in London last year was a den of heroin. There were a few arrests and drugs found. But he got away before anybody could pin him with anything, and he came back home, here. Most people in the village just think he left London for his grandfather's funeral, here. That just happened a few months ago. They figured he chose to stay around after that. That's okay. It gives him a second chance. He seems to be doing okay, now, holding down a job, staying out of trouble so far. He's had such trouble in his life."

"He has?"

The constable nodded. "As a kid he was all a-cock. All mixed up. His father disappeared. His father had racehorse problems but nothing that got him in trouble with the law, but maybe the OC was after him…organized crime. And Roderick Stuart had mental problems as a kid. But I can't talk about that at all. Seriously. I'd get fired in a bloody heartbeat for discussing the case of a juvenile, at all. He's getting a second chance now…that's all I dare say." The constable looked uneasy and hurried out the door.

Alone, Joan said to the door that he'd walked out of, "Bless you." She fumbled at a collection of lipstick tubes and then swore when she couldn't decide on one. "Everybody's crazy!"

* * * * *

As Roderick Stuart drove Joan back to the hotel, she enjoyed the summer breeze blowing on her face from the open window, and enjoyed the smell of the countryside. Joan finally said, "I heard there was an All Monster Film Festival in London that you were involved in. I'm impressed with young people who get involved in promoting Hollywood abroad. I assume those were Hollywood films?"

Roderick Stuart made a haughty face. "Oh yeah, the Universal classics. Hollywood and British films are the best! The French films are awful. The French New Wave was such a pile of crap. *La Jetée* was nonsense. Pretentious. *Hiroshima Mon Amour* was worse. They keep saying we all have to bow down to Truffaut's *400 Blows* and Godard's, *Breathless*. I think it's all stuffy crap and needs snored at."

Joan nodded. "Hollywood and England is best. I agree. Films should entertain *and* inform. And they should look professional. Some of that art film looks merely amateurish and shoddy. That would be fine if they just *called* it a home movie and showed it in the basements of the homes of bohemians."

He added, "At the movie theater those kinds of movies only put us into an existential coma. There just wasn't enough there to be a real movie."

Joan added, "The emperor has no clothes. And the stars nowadays, too. And I heard there's a lot of hippies at those things?"

"Yeah, it bummed me out when near the end of *Frankenstein* everybody started to sing, 'All You need is Love.' Actually…it was kinda funny."

Joan raised her eyebrows. "And I heard there's lots of drugs at those things. I hope you don't get involved in that sort of business. It's not safe. And it only feels good until it ruins your life." Joan's tone got harder. "Don't let drugs ruin your life! A ruined life is no fun at all!"

It didn't seem like he wanted to talk about that. He said, instead, "The French don't even like their own movies. At the art theater there's always *Sunset Boulevard* and *Johnny Guitar* when they're not showing Jerry Lewis movies. I try to make it to France at least twice a year to see *Johnny Guitar*. That movie is really something and I can't get enough of it! I don't care much for westerns but I sure love that movie! Boy you sizzle in it! You make me so hot when you come down the stairs with your gun out and you tell everybody to sod off."

"Joan Crawford in pants." Joan rolled her eyes.

"It was great! You looked hot!"

"Bless you."

"Tell me all about it! Tell me about filming it! It's such a classic now! It's become such a cult classic! The next time I'm in France for it I want to be able to tell everybody what you told me about it. They'll let me be a special speaker if I can do that! So tell me about it. I beg you!"

Joan grinned. "Oh, bless you…it was marvelous fun. There was always half the town of Sedona there to watch. No matter where we went to film in the desert there was always a huge crowd wanting to see us film. They were such lovely people. So kind. In no time at all I felt like a neighbor and friend in town. My kids played with their kids. I gave birthday presents to those who had birthdays while I was there and we had so much fun with that. I danced with people so they could say they'd danced with Joan Crawford. I'll not be called *stuck up*…not at all costs! I brought cases of vodka with me and I always entertained everybody. I'm sure Joan Crawford was the biggest bar in town while we were there. We had big cowboy cookouts on open fires with everybody too. The kids all had such fun! We were far from Hollywood so I put the girls in blue jeans and let them get dirty. It's the best way to go camping!"

"Tell me about how you filmed it."

Joan took a deep breath. "I suppose nobody cares about family stuff. They just want to know about what they saw on the big screen. Well…let me think. We were mostly at Grasshopper Flats in Western Sedona. That's in Arizona. It seems like we were going out to the middle of nowhere to film. But it wasn't. Not only was there that nice town there and the lovely Old Cedar Hotel, but there already was a permanent cowboy town built there in 1946 for a John Wayne movie by Republic Studios. So the place was once famous for that. And now it's even more famous. Joan Crawford filmed there, too! The town was so thrilled and made it so exciting for me—huge crowds followed us everywhere we went. They did get in the way sometimes. Once I finished shooting a scene in the desert and I couldn't find my car anywhere and they needed me back for a costume change. I pushed my way through the crowd looking around until I just gave up, and so I hiked up my big white skirts and ran down the trail to my dressing room, instead. I always jogged to keep fit so that was no big deal but I'm just not used to doing it on a cow trail in a full puffy skirt. Poor Frenchy was running after me trying to keep up. And it was nighttime. And we didn't even have flashlights with us—that's what you call *torches*. But I could see—the trail was lit up by the light of the moon. When I ran off again back to the desert to shoot in my Levis and cowgirl shirt I told Frenchy to wait for a ride. She was so tuckered." Joan chuckled at the memory. "Once, so many people wanted my autograph and I'd just finished filming my scene swimming at the waterfall. It was icy cold and after we were done and I was trying to make my way to my car I did my best to autograph for everybody while my teeth were chattering and my hand was shaking." Joan shuddered at the memory. "The waterfall gateway to the secret hideout there was actually just a tunnel under a highway. The water all came from an irrigation ditch diverted from a farm. That was a lot of work to arrange and set up that waterfall."

"Fascinating. I never knew that. I thought that was a real waterfall."

"Uncanny, huh."

He asked, "Was it true you punched out Mercedes McCambridge a few times?"

"Heavens no! I should have. She deserved a few good slaps for her horrible rude behavior! And my co-star's wife threatened to slap me—she said so out loud! How dare she. Her husband was an actor and there he was in a Joan Crawford movie and she wasn't grateful. How does she think he pays her bills? Acting! If it wasn't for me he wouldn't have had that movie at all. And his character's name was Johnny Guitar and the movie is called *Johnny Guitar*! What more did she want? Didn't they both know it was really a Joan Crawford movie? They all fought to take the movie away from me. So all I got was rude behavior from her, too! She was damn mad at me, well too bad, I was damn mad at her! How dare she treat me like trash! Just because she didn't have to work for a living, just because she lived off her husband, didn't make her better than me!"

"What about Mercedes McCambridge? Boy they tell stories about you two."

Joan shook with emotion as the car bumped along the unpaved road. "I don't want to think about that damn rude bitch! She just thought everything was about her! She had absolutely no respect for me! That monster brat! Fuck her!" Joan fumed as she silently thought about the time she tossed all McCambridge's clothes out into the desert. Joan would have burned them all if it wouldn't have set the production schedule back. McCambridge had been extremely impolite and mocking to Joan during the whole shoot as if that was the normal way to treat a top Hollywood star. In the 1950s the word *Joan Crawford* meant *top Hollywood movie star*. McCambridge didn't respect Joan's accomplishments—she acted the way many teenagers treat their parents when they think they're so much better just because they're young, cool and new on the scene. Instead of being respectful to Joan Crawford for getting to be in a Joan Crawford movie at all, the whippersnapper acted as if she was the star of the show, still swollen-headed from all the awards she won for *All the King's Men.* She constantly antagonized the genuine star of the show. McCambridge wouldn't have even had the movie if it wasn't for Joan buying the film rights to the book before it was even published. Joan didn't expect it to ever be published or the film to ever be made. An old friend of hers who had once written some Tarzan scripts wrote the novel and needed money. Once Joan bought the film rights to it, he was able to use that to get it sold to a New

York publisher. Joan Crawford was a big powerful name. Then Republic wanted it because her name was on it. It took a long time to fashion the book into a screenplay and then Joan still finally had to steal some lines from other characters to make the role into a Joan Crawford movie.

Joan started to talk aloud to her driver again, "Nobody mentions the good things I do. A crewmember had a heart attack on the set. I sent for my own doctor to be flown in from Hollywood and I paid for everything. I did my own stunts but always kept my stunt double on hand so she would get fully paid everyday. I put up with all the crowds while I tried to film because I knew they'd just think I was mean or stuck up if I insisted they keep their distance. It isn't like live theater where people just know they're not supposed to all wander up on stage, they just pushed closer and closer. I worked damn hard on that movie to give every scene my very best for all of my fans the world over, working night and day in the desert! But everybody thinks I just want to hurt people. I only hurt those who go to war against Joan Crawford first—and Hollywood is full of upstarts all the time. They always want to pull you down so they can climb up your back. When I go to war I make sure I win! Nobody is going to pull down Joan Crawford! I'm not somebody else's stepping stone! I'm not somebody else's doormat! I am not yesterday's trash! I'm not to be scorned and thrown out like some expired cabbage! Everybody tried to take that movie away from me, treating me like I should be yesterday's news. Everybody wanted to use me. My costars tried to steal that movie out from under me and make me look like I was in a bit part for has-beens. They thought that because it was a western I wouldn't mind and would let it slide just this once…but I wasn't born yesterday! I showed them! I stayed on top in spite of all the dirty tricks!"

As he turned off the side road onto the highway, he asked her, "Can you still do stairs okay?"

"Of course!" Joan gasped. "I'm not an invalid! What a terrible question to ask Joan Crawford!"

"I remember last year I saw you in all the newspapers in a cast. You broke your leg? I just wondered if that was all better? We all talked about it at the All Monster Film Festival…"

"…talked that Joan Crawford was stoned and tripped since you were all so stoned? Did you all laugh about it? It was a simple accident in my own home." Joan took a deep breath and looked down at her long slim legs. She calmed. "Yes. I sprained my ankle last year. I'm fine now and I can do a dance number up and down stairs with Bo Jangles if need be, again. Bless you for caring. Bless the papers for all caring so much. I'm touched everybody was so concerned. Everyone was so kind." Joan thought about how she received piles and piles of get-well cards from fans from all over the world. She personally answered every one on Pepsi stationary.

Roderick Stuart said, "Yeah, it was big news, at least to those of us who knew who the real stars were."

"Why ask if I can do stairs?" Joan asked. "Where did that come from?"

"When do you want to see *the chosen*…my mummy? You have to go down stairs to see that. That's why I asked. I want to take you down to the secret room. When do you want to let me show you? I can show you how she can inspire our next great movie! Hammer's next great mummy movie…*Blood from the Mummy*, or whatever it will be called! The queen will walk again! She is *the chosen*…"

"*Our*?"

"I control Hammer Films. I know where the queen is hidden. She isn't just any prop mummy. She's real. She's many thousands of years old and brought back from Egypt. She's the queen of queens waiting to rise again. Hammer Films is mine! She will bring me great riches!"

Joan tried not to smirk. "Roderick Stuart, love, I'm sure I would love to see your monkey…I mean *mummy*. But not tonight."

"You don't want to. You think I'm making it up! You don't think the ancient queen could make a great horror movie for us."

"I don't do horror. I am a serious actress."

"Don't you want to make another horror movie? They're the best kind and you're so fantastic in them! You're so serious and dramatic and you make everything so suspenseful. You could play the archeologist! That part is usually played by a man but if you did it then nobody would think it wrong. Horror movies are my favorite, so much drama and suspense. Those are my favorite of yours, you do them like nobody else. I saw them all many times. I love *Straight Jacket* best. I love how you chopped their heads off with the axe. And nobody knew who cut the heads out of all the family photos. It was such a creepy movie and you looked great in it! You were so vicious with that axe! You really did it like you meant it!"

Joan finally chuckled.

He grinned big. "I loved the scene when you flirted with your daughter's boyfriend. He should have dumped her for you in a heartbeat. You had sass. You really gave me a boner. I wanted to come to you in your sleep and diddle you and diddle you and diddle you and tell you stories about princesses and castles and dragons until I got tired of diddling you." His cheeks turned red.

Joan grinned. "I tell you what. I don't have any *Trog* scenes for most of tomorrow. They're filming with others. I was hoping to tour Windsor Castle but I suppose that'll always be there. I can go another time. I met the queen and would like to see her castle someday, and now that I'm shooting right next door to it…"

"I can show you that, too. It's only right to first see *the chosen*…the greatest mummy queen of the world, and then the greatest castle in the world, before she rises and takes over the world and does it all from Windsor Castle. There should be time to see something of it, later. Not the whole place, of course. It's huge and it would take a month to see it all. I wonder if Queen Elizabeth has even seen it all. I wonder if she just walks around it all looking into all the rooms, just to see them because they're hers. I wonder if she loses track of what rooms she's seen yet and what rooms she needs to look into yet. There must be a thousand rooms. I hope we can see the Changing of the Guard. The Windsor Changing of the Guard is a far grander experience than the London version. Everybody is just a bunch of poseurs in London. At Windsor, the guard marches through the village. Once *the chosen* has been turned into the real queen again she should like to see the big castle. After thousands of years of rest she should like to see it very much! It's something the mummy queen should see!"

"Bless you. If I could just see the dollhouse that's there I'd be thrilled. I'm sure it would make me feel like a little girl again to see it. I hope I can arrange to take the child actress with us, too. It's always best to see a dollhouse with a little girl." Joan looked out the window, wondering why her driver sometimes had moments where he babbled on making absolutely no sense at all about his movie monsters. "You can pick me up first thing in the morning and take me to see your mummy. But I won't go if it's far. I don't want to get too far away from the studio. I'm not going into London tomorrow at all. I still want there to be time in the day to see something of the castle. I hope it's nice and cool inside."

"It's *in* the studio, the mummy, *the chosen*. It's in a secret room in the main house of the studio. And it's not a movie I'm thinking about. This is real. I've grown sick of shadows—shadows of sound and fury—a poor player—and then is heard no more. This isn't some prop either. It's real, it's thousands of years old and it's in one of the secret rooms of the old house, Down Place. It's in the basement. And there's stairs. It's under the main basement. The mummy has her own tomb. Stairs go under the stairs."

Joan shuddered. "That basement has a spell on it of some sort. Vincent Price and I were down there and…"

"Vincent Price? You saw Vincent Price? Man-oh-man! He's my very favorite! I love his Richard III, he was born to play that part! Man-oh-man! He's best when he makes movies about England!"

"Of course I saw Vincent Price! In my Hollywood swimming pool!" Joan thought about how everybody wore swimsuits that night but it was still so exciting. "And the other day I crossed paths with him again. Of course I saw Vincent Price. I'm Joan Crawford."

Roderick Stuart sounded very excited. "He's in town?"

"In a town nearby filming his own movie right now. And he stopped by to say *hi* and we walked around down in the basement together to look at all the antiques, and as I was saying, time acts very oddly down there."

"I know. It's the mummy. The mummy warps all time around her. But it's safe. Just don't wear a watch. It might break your watch. And it might crack your mirror."

Joan griped, "*Now* you warn us. Vincent's watch broke. It'll cost me a pretty penny to replace it but he should have a watch from Joan Crawford anyway. We poked our noses into many rooms but didn't see a mummy."

"It's not in a room you'd walk into if you don't know how. To get there I know all the secret rooms and passages. I know that place like the back of my hand. It's my real home. It's my studio. It's all mine!"

"Are you going to have a *mummy unwrapping*? I'm not sure I'm up to all that. And not on my account, anyway. Maybe for your young friends this Halloween?"

Roderick Stuart shook his head. "Oh no, we'll do nothing like that. The mummy is not to be diddled with…I mean…" He put his nose in the air. "…*violated*. We'll visit her as if we're the slaves. We're visiting the one and only queen who will reign forever and ever. Queen of queens. *The chosen*! And I'll read to you from a book that's there. It's a translation of the scrolls that were found with the mummy. It's in Latin."

"You can read Latin? I'm most impressed. There *is* a fine young man in there!" Joan smiled in relief and couldn't wait to hear him read to her in his fine voice. "That would be nice to see the studio like that. It's a date hidden away in the dark, Roderick Stuart. Do you dress up Egyptian for it? Do you paint your eyes and wear sandals and a little loin cloth?"

"No nothing like that. No diddling! No diddling!"

"It will be nice just to be read to. You have such a fine voice. So please talk to me the entire time, explain everything to me. I'm most interested in old traditional English hobbies. I'm impressed that a young man like you is keeping old traditions alive."

"So you'll come and see my mummy?"

She nodded. "I look forward to it. It will be nice and cool down there."

Chapter ten

That night when Joan walked into the hotel lobby a few people were waiting for autographs. She gladly signed them. Greeting fans cheered her up.

A young woman dallied behind. After everybody else had left, she approached Joan again. "I'm from London and may I interview you for my college paper? It's Bedford Women's College at the University of London."

"I'd be delighted." Joan sat at a couch in the lobby and when she saw that nobody else was looking, she quickly finished the flask in her purse. "I'm glad to see all you college kids aren't on drugs so much you can't still run a school paper. Or maybe women's colleges are more sensible."

The student sat next to her and asked, "Why didn't you play Scarlett O'Hara?"

Joan lit a cigarette. "Oh my. You go *way* back. I didn't play the part because nobody asked me."

"How come you haven't been in any Disney movies?"

Joan sucked hard on her cigarette. "Nobody asked me. Although Disney I were such friends. So I don't know why. He told me that he fashioned the queen from Snow White after me. I think that's hilarious. And we've worked together…with Pepsi. In 1964 there was a World's Fair. I asked my dear friend Walt Disney to have the Disneyland folks design a ride for it that Pepsi would sponsor. I was on the board of directors of Pepsi and I wanted it to stress a global theme since I was always taking Pepsi to the world—South America, Spain, West Germany and Africa. And since I loved dolls so much I asked that it be all about dolls. So I asked if it could be about all the children of the world and that it be all done up in hundreds and hundreds of dolls…every child's dream! I wanted it to be like a ride through a dollhouse. Disney and his team came up with the It's a Small World ride for me. I was so excited. They dropped the dollhouse idea because when you go into a large sized dollhouse it just looks like a regular house, again. But they made it a world of dolls of children—children all singing in all the beautiful languages of the world. When I presented it to the rest of the board they came up with all sorts of reasons not to do that. But I wanted it badly. Disney had already done all the work planning it! That board was so unappreciative of Disney! So I twisted all their arms to do it. They were so difficult. I finally just blew up and yelled, '*Don't fuck with me fellahs*!' They still dragged their feet but then finally decided to do it just because they didn't have anything else, so I don't know why they were being so difficult with me at all…men just don't appreciate dolls. I did *all* the work for them. I'm glad I won. The ride was the most successful one at that World's Fair. So the Disney people came in when the fair was over and boxed it all up and set it all back up again in Disneyland. It's a shame the ride no longer gives any credit to me or Pepsi for it…that's a shame. But I can see where Walt didn't want you to go to Disneyland to ride Joan Crawford." Joan winked sardonically.

"Are they always so mean to you—the people on the board of directors of Pepsi?"

"No. I shouldn't make it sound like they are. Bless them for what they did for me. After Al died, *Mr. Pepsi*, my last husband, I was flat broke. He was in such terrible debt from building up Pepsi to where it rivaled Coca-Cola so he finally borrowed all my money and before he could pay back a penny he dropped dead. So we had just literally cancelled each other out, and all for Pepsi. For a few months I had to borrow money from old Hollywood friends just to pay the mortgage and buy food. I scrambled to land a movie role and was so lucky to get a juicy part in *The Best of Everything* all filmed in New York. I wasn't on the board of directors, yet. So far, with Pepsi, I had just been the movie star who opened bottling plants all over the world for them. It was one gig at a time. That worked out great when Al was alive. But with him gone it wasn't a job anymore. Only Al had hired me. But then he died." Joan dabbed at both eyes. "Then I got lucky again as the board of directors felt sorry for me. They felt so bad that they finally voted to put me on the board. I was so surprised and thrilled…and grateful. I cried and cried for joy when I first learned what had happened on my behalf. I thanked them and thanked them. Joan Crawford is always grateful for the kindness and generosity of others. At first people made fun of Joan Crawford in a job like that, thinking I was in over my head, thinking only men could do that work, could be so bold. But I worked hard and learned business well. And I had my own ideas. I was always full of bold ideas for how to expand the Pepsi market. I was never afraid. I had an income again."

Joan smoked in silence as the woman wrote in her pad for a while. Joan thought about how her movies had gotten so spotty, maybe only one a year, and the pay from them less and less. She needed the steady income and perks Pepsi gave her. That caused some trouble over the years, working on the board of directors. Joan was not the president of Pepsi but everybody thought so. The president hated that. All the mail to the president's office, even the bills, were addressed, 'Joan Crawford President of Pepsi.' So the president was always plotting how to get rid of her, for his own ego. History would always be on Joan's side, though. No matter how successful he would be in crushing her, nobody would know his name.

Then the student said, "Wow you started something new!"

"A feud with an international corporation? Is that new?"

"Disney's top ride!"

Joan looked pleased. "Oh, yes, that. And that was not the first time I've done that. And I hope not the last. So much of what we get in show business is from luck. Sure you have to be ready, when your time comes, to back luck up with looks, talent, and hard work. But without luck you're out of the game entirely. I want to help others. I want to be that luck for somebody else as others have helped me and made me lucky."

"Who have you helped start?"

"I helped start Steven Spielberg. Look for his name. He's a new director. I worked very intensely with him on his first major project to make sure he looked perfect. First impressions are everything. His résumé is a Joan Crawford TV movie—it doesn't get any better than that. I have connections, you bet. And I helped start Fred Astaire. You already know him, of course. I started him off in style. He danced with me in his first movie. It was a very big movie, a Joan Crawford movie when I was on top, when my stardom alone was financing most of MGM. Clark Gable was financing MGM, then, too, and he was in the same movie. *Dancing Lady*. It was 1933 and it was MGM's biggest release of the year. Fred was my dance partner during an entire big long dance number at the end. It was the most important dance number. It was the grand finale of the film and it had to top everything. After that, everybody asked about who he was. The rest is history."

"Fred Astaire could do that, for sure, dance real good!"

"I'm glad I danced with him first, that I chose him. We could have used somebody who was already famous. It was MGM's biggest movie of the year. Or we could have used somebody else who was also unknown. We weren't stuck with Fred—he was a nobody. Back then Hollywood was full of people tap dancing down all the streets trying to get noticed. There were many great dancers around not getting star parts. There weren't enough star parts for everybody. We could have used somebody more attractive. Fred looked funny in a Laurel and Hardy sort of way, but nothing distracting. The producers didn't like him and they fought me but I thought he was special. He was good and he was adorable. It was fun to gamble on an unusual unknown talent and then see him rise to the very top of stardom. He might not have gotten another chance if I didn't put him in my movie. I wasn't able to provide another opportunity like that, after that, for anymore unknown dancers. Hollywood is not fair. Life isn't fair."

The student asked, "Do you think this movie you're making now is going to be a good movie?"

Joan's face tightened. "I think it is. It's about science. Topics of science have become very popular in serious films now and I hope it inspires the young people who go to see it to become interested in scientific study. All college students should see it, certainly. I think this film will be another example where Joan Crawford can say she had another positive influence on the world. We need more good in the world. I hope that after people see this movie they'll have a conversation about history and what makes humans so special in it. I hope the answer is love and kindness."

"Thank you Joan Crawford. I'm sure I have enough for a nice article in the paper."

"Please be kind in choosing a photo."

"Since it's a college paper, and since I have so much here, I don't think I want to use a photo. It takes up too much space, I want it all to be your words."

Joan stood up and shook her hand. "Bless you. I *really do* appreciate being taken seriously!" Joan walked her to the front door to see her out and then went to the stairs.

When Joan got to her hotel room she poured a drink then opened the windows to let the cool night air in, and watch distant lights glisten off the Thames. She did her leg exercises that the doctor told her to do to keep her ankles strong. She crab-walked around the room. She had recently fallen over a sheet in her apartment that she had put down for a cleaning project. Her bedroom slipper caught on it wrong and she was unbalanced, holding a cigarette in one hand and a bucket of water in the other. She refused to let go of either as she went down. That put her in a big plaster leg cast for a while. She had sprained her ankle several times in her life. When she was small she cut her foot badly and the doctor said she'd never walk normal again. She marched back and forth until her limp went away. And then she took up dancing. Dancing was what had first brought her to New York and then Hollywood. She won all the dance contests in the 1920s. When she had recently been on the Lucy Show they were to have a longer dance number but just as Joan learned it, Lucy changed it, cutting it much shorter. The dance number was all to be a homage to the 1920s. "Damn you Lucy robot bitch! Dirty pool!"

Even though Lucille Ball had annoyed Joan into anger they were really two peas in a pod. Lucy had also toiled to keep working and had great business success beyond acting. Lucy was the first woman to own and run a major Hollywood film studio, Desilu. "Desilu" was taken from a combination of "Desi", her husband, and "Lucy". The company started in 1950, grew, and eventually bought

RKO Studios and in 1957 had a few more sound stages than Metro-Goldwyn-Mayer and Twentieth Century-Fox.

Lucy was mostly just the artistic side of things until 1962 when Desi Arnaz quit as president and sold his holdings to Lucy, so she became the one who called all the shots. This made her the first woman to head a major studio, and so, the most powerful woman in Hollywood at that time. Lucy was "President and Chief Executive Officer of Desilu", while also starring in her own weekly series. Those were two huge full time jobs. Eventually tiring of the stress, in 1967 Lucy sold the company to Gulf+Western, which merged it with its film studio, Paramount Pictures, that was just literally next door, anyway, and renamed it Paramount Television.

Desilu's six TV series in production in 1967 were *Mission: Impossible*, *I Spy*, *Mannix*, *The Andy Griffith Show*, *The Lucy Show* and *Star Trek*. Those shows then changed later into Paramount productions after the buyout. In 1966, *Star Trek* and *Mission Impossible* were Desilu's first hour-long dramas. Until then, Lucy had been producing half hour comedy shows to great success. She was warned that she would fail with *Star Trek* and *Mission Impossible*—they were just too different for her and the studio. But Lucy reluctantly gave the green light, and even let Barbara Bain be in *Mission Impossible* even though Lucy didn't like her. But Barbara Bain's husband was Martin Landau who was in the show and Lucy liked him and had a soft spot for husbands and wives acting together. Barbara Bain would go on to win several Emmys for that role, which certainly shut Lucy up.

As Joan thought about Lucy's wild successes she swore she must work harder as she sat on the floor with her legs straight out before her and did her exercises that kept her butt fit—she walked forward and backward across the floor just using her left and right butt muscles. "Lucy, damn you, my butt's going to be better than your butt! I have Pepsi. I have something too! I have things too! I'm a success too!" She decided she needed to do more.

After a half hour of wiggling across the floor, Joan did some jumping jacks, did some stretch moves and then fell onto the bed. Catching her breath, sucking on a cigarette, she thought she heard wind. She jumped up, made another drink and went to the window. She heard wind moaning but didn't see the curtains move. She put her hand up and didn't feel anything. She noticed her cigarette smoke didn't appear caught in a draft. She grabbed the phone book and flipped through it. She called the Spiritualist Society.

An old woman answered. "Hello? This is the Helen Duncan of Windsor Castle Spiritualist Society."

Joan asked, "Are you Helen Duncan?"

"No, this is Mary Winklehorn. Helen Duncan has passed on…she was a famous Scottish spiritualist and our society is named after her. We admire her work. Are you interesting in joining our society?"

"No, I can't do that. I'm only in town a few weeks. Only in England a few weeks. This is Joan Crawford and I'm filming a movie at Bray Studios now."

"Joan Crawford is calling me? Joan Crawford? Oh my God! I was doing my tarot cards just now and they suggested to me I'd get a delightful surprise, and here *you* call! Do I win a Pepsi prize? But I forgot to answer saying *Pepsi Please*."

"No I'm calling you about something else. Something about the society."

"I thought you sounded like Joan Crawford. I just knew it! I could only hope. And what's that tinkling sound? Do I hear bells? Are you Buddhist?"

"Bless you. And, no, that's my ice cubes making that sound, sorry. My ice in my Pepsi. I drink Pepsi, of course. You say your name is Winklehorn? Are you related to Vanessa?"

"No, not by any recent family tree. It's a common name in town. There's even a road here by that name. It goes through Winklefield."

"I love the names of places in England. It all feels so rich with history and tradition. Sometimes it just seems downright magical. Hollywood was named after holly bushes. They planted them to try and dress the place up a bit, back when it was just a real estate scheme. The bushes died right away but they pretended they hadn't, painted them green, and kept the name anyway. That's Hollywood. British names are better."

"Miss Crawford, where are you calling from? How can *I* help you?"

Joan took a deep breath. "I've a question. If a Jewish woman killed herself with poison, but it might be murder, can she still be contacted from beyond the grave? Can we ask her if she was murdered?"

"You're speaking of Vanessa! You think she was murdered? Why?"

"I have...reasons. Do you believe in ghosts?"

Mary gave a chuckle. "Love, this is a spiritualist society. Yes, yes I do."

"Can I ask you to have a séance for Vanessa? Just to ask her."

"We were already planning one. You may join the séance if you'd like, since you have such an interest, and you're Joan Crawford and I'd be so thrilled to meet you. But otherwise we are a closed group. But I would love to help you in any way that I can. You helped me so much in my life."

Joan asked how.

"Your movie *Susan and God*. I saw that at a time in my life when I really needed to see that. I had become just like Susan in all the wrong ways. You really opened my eyes...and my heart."

"I am honored."

"So please come but please don't bring any friends with you. We are not the evening fun and games."

"So you think she was murdered, too? You want to ask her what happened, too?"

Mary explained, "She was a member of our spiritualist society. Now that she's died we're curious if she wants to talk to us. We'll certainly ask her if she was murdered...if that's what you want to ask."

"She was a member? But she was a Jew."

"Her mother was a Jew and she remained one herself but she also explored other spiritualities. She was a devoted member of our group."

"Oh, that's a surprise. I suppose I don't know as much about spiritualism as I thought I had."

Mary asked, "Do you have anything against Jews?"

"Hell no. I'm Joan Crawford. I'm a product of Hollywood. Hollywood is a creation of the Jews. They're hardworking people. They turned the desert sand into movie tinsel...America's biggest dreams. They told America stories about itself. What stories would America have about itself without Hollywood movies? I should call myself a Jew, today, just out of gratitude for the movie star life I've had. I am always full of gratitude. My real father was a Jew, if you consider the head of MGM my real father. I do. But that might be going too far. People don't usually choose their religion that way.

Vanessa was a Jew because her mother was a Jew, I was a Roman Catholic because my mother was a Roman Catholic."

"I hope you weren't offended that I asked. I just wanted to make sure. We can't do a séance with negative vibrations."

Joan shook her head as she said into the phone, "Not offended at all."

"When we have a séance we want it to involve positive people, people who are positive to all aspects of the dear departed. It has a greater chance of success, then."

"I completely understand. Can I bring my driver, John Winklehorn? Otherwise he'd just be alone in the car whistling Dixie."

"He's already a member of our society."

"He is? Are you all named Winklehorn?"

Mary said, "Just one other in the group is. It's a common name in town."

"Are you sure this'll work?" Joan asked. "Are you sure Vanessa will appear to us all? I'm very busy and if nothing is going to happen I probably should be doing something else."

"We can't guarantee results. Only the fakes with hidden bells and projectors can promise to give you something to hear and see on cue. In spite of the law that is against us, we insist we are genuine. But don't tell anybody I said that. I don't want to get in trouble with the law again."

"What? You're doing something against the law?"

"To be legal we can only call this entertainment. The courts passed the Fraudulent Mediums Act of 1951. That prohibits a person from claiming to be a true Spiritualist. It forbids any money to be made from...*the deception*."

Joan gasped. "The cops can raid our séance?"

"They won't bother, because if they do then we'll just tell them that it was all for entertainment purposes only. *That's* what is legal. For entertainment purposes only. As long as the room is rented and refreshments are provided then we can say the money that was donated that night was to cover those costs, only. If the cops come we can say it was all about you—we were entertaining a Hollywood movie star with our eccentric village fun and games...if you don't mind."

"Bless you for blaming me. I'd be so honored. How mean of them to pass a law like that against you all!"

Mary chuckled. "Actually this law is an improvement on the law before it. This law gives us all the wiggle room we need to still function. We can always call ourselves *entertainment* in a pinch. Otherwise there was the Witchcraft Act of 1735 that insisted we were all to be punished as vagrants and con artists no matter what."

Joan suddenly realized that laws in an ancient land must go back a long ways and so might get weird on occasion. "Gotcha. Do you meet in Windsor Castle? I know where that is. It's the first thing they showed me on the way to Bray Studios. What door do I use? There's a lot of doors there! There must be a thousand!"

"No, they don't rent rooms like that, there, we use that place in our name because it's the most important place in town. It's one of the most important places in the nation. We're so proud that we live in Windsor. We meet in Old Warf Cottage across the river from Old Windsor. It's on Friary Road just north of Wharf Road. Your driver knows it, of course, so no need to write this down. You'll enjoy visiting just to see the cottage. It's a very large thatched cottage built to look medieval but was built in the Edwardian era, influenced by the Arts and Craft Movement. We're very proud of that, too, even though we're just renting. We're proud of having such a building in our town."

"England has such treasures of quality. Hollywood was built with things like that, castles and medieval cottages…but in stucco. They were already crumbling by the end of the 1930s."

Mary said, "Our next meeting is this Saturday night. Your driver knows all about it so if you have other questions until then he'll probably be able to answer them."

"Bless you. And please always serve Pepsi at your gatherings." Joan realized she was sounding too much like a Pepsi commercial again, so she added, "And if Bella Lugosi shows up I'm going to scream like Faye Wray."

"Me too, love!"

Joan gave a husky laugh and hung up, then she looked out her tall window and saw the full moon peeking out of thick rolling clouds. She shivered as she dressed into her pink pajamas, then crawled under the bed's thick cozy floral duvet. She put her script over her lap and started knitting.

"Once upon a midnight dreary, while I pondered, weak and weary…while I nodded, nearly napping, suddenly there came a tapping, as of someone gently rapping, rapping at my second floor window."

She opened her script to the next scene she would shoot. "That's not what it says!" She laughed, she had been reciting Poe, sort of.

She started to knit and nodded off. She had a dream that she was in the cemetery and she turned away from the fresh grave of Vanessa. She started to walk back toward the gate, her flashlight lighting up the ground at her feet. A cold mist blew over her face. She raised her light to see a billowing fog roll in around her. It felt as cold as ice. Joan shivered and thought she felt a finger on her shoulder. She turned. A woman in black was suddenly standing beside the grave as if she had stepped out of the fog. Joan couldn't see the woman's face. She tried to point her flashlight directly at it but she couldn't get it to show up. Joan called out, "Hello?"

The woman didn't say anything.

"Hello? Are you a friend of Vanessa?" Joan turned around and called out to the driver. "Where are you? We're not alone." A strong wind blew on Joan and the fog blew away. "Hurry! A terrible storm is coming!"

Joan jolted awake with the horrible realization that that wasn't just a weird dream—that had really happened. She really had seen a ghost in a cemetery at night. She heard a feminine voice at her side whisper, "Thank you." It was so soft she wondered if she'd really heard it at all. Joan slipped deep under her duvet and shivered.

Chapter eleven

The next morning, Roderick Stuart drove Joan back to Bray Studios. She was prepared for old dark house adventures, her hair prudently hidden behind a scarf in case she should stagger into dirty dusty cobwebs.

He asked, "Did you have a magical dream last night?"

Joan lowered her eyebrows. "Why would you ask me that?"

He said, "The stars and planets are now in a magical alignment. Today is a day for stronger magic yet. This is a perfect day to see the mummy. Are you ready for your magical mystery tour?"

As they pulled up to Bray, a thick fog was rolling up from the Thames. The buildings were grey shapes. Joan commented, "Everyday is like Halloween in England."

In the side door of Down Place, Joan said, "Let me just check my dressing room for any messages before we go down." Once in the room, the phone rang. Joan answered it. It was Gloria Swanson. Joan said, "How did you know I was here?"

"I had a premonition. And the hotel told me you were here."

"They told you where I was? They shouldn't do that, for my privacy."

"I told them I was Gloria Swanson. Anyway, I had such a premonition. I had a dream Cecil B. De Mille was going to film in Egypt again."

Joan turned to Roderick Stuart and wildly gestured for him to wait for her outside the door.

Gloria continued, "And I was holding John the Baptist's head on my lap the whole time as he planned it, on a platter. But he was going to make *Cleopatra*. Dreams get things so mixed up!"

"Egypt? Interesting. I'm about to see a real live mummy."

"Alive?"

"A dead one, but a real one, you know what I mean. Maybe your dream had something to do with that?"

Gloria gasped. "It was a premonition!"

"Or…you're just thinking about Cecil again. I understand why you miss him, so. He was as good as your papa when you were still just a kid, like Mayor was a papa to me."

Roderick Stuart stuck his head in the door to ask if she was coming.

Joan snapped at him, "Shop talk!" She gestured him away again and continued on the phone. "Your dream of a Cleopatra remake is fascinating but isn't the Twentieth Century Fox remake big enough?"

"Poor Elizabeth Taylor." Gloria snorted. "She couldn't even ride in the backseat of the limo without having a drunk accident. The driver stopped and she fell off the seat onto the floor and needed a hospital visit for that, even. What did she do, try to poke her eye out on the way down? That takes talent. You're a much better drunk."

Joan gasped. "I beg your pardon?"

"You are a functioning drunk. You can drink and walk. You don't have accidents. Well, except there was just that one last year when you tripped on your own floor. Were you drinking? Well of course you were. You were awake. How does Liz get insured with the way she slurps and tumbles. They won't put up with that forever, you know. Maybe they already have closed her down. Her films aren't what they used to be."

Joan decided to change the topic a bit. "They were testing Joan Collins to play Cleopatra. I wonder how much cheaper the film would have been if they'd done it with her all on the studio back lot? Then the film would have made a good profit."

"She would do. She's a poor man's Elizabeth Taylor but at least it would get done on time on budget. Can you imagine a film taking that many years and at that cost?"

Joan said, "And like Elizabeth I can imagine Joan Collins as a Lady Macbeth. Good thing they followed the Shakespeare script and made her the Lady Macbeth of Egypt."

"Cleopatra is Lady Macbeth?"

"Sure. She pushed her men too hard. She brought out the monster in them, the monster in all of us. We all could become Macbeth if we let ourselves go—if we let everything fall out of control. It's a thrilling story. Not like that George Bernard Shaw Vivian Leigh *Cleopatra* that's just *Pygmalion* all over again. *Pooh*!"

Gloria asked, "Who taught you your Shakespeare?"

"My first husband. And my second husband, too. Franchot Tone called me Lady Macbeth sometimes when I pushed him too hard. I always pushed him too hard. I was just more ambitious than he was. But no matter how hard I pushed for myself I didn't get the expensive movies. I was the one with the cheap movies that made all the profits for MGM. Me and Clark Gable made all the money for MGM. And Judy, too."

"Yeah, and I paid for Paramount," Gloria said. "And Frankenstein paid for Universal!"

"We paid for Hollywood, you and I, and that Frankenstein. They couldn't let us go, not for one minute. There was a time where we were making three movies a year plus all that promotion."

Gloria grew annoyed. "We were the geese that laid them golden eggs and they almost killed us to get more and more, always pushing it, pushing their luck. Yeah, Judy Garland got the worse wear and tear."

Joan nodded furiously. "They were always sniffing up our skirts to make sure we weren't pregnant. And if we were they made sure we got the operation right away before we wasted them a minute." Joan didn't want to think about what MGM's secret backroom operating room put her through, so she only thought about how Gloria's abortion almost killed her, and all to keep the career going. Finally Gloria invented the rubber girdle so she could keep her next pregnancy a secret until she could have that baby after the shooting was all over.

Gloria quickly added, sounding shrill, as if she wanted to change the painful topic, "And the mummy! Boris Karloff paid for Universal. And Lon Chaney Jr.!"

Joan nodded as if that could be seen on the telephone. "He was the king of them all. Nobody played so many different monsters as Lon Chaney Jr. He was supposed to have played Quasimodo in the remake of *The Hunchback* but lost it out to Laughton in the end. Then he would have played even more monsters. It's a shame they didn't ask him to play the part of Trog. That kind of part is right up his alley these days. They say his voice is going and he isn't well. Is that true? He still does several pictures a year. How does he do it? What have you heard?"

Gloria moaned. "Oh Joan, it's serious. He's drunk his life away. They say he has terrible throat cancer. Yes, if Trog doesn't have too many lines then that part would be good for him."

Joan sucked fretfully on her cigarette. "Trog doesn't talk at all. As dinosaurs don't talk. And he doesn't have any scenes out on the moors like I do so they wouldn't have had to rent him his own trailer. He wouldn't have cost that much. I would have given him my salary. I'm only here making this movie to keep the juices flowing, and keep Herman Cohen going. If we all pull together we all just might get somewhere. It's always good to work."

Gloria added, "And they say Lon can't shoot any scenes after noon. He's too drunk to move. Sometimes they just let him sit in the corner on the set as he drinks. He gets so drunk he can only move enough muscles to sip. He's very behaved when he drinks—a pickled kitten. Did you see when he was on TV playing the Frankenstein monster? At the end he had all those break-away props and doors to smash up but he was so drunk he just couldn't bring himself to do it. He ruined the whole show. At the end the monster just walks around and pretends at things, mumbling things like, 'I'll have to break this later,' as if that bothers him."

"Yes, I heard about that. Everybody talked about that. Poor man. That's a shame he's in such terrible shape. It's a shame he doesn't have more self-control. Men. It's a shame Lon can't be here so I could help nurse him between shots. I'd make him dilute his booze with Pepsi, as everybody else does. He'd have made a perfect trog and the film poster could have bragged that he plays yet one more famous monster in his great monster career. When I get back to New York I'll make phone calls and make sure he sees the best doctors. When they make a sequel to *Trog* I'll make sure he gets the part. He's so famous for monster sequels it'll get such good press. Any producer will love it! We all owe people like him a great deal. There would be no Hollywood if you and me and people like him didn't bring in all that money for the studios to spend on everybody else."

Gloria said, "I once had a crowd so big gather for me that they threw flowers at my car. The top was down. In no time the car filled up with so many flowers I couldn't even sit down. I was buried in a mountain of flowers on wheels. It was thrilling!"

"My fan club is the biggest and always was but then I made that one of my full time jobs. Fans want stars who care right back. Us winners also paid for the losers, and the fat cats in the banks, and just those many other nice stars who didn't get so big who didn't have box office. We were a team. Hollywood was such a company town. I better go. I'd love to see Boris Karloff or Lon Chaney Jr., they're both so gentle and kind and charming. But I'm going to see a real mummy. A real one. Isn't that a change of pace for a star to ever see something real, to see something that wasn't wheeled out of the prop department?" She chuckled. "This one's very old. It isn't spray painted to look very old."

"Sounds dusty. And be careful, Joan. I had a dream about an Egyptian movie for a reason. We have dreams for a reason. Dreams tell us things. Sometimes they have to scream at us because we just forget all about them the second we wake up. For most of them anyway. And you weren't even in it but I thought of you immediately and I just had to call you to tell you all about it."

"Bless you." Joan waved at the door. "I have to go now anyway or my tour guide might find something better to do other than show Joan Crawford a good time."

"You're also going to have sex?"

"Gloria, you have such a dirty mind. Of course not. Unless he proves to be unbelievably romantic and charming and lusty and forceful. But I doubt that. He's so moody, really. And full of self doubt."

"He's queer as a bed bug?"

"No. I think that went out with DDT. He's not homosexual either, I don't think. He's just a typical nutcase, I think. Typical of boys his age. No worse than my boy, different, but no worse. At least this one doesn't slug me every time he comes within arm's reach of me. Boys are hard on the nerves, and the whole body. Oh, he's right here and he hears me talking about him. I must go or he'll think I'm the one who's rude." She hung up. "Coming, coming, coming, hold your horses!"

Joan redid her lipstick, poured a drink in her large Pepsi glass, and then an impatient Roderick Stuart took her to the basement. They both held hurricane lanterns. He had a bag of his provisions; she had her purse clamped under her arm under her armpit, her hands full since she took her drink with her—ice cubes clinking in it as she walked. "I hope this ice isn't taking up too much room. I hope we aren't gone long."

He said, "I heard you talking about Lon Chaney Jr. You knew him, too? Wow, man. He's my very favorite! All those monster movies!"

"Of course I know him. I worked with his father. Hollywood was a company town and I saw him at all the parties. He was always a peach. So handsome and kind."

"Wow. Man-oh-man!"

Along the way through the basement, he showed her several rooms and items of interest, impressing her with his knowledge of some of the old film equipment that was broken and discarded, waiting for spare parts and spare time.

He asked, "Tell me more about Lon Chaney Jr. He's so cool! He's one of my favorites. Oh the many monsters he's played. You knew everybody!"

"He's a very nice man. He's a very hard-working man, sick with cancer and still making several pictures a year. When he dies I hope Hollywood gives him a great tomb. I hope it's surrounded with statues of all the monsters he's played to make Hollywood rich. Hollywood needs to do a lot more to honor those of us that made it rich."

"Wow! He's so cool! Did you ever shag?"

"Bite your tongue!"

"Wouldn't it be cool to diddle a movie monster?"

"A what?"

"By a werewolf!"

Joan stomped her foot. "Enough of this vulgar nonsense!"

"Just trying to chat a bit along the way."

"We can only pray the conversation improves." Joan nudged him with her elbow. "There's a fine young man in there when you want to be." She looked around. "Are there any Egyptian antiques down here left over from *The Mummy's Shroud*? I hear Bray Studios became a museum in Egypt for that movie."

"They would have sent those back years ago now."

"You're not taking me to some old prop from that movie?"

"No way. This is all mine." On a wall he pressed a spot on it. The wall panel flipped out and he walked through the opening. Joan followed. At a landing, he put his hand out cautiously. "Watch your step. There's a drop off if you don't turn. No railing. Find the steps."

"Oh, it's so nice down here," Joan commented on the cool temperature. They went down another set of narrow stairs that ran alongside a secret room. In the middle of it was a stone coffin. "Oh shiver me timbers!"

He pointed at it. "See? I'm not just a silly dreamer. I don't just live in movies that I make up in my head. I don't just live in shadows on the screen. I'm making my dreams come true in the real world!"

Joan nodded as if she was impressed, and then said so. He placed his lamp on one table along one wall and she put hers on a table along the opposite wall. Then he took six red candles out of his bag, lit them, and set three at each lamp. She put down her drink and lit a cigarette with one of the candles. When he gave it a dirty look, she gave an extra puff and said, "It smells so old in here. I'm just freshening the room up a bit with some fresh smoke. Unless you brought incense."

He opened another door. Joan stepped to it and saw it led to a tunnel. Her cigarette smoke sucked into it. "Where does this lead?"

"The river. I bet we're actually below the water level of the river right now."

"Water can come crashing in?"

He shrugged ignorance then grabbed a green jasper stone on a string. He handed it to Joan. "Put it on around your neck. It must be over your heart."

Joan looked at it closely. She blew on it a couple of times. "Old things always look so dirty, don't they? What is this? Village fun and games? What are we doing? A séance?"

Roderick Stuart referred to the green jasper stone. "It's an Ab, or Heart Amulet. It was buried with the queen. The heart is the center of all knowledge and spirit."

"Not the brain?" She put it on.

He shook his head *no*. He took a tall jar from a side table and waved it around him. It had a dog-like animal head on top of its lid. "The canopic. The jar holding the heart and liver, the center of all thought and soul. Protected by God Duamutef."

Joan looked at the tiny hieroglyphic carvings on her green necklace stone. "Is this all that was buried with her?"

He put the canopic jar back on its table and told Joan, "Put it down. You don't need to look at it. Keep it down against your heart. There were thousands of jewels buried with her. The most important weren't made from the most precious of stones. All that's left now are the two pieces that are *really* important…those that will help complete the magic circuit…and complete the ancient spell."

Joan didn't see any other jewelry lying about. The coffin lid was bare. "Two?"

"I sent the ankh on ahead to the queen."

"Queen Elizabeth? You sent it to her in the mail?"

"She must have it, she must hold it when the stars align and the magic circle then comes complete."

Joan asked, "What makes you think Queen Elizabeth will hold an old ankh at the time you wish? It must be in a big pile of mail right now. A secretary probably hasn't gotten to it yet. Unless she is as efficient with her mail as I am. And even then, what makes you think the Queen of England would keep it with her? She must have so many nice things sent to her."

"It's magic. She will feel compelled to hold it at the right time. Nothing will stop it. The queen will be moved by the queen!"

Joan proceeded to explain how she gets all her mail processed quickly and orderly, until he interrupted her and then with brief directives she helped him slide the thin stone lid off the coffin and set it out of the way. A waft of rotting but sweet odor blew at them from within. He moved the six candles in closer, setting them on the edge of the coffin.

Joan peered inside and wrinkled up her nose. "England is not a good climate to keep mummies. I thought you said she was in a time warp, or something." The flesh and cloth had all but rotted away. The mummy was a brown fuzzy skeleton that had collapsed and was only a few inches high along the bottom of the coffin. Even the skull had fallen apart where it lay.

Roderick Stuart pointed at it. "The distortion in time has been enough to keep her with us long enough. Just enough. A year more and she'd be gone from us forever. See the hands?"

Joan moved closer. "No."

"Right there. On the left hand is six fingers."

"Are you sure? It's a bit of a mess down there. A dead raccoon could be down there in with all that and I wouldn't even be able to tell. Sad that it can't be all cleaned up somehow. But then I guess that's just the nature of mummies."

"Do you see the chain and bracelets? It's not gold. It's a strong metal. This cannot be taken off of her. Her hands are chained down to her sides. Her hands are kept from reaching out into this life. Her hands are kept from touching. And killing."

"She?" Joan nervously touched her own neck. "Are you sure? How can you really tell, anymore? How can you even tell it's a woman?"

"Queen Kera."

"You know her name?"

He pulled a slim book from a cabinet at the head of the coffin. "It's all written here. Written by hand. Somebody translated everything into here in Latin." He opened it up and rested it on the edge of the head of the coffin. He instructed Joan to stand at the feet, then said, "This first part is from the Ani Papyrus, one of the Books of the Dead, the most ancient holy collection of books. This chapter is the most important part of all of them. It's the spell to give the deceased a voice when they rise again. They must regain their voice so they can speak." He let the book rest on the coffin as he took a chisel and placed it where the mouth probably would have been on the mummy before it fell apart so badly.

He left it there and then picked up a Y shaped sistrum from a side table. It was small bells on rods between two angled sticks. They joined in one stick at the bottom to make the handle. He shook it and then put it down. Then he read from the book, translating it into English as he read, "I have risen forth from the eternal egg which is in the secret land. May my mouth be given to me that I may speak wherewith before the One Great God, the Lord of the Otherworld. Hail to thee, Lord of Brightness, He who is head of the Temple Above, the Lord of Twilight. I have come unto thee. I am glorious. I am pure. My arms are about me. Give unto me my mouth that I may speak therewith. Guide my mouth with my heart in its seasons of flame and night."

Joan closed her eyes and put her fingertips against the foot of the coffin to steady herself as she listened, loving the sound of his warm voice as he read this ancient poetry just for her.

"I shall ride the Solar Boat until I wake up in contentment in the Lake of Lilies. I shall not putrefy. My intestines shall not perish. I shall not suffer injury. My eye shall not decay. My ear shall not become deaf. My tongue shall not fall away. No evil defect shall fall upon me to wither me."

Joan opened one eye and regarded the bones. "Are you sure?"

He continued, "I, Queen Kera, Jewel of the Six Stars and Jewel of the Eternal River, shall rise again when the stars and waters bring me forth from their eternal womb where I never died but only rested waiting for eternal awakening, like a star plucked from the night sky like a jewel and returned to the earth like a seed. I will awaken when my soul meets the One Who is Waiting. The One Who is Queen and Still Lives. It is the Time of the Gods and Goddesses. It is the Time of Queens. It is time again for Queen Kera. The One Who…"

Joan interrupted him. "Is that a heartbeat I hear?"

He nodded. "She lives!"

Joan looked up at the cobweb covered ceiling. "Maybe it's just the pipes."

"It's her heart! The heart of her soul! She lives!"

Joan started to see swirling patterns before her eyes that was like the psychedelic paint on her No. 2 pencil. "It sounds angry!" Joan blew out the candles on her side of the coffin, walked to her lamp and picked it up. "I'm getting frightened now, and dizzy. I started to smell roses and my ears started to buzz. And those heartbeats! I felt something pull on my heart! I hope it was just my imagination. Time to leave. Drive me back to my hotel." She took her Heart Amulet off from around her neck and left it on the foot of the coffin.

"But…but. The soul transference hasn't happened yet. Queen Kera hasn't entered the body of a living queen yet, to live again. The fit offering has not been taken."

"That all sounds very rude. I'm not ever going to be Queen Kera. I am Joan Crawford and there's no room for anybody else in here." She thumped her own belly. "It's a tiny body."

Roderick Stuart stamped his foot. "Queen Kera will strangle you now with her six fingered hand!"

"Queen Kera is dead. If *you* try to strangle me I'll put your eyes out. Don't think I won't. I know how to fight—I've had husbands."

He put his hands up in the air. "*I* will not touch you. The mummy's curse is not from me."

Joan impatiently rolled her grand eyes. "You've watched too many horror movies. Drive me home or I'll just ask somebody upstairs now in the studio to do it, and they'll wonder what's wrong with you that you can't do it. Coming?" She went up the stairs toward the trick panel in the wall

He slumped. "Coming."

* * * * *

Outside on the lawn between Down Place and the car, a bizarre churning shadow passed over Joan. She shivered and felt as if she was in a tomb—she suddenly felt such despairing cold. She looked up and saw a swarm of bees passing between her and the sun. Then she couldn't breathe. She grabbed her throat and choked.

Looking terrified, Stuart grabbed her and carried her to the car. He sped to the village doctor. After the doctor gave her several injections she saw Disney's cartoon skeletons dancing around her. When Judy Garland and Gene Kelly started square dancing with them she realized she was dreaming. In real life, Disney and MGM would never do anything together. In disgust she walked out of the room into the Egyptian desert.

She walked up to a cliff and entered a cave. Inside was a great tomb. A bell rang. She loved the echo so she struck a grand *Torch Song* dance pose and loudly sang, "*All mortals who live on the boundless earth, Thracians, Greeks and Barbarians, all express your fair name, a name greatly honored among all, but each speaks in his own language in his own land. The Syrians call you Astarte, Artemis, Nanaia. The Lycian tribes call you Leto the Lady. The*

Thracians also name you Mother of the gods and the Greeks call you Hera of the Great Throne, Aphrodite, Hestia the Goodly, Rhea and Demeter. But the Egyptians call you mighty Isis because they know that you, being one, are all other goddesses invoked by the races of men. Mighty one, I shall not cease to sing of your great power, deathless savior, many-named, mightiest Isis. Hear my prayers, oh one whose name has great power to forgive. Prove yourself merciful to me and free me from all distress!"

Then Joan stopped singing to notice Queen Kera sitting within the tomb on a bench made of solid gold. Joan said, "So you thought you'd kill me with a swarm of bees? Maybe in your time you could have pulled off that kind of nasty shenanigan but that doesn't work like that anymore in modern times."

The Egyptian queen said, "The bees weren't sent to kill anybody. The bees were merely sent away. I cannot abide by bees. Honey is poisonous to the dead. They had to go."

"But...my throat!" Joan said. "I was surely stung!"

"Stung? No, strangled. I strangled you with my own bare hands!" She held up her deformed six fingered hand. "How dare you ruin the spell to let me come back again!" The queen bared her vampire fangs. "I will finish you off."

"Oh, so that's who you really are, in the end. So that's the game you want to play!" Joan walked up to her, knocked her tall fancy Egyptian hat off, and grabbed her by her hair. "How dare *you*!" Joan dragged her kicking and screaming to the mouth of the cave and out into the sun. As its hot holy rays hit her, the undead queen burned away into smoke and ashes.

Joan woke up. "Where am I? Am I dead?" Joan's hand shot out, fumbling at the air for her purse. "Where's my lipstick? How do I look? Am I okay?" Joan glanced about to see if cameras were aimed at her. She saw none and was relieved, thinking of a line she said in her 1952 movie *Sudden Fear* where she almost was killed, "I haven't even got my lipstick on! A woman has to wear lipstick. I'd feel positively naked without it!"

A nurse smiled down on her. "You're okay. You were just stung by a bee and you had an allergic reaction. And in your sleep you sang an entire hymn to Isis. Rather loudly. It was remarkable. Did you once do a screen test for *Cleopatra*?"

Joan looked at her, puzzled, feeling itchy.

"You sang very nicely...for somebody knocked out."

"I don't understand. I would've made a marvelous Cleopatra. I can play parts with such depth and changes in emotion. I'd have made her so sympathetic, a real Lady Macbeth. But I didn't ever screen test for anything like that. That was Paramount that did that movie. I wonder why Cecil didn't use Gloria Swanson. She sooo needed a comeback in 1934. And she's weird—in a good way—you would have believed she was the queen of Egypt. And I don't know anything about any songs to Isis. I have no idea what you're talking about. Why am I talking about this? Why am I talking so fast?"

"Oh. Well that was the most amazing allergic reaction. We thought you'd die but the stimulants seem to have brought you back just fine."

"How do you know it was a bee? A bee? How do you know?"

"Because your driver said there were bees swarming at the time you fell ill and you couldn't breathe. And so the doctor gave you an antidote. And then he gave you a tranquilizer. And then some stimulants. And it seems to have all worked just fine. So that must have been what it was. A bee."

"Yes it has. I can breathe. Look at me! I can breathe in the whole room! Is my driver still here? I wonder if he wants to dance with me? I mean…"

The nurse shook her head. "He left. We sent him off since you should stay, at least until morning."

"How can I get back to my hotel? I'd like to go to bed but I feel so oddly awake. Where's my driver? I wonder if he wants to take me to bed…I mean. Not that! I don't know. And I must leave. I shouldn't be here. I don't pay taxes here to pay for British healthcare so I'm really in your way. I do a lot of charities in America for healthcare since most Americans can't afford it and do without. It upsets me. I promise I'll donate children's books. I do that all the time. Oh damn, and I was going to go see Winsor Castle this afternoon. But I'm too late now. But I'm not sure. What did I just say? Why do I feel like I need to tap dance? Did you know Lucy is a robot bitch? She cut my dance number! Why am I talking about Lucille Ball? How many stimulants did you give me?"

"We can arrange a ride for you to your hotel, Miss Crawford. You can rest there, and it's nearby incase you need our help again. We'll call somebody from the hotel to pick you up and keep an eye on you there. Then you will feel more comfortable and that's what's most important for you now. Maybe you need another tranquilizer."

"Bless you. But just get me back to my bed at the hotel."
"You tired?"
"I feel a crazy urge to jump on my bed like a little girl!"

Chapter twelve

On the way back to the hotel, Joan changed her mind, so told the driver, "Take me to Bray Studios. I've decided I need to go there first. And on the way, could you drive by Windsor Castle so I can at least get a look at it, again?"

"Easy peasy."

To Joan's delight, when the car came near the sprawling Bagshot Heath stone castle that covered thirteen acres, the Changing of the Guard went by. A deafening full regimental band accompanied by a hundred soldiers paraded up High Street and headed back into the castle main gate, stopping all traffic. When they had all passed, Joan applauded, tears in her eyes. "I can now say I saw the Changing of the Guard! And I didn't even have to stand around for it!" Then inside her head she heard a boy's choir in a vast cathedral singing *God Save The Queen*. She shuddered. She suddenly had a horrible feeling that the queen was in grave danger. She imagined Queen Elizabeth fighting to hold on to her very soul! She hoped the queen wasn't holding the ankh he'd sent her. "Hurry to the studio! Step on it!"

Traffic remained stopped by a follow-up parade—war protestors. Many dour looking people held large signs that read, "British Counsel for Peace in Vietnam."

Joan commented, "Those hippies look so much nicer than the ones we have in America." Many of them looked middle aged and very conventional.

The driver said, "They're usually doing this at the American embassy. They must have wanted a change of scenery." When the last of the protestors were gone he pulled ahead.

Joan got out of the car at the studio and ordered the driver to return to the hotel without her. She entered the basement of Down Place, lighting her way with her silver cigarette lighter, and pushed her way through the secret panel into the hidden room beneath the basement. The mummy was still exposed—the coffin lid had not been put back on yet. Joan lit the candles. She poured the fluid from the two hurricane lamps onto the mummy. She tossed in all six burning candles.

"Burn, you wicked witch! You're no longer a queen. Your war is over! The queen is the queen! You're through! Leave us, in this time and place! Leave us alone! Queen Kera! It's time to move your Ka Ka. *I mean* Ka! Your soul must move on! Let the astral beings who have died before you intercede for you and guide you into eternity. Let them take your Ka away from here where it no longer belongs. Your earthly body is done with! Be a Ka!"

She wished Gloria Swanson was here to help her move the lady's Ka along, as she watched the bones burn. She added the book of the Latin translation of the Egyptian spells to the fire, to help keep the flames going. She noticed the room was filling with smoke. She opened the door that led to the river and the smoke sucked into the tunnel.

Roderick Stuart ran into the basement room. "*Man*! What are you doing? Oh no! *Fuck*!"

Joan stood proudly. "Enough of this! It had to be destroyed for all time."

He swore at her.

Joan stiffened her posture even more. "This was dangerous. Don't play with mummies!"

"But...but the soul transference. Now Queen Kera is dead forever and ever!"

Joan nodded. "As it should be when you die. And a soul transference with who? The queen for a queen? I may very well have just saved Queen Elizabeth from your horrible childish pranks!"

He pointed at Joan. "*You* were the queen to be the new Queen Kera!"

"Make up your mind, I'm only a movie queen. I'm sure this ancient Egyptian queen would have wanted at the real thing...if a soul transference can really happen. I'll have to ask Gloria Swanson about this. I wonder how much danger you put Queen Elizabeth in! That poor woman!"

Roderick Stuart began to weep. "My mummy! That's a great thanks for my saving your life. You burn up my mummy!"

Joan slapped his face. "You reckless fool! You wouldn't have needed to save my life if you hadn't risked it with your frightening warlock show! They say I was stung by a bee. I wonder, now. I think this bitch tried to strangle me! Who knows what Queen Elizabeth just felt! For all we know she just tripped over one of her corgis and she's laying at the bottom of the stairs now with her head on backwards! We have to check to make sure the queen is okay! I can't wait to see the morning paper!"

They saw a spinning sparkling purple flame that looked like a belly dancer, for a moment, within the other orange flames. Roderick Stuart pointed, "Look! She's making fists! Queen Kera is alive!"

Joan didn't see it. "All I see is an old mess." After the fire burned out, Joan began to scoop up the ashes and dump them into the canopic jar holding the heart and liver.

"What are you doing?"

Joan looked him up and down. "We're going punting down the Thames. You do know how?"

"Of course."

Joan raised her chin. "We're giving her a final burial in the river. It'll be dignified enough. I know she's used to more, being a queen…but too damn bad."

With a vase full of ashes, they walked out the front of Down Place where exteriors of the first Hammer mummy movie had been filmed in 1959. They preceded to the riverbank that lay just a stone's throw before it. He took Joan's hand and helped her step into the wooden boat, staring in alarm at her high heels, calling out warnings.

"One of these days I'm going to kill myself with these heels, but they do act like a ramrod up my spine. When I don't wear heels I feel so slouchy. I don't feel like Joan Crawford."

"Yeah, yeah. Just sit down before you fall into the drink."

"In this designer dress? Not on your life."

As Roderick Stuart punted down the Thames by pushing against the riverbed with a pole while standing near the back of the flat-bottomed boat, Joan sat in the front at the square-cut bow. After she redid her lipstick she silently spooned ashes into the water. She asked, "Is there any good Shakespeare for a moment like this? It's a Shakespeare moment, don't you think?"

"Let's talk of graves, of worms, of epitaphs…make dust our paper. And with rainy eyes write sorrow on the bosom of the earth. For God's sake let us sit upon the ground and tell sad stories about the death of kings." Then Roderick Stuart began to sing words far more ancient, so ancient the author was long forgotten, *"The river of*

Khemet is empty and men cross over the waters on foot. The sky will no longer be of a single wind. Chaos reigns."

"You have a lovely singing voice!"

"*A foreign bird will be born in the waters of the delta having made its nest on the bones of the people. A foreign bird will sing and the bones will not know the song.*" He stopped singing to say, "You have to pull your hair out, too, while you're doing that."

Joan paused. "I beg your pardon? Pull my what out?"

"To show you're sad. It's what the women do. The queen is dead. You must pull out your hair in grief."

"Joan Crawford does not pull her hair out."

"Show how sad you are or else we'll both be cursed."

Joan selected one hair and gave it a tug. She tossed it into the water. "We don't want that."

He continued to sing, "*Foes are in the West. The foreign bird shall hatch many eggs. Their tongues will be like serpents, pretending to speak in the language of the Nile. Sleep shall be banished from mine eyes and I will lay there and say how awake I am in the dry desert that once was the waters of all the earth. All will be made dust as they eat our land.*"

When the canopic jar was empty, Joan said, "That was an interesting song for the occasion. Something you learned in school? Is that from the Bible?"

"It's from the Khemetian Book of the Dead."

Joan lowered her eyebrows. "How frightful. Was it about dead evil queens and their curses turning all the lands to dust, just because we didn't let them rise and take over again?"

"I don't think so. I think that back in its day it was just mainly about how much they hated the Libyans."

Joan complimented him again on his warm singing voice, then looked deep into the jar. "Where's her heart and liver? Oh well, it must have become powder, too, and it's all in the river now. She has become the river." Joan tossed the jar into the water and watched it sink out of sight. For a moment she was sure she saw the bed of the river as a carpet of underwater crocodiles, watching and waiting to surface and attack. She jolted. The boat rocked. Joan grabbed on. "Roderick Stuart stop that!"

"I'm not doing that!"

"Stop it anyway. You're really spooking me. You have such a contagious imagination! I was hoping to imagine we were looking like a Pre-Raphaelite painting out here like this on the river, not a clown show!" The boat calmed again.

"You're just not used to funerals."

"Nonsense. I'm getting good at this by now, spooning ashes into the water. I just put the ashes of my dear second husband Franchot Tone to rest forever in Lake Muskoka in Canada. That was his true home, not Hollywood. Hollywood was terrible to him. That lake was very good to him." Tears welled up in Joan's eyes. "That was just last year. It seems like just yesterday we were both so very young. We stayed close friends our whole lives. Never let divorce ruin your life. Never let a divorce leave you with hard feelings. Stay friends. Don't run from your mistakes just learn from them. The more personal the mistake the more you can learn. That's what mistakes are. Lessons. I've had a lot of life lessons." Then on her orders he took her back to the hotel by car, even though the hotel was on the same river and he wanted to continue by boat. On the last stretch of road to the hotel they saw fire trucks pass them.

Roderick Stuart wondered aloud what the trucks had been up to.

As Joan entered the hotel lobby the desk clerk ran to her as soon as he spotted her. "Miss Crawford! Oh Miss Crawford! I'm so sorry but we had to move all your things to a new room. All forty pieces of luggage have been moved. There was a fire on your bed! Most mysterious. The duvet is ruined and it might take a few days to get all the smell of smoke completely out of the room so we moved you to a new room. We're so sorry. Most mysterious that fire was!"

Joan shuddered. "I'm not superstitious. It wasn't mysterious at all. It has to have a logical explanation. I'm sure it was just a cigarette I left on the bed. It must have fallen from an ashtray. There must be a logical explanation. I'll pay for it all. Add it to my bill. It's certainly all my fault."

"Miss Crawford, no need to get so upset. The hotel's fire insurance will take care of it. And only a duvet was ruined. It was the oddest fire. Odd that duvets burn that way…with a spinning sparkling purple flame that looked like a belly dancer for a moment, within the other orange flames. And the ashes ended up looking just like a skeleton. It was the oddest thing."

Joan was shown to her new room. After she rearranged her luggage to her liking, she sat on the bed and took a swig of her vodka then spotted the black Egyptian cat sculpture on a small table. It was staring at her. It loudly furiously hissed. Joan rang up the main desk. "Please remove the antique Egyptian cat from my room. I don't know why you brought that over with my luggage."

He insisted that they hadn't.

When Joan looked back at the cat it wasn't there anymore. There was just a black vase on the table. She let out a sob. "I must be hallucinating. It's not here at all. I've just been at the doctor's office and I was shot up full of tranquilizers and stimulants and god knows what else. I must have just imagined it."

"We'll bring you tea, Miss Crawford. That will make you as right as rain."

"Bless you. And call me *Joanie*. We're practically old friends by now."

* * * * *

That night, Joan entered Old Warf Cottage wearing a fur-trimmed turban-shaped hat and a sleeveless mini-dress covered in an ankle-length gossamer yellow vest. She carried a glossy orange purse containing glasses, pencil and pad, cigarettes, matches, a silver cigarette lighter, toothpicks, many lipsticks, tissues, rose papers, a cross necklace, her earrings, and two flasks of vodka. She wore round wide-rimmed sunglasses even though it was night so she wouldn't have to put the eyelashes on again. When she saw a few cameras she turned away from them and quickly redid her lips to gloss them up then pressed a small sheet of rose paper against her nose so that it wouldn't shine. She turned and smiled, ignoring the flashbulbs, holding still or stiffly hugging others until everyone was happy that they got all the snapshots they wanted.

Joan regarded the meticulous pink and yellow floral wallpaper, wondering how it would clash with her outfit. "Sorry I'm so late but I decided to change at the last minute when I realized I had looked like I did for the *Rosemary's Baby* premiere. What a faux pas…I'm pretty sure. The devil has nothing to do with what we're doing here." She crossed herself.

Mary asked, "Where's your driver? Roderick has a book he owes me. He couldn't even come in to give me that while he's here?" She went to the door and watched the car pull away. "Bastard."

"He said he couldn't make it tonight," Joan said. "He must still be sore at me for burning up his mummy. And I mean an Egyptian mummy, not his mom. Don't ask. Long story. He said he'll only be away for an hour. I told him an hour was plenty of time. He's not going to be involved in the séance tonight. He said everybody would just talk about him. And he mumbled other things that made no sense to me about diddling and diddling and diddling."

Mary frowned. "I know. He quit the club. He just called me up, cursed me out, and that was that. He must be sore at all of us. So we won't have him back…maybe ever again."

Joan furrowed her brows sadly. "He must be upset. Vanessa must have been important to him in a way the rest of us don't understand. Maybe you can talk to him about it later and he'll become all the closer to you all for it. He seems like such a nice young man…sometimes. Don't let him burn this bridge, for his sake. He needs to belong to something nice."

Mary nodded to Joan to humor her then turned and instructed everybody, "Stay in the foyer, for now. We must take all flash photos with the movie star outside the room that we'll have our séance in. No flash lights where it'll disturb the ectoplasm."

Joan said, "Trog doesn't like flash lights, either. Flash photos. It makes him aggressive. Does the ectoplasm become aggressive too?"

Mary explained, "Ectoplasm disappears quickly in the presence of any sort of light, even a flash of it. So the curtains must be drawn so lightning can't even harm it. We dare only use one candle, to see. The famous Scottish medium, Helen Duncan, was killed that way. She was in a trance and journalists started taking pictures of her. The ectoplasm vanished so quickly back into her that it burned her. After her death, soon after, burns were found all over her belly. If a ghost or glowing bubbles or phantasmal shapes do appear it'll be in the form of ectoplasm that is extracted from all of us who are participating in the séance. It'll come out of us slowly and must be given just as much time to return after we're all done. Hasty ectoplasm isn't safe."

After a few more last minute flash photos were taken with the movie star they walked into a dank library room featuring a massive brown globe of Earth on an ornate pole. Joan noticed that there was no room for wallpaper. The bookshelves went to the ceiling, the top shelves accessed by a ladder on a track and wheels. She regarded a long narrow black table in the center that could easily seat ten. At one end of the table was a full windowpane sized sheet of glass. On the other side of the glass was painted the alphabet, and *yes* and *no*.

An empty wine glass sat on it. Spotting it, Joan licked her lips and resituated her purse in her hands. She looked around for a bar. She excused herself to the bathroom and drank some of her vodka.

Joan returned and sat at the table at the other end from Mary, who was at the end with the alphabet on glass. Even though it was dark with only one candle lit near Mary's end, and the photo taking was finished, Joan kept her sunglasses on. She didn't want anybody to see her without all her eye makeup and become disappointed that she didn't really look like a star. She looked over and under her glasses long enough to search out an ashtray. She frowned when she didn't see one anywhere in the room.

They began. After introducing everybody again, Mary said, "This is a time of great astrological alignment. Planets are now in the tightest five-body longitude in over 700 years. There's a full moon and there's the Grand Cross. That's the alignment with the sun opposite the moon, and Uranus opposite Neptune. They make a perfect cross and a square. The planet is in the middle of the cross and is penned in by the square…and so we're very safe."

A man next to Mary asked, "What does that mean for us?"

Mary said, "The soul grows longing. We revisit our own past lives and learn from them about who we are today. We find old things that have been lost and forgotten. The soul remembers past mistakes. We discover the whereabouts of stolen goods. The soul finds lost energy. We dream at night that we're flying. We see the future. The soul is free. We're closer to the spirits who are dead and haven't reincarnated, yet. It's a good time to get into the stock market." Mary slowly turned the wine glass upside-down over the alphabet letters. She lightly touched both fingertips to it at the stem. "Now it makes a vessel for our plasma, if this is how Vanessa chooses to speak with us. It's hard for the dead to speak but this makes it possible." She said to the two sitting next to her, "Touch my elbows." To everyone else she said, "Take each other's hands. We must make a circle of power. All of our isolated pools of internal ectoplasm must become one. Together united we're a greater power and it must not be broken."

Joan tossed her lighter into her purse and took the hands of those sitting next to her as she wondered how she would light up a cigarette while holding hands like this. She had used her open purse as an ashtray in emergencies, before.

"Everybody concentrate," Mary said. "Listen to the words I say, and ask what I ask." Mary called out into the room, "Vanessa, can you hear me? We're asking that you visit with us."

In the silence that followed, Joan thought about how she was dying for a cigarette. As Mary called out more and more and nothing was happening, Joan wondered if she should just ask them all to take a cigarette break. Joan became sure that Vanessa would be happy with that. Joan told herself that since everybody smoked these days certainly Vanessa did too, no matter how young she might be, and that maybe Joan could have a cigarette now for Vanessa, and then maybe it would help Vanessa cooperate. She wondered how she would interrupt Mary and change the plans and not sound rude. She decided she needed a cigarette enough that it didn't matter if it seemed rude or not.

Mary called out, "Move the glass to *yes* if you can hear me."

They waited in silence. Joan was about to let go of the hands beside her and pull her cigarettes out of her purse when she decided that would make her seem like she wasn't concentrating enough on their group effort. So Joan blurted, "Knock!" She finally decided it was safe to declare a cigarette break since nothing was going to happen.

They heard a knock.

Mary called out, "Knock two times if you hear me!"

They waited in silence.

Joan impatiently called out, "Knock two times if you hear Joan Crawford!"

They heard two knocks.

Joan shivered, suddenly getting the heebie-jeebies. "Why do you respond to *me*?"

They waited in silence.

Mary told Joan, "Ask her to knock two times if she is responding to only you, for a reason."

Joan asked Mary, "Would Vanessa mind if I have a cigarette? Vanessa do you mind? I'll blow some smoke your way."

Mary looked irritated. "Later! You must not let go of anybody's hands. You must not break the circle."

Joan took a deep breath and called out, "Knock two times if you're responding to only me, for a reason."

They heard two knocks.

Joan called out, "If you were murdered, knock two times!"

They heard two knocks.

Joan called out, "Can you spell the name of your murderer?"

There was silence and the wine glass did not move.

Joan looked about. "Where are you knocking from?"

They heard a knock. Joan looked up. A piece of the plaster ceiling fell down that was the size of a dinner plate. As it crashed to the table it smashed the wine glass and sheet of alphabet glass. The candle knocked over and went out. Everybody jumped up, knocking chairs back. In the dark, while Joan backed away from the table she dug into her purse and lit a cigarette. Mary said, "Thank you, love, for the light." Joan sucked on her cigarette as she rushed to the candle and relit it. Mary cautioned, "Don't let there be too much light! That's too much light!"

Joan closed her lighter so there was only the one flame again. Joan said, looking up at the hole, "That's terrible!"

"That was amazing." Mary shuddered.

Joan nodded. "Yes, it was. But what did it mean?"

Mary said, "It means we made contact. It means there are spirits that can hear us."

"I thought you already believed that." Joan yelled out, "Knock three times if you're trying to tell us more!"

More of the ceiling fell down hitting a bald man on the head. He fell backwards out of his chair. When the men next to him helped him back up he had blood dripping down his face. They helped him out of the room and to the bathroom.

Joan yelled, "What does this mean? Knock if this has meaning!"

Nothing more happened. Mary said, "We broke the circle."

Joan said to those who remained, "Hurry, everybody, hold hands again!"

Mary shook her head. "We *really* broke the circle."

Joan went to the front door to look out into the night, and sucked on her cigarette. When Mary joined her, Joan said, "I wonder if Vanessa wanted to tell us more and the ceiling breaking was just an accident on her part. Maybe she didn't mean to knock so hard. But the blood! The blood! Seeing it run down the front of his face like that was so…so ghastly! What does that mean?"

"I hope he'll be okay." Mary sadly shrugged. "We'll never know about Vanessa until we try another time. But for now we're too rattled. We need a break. Another night. My heart is still racing!

That poor man! I'm sure his heart is racing, too. We need to be calm to try it again."

Joan looked at the red lipstick on her cigarette. "Will that poor man be okay?"

Mary nodded. "I think he will. He just got a few small cuts on his head."

"Oh? Is that all it was? At first, from where I was standing I thought blood was dripping on him from the ceiling as some horrible sign. I thought the whole house was bleeding!"

"No, he was cut."

Joan made herself laugh. "I thought it looked like some silly horror movie. It scared me to death!" Joan showed Mary her hand. A few fingers were still shaking. "I was terrified. I wasn't expecting the room to drip blood. And of course it didn't. But still. I hope he's going to be okay!"

"That would have been even more incredible if the room dripped blood, too. Part of the ceiling dropping on cue was bad enough! Vanessa may have found some weakness in the plaster."

Joan threw her cigarette out the door. It landed in the driveway—a glowing red dot in the dark. "Damn, my drive isn't back yet." Joan wearily sat in a chair near the door as Mary continued watching down the driveway. Joan asked Mary, "Is he on drugs? I know that all young people these days are, but...but he seems odd and I can't put my finger on it."

Mary said, "I'm not sad that he left the spiritualist society, I have to admit."

"He didn't believe?" Joan redid her lipstick. "He is full of self doubts. Always brooding and full of worry. He's so morbid. If he was an actor he'd make an excellent Hamlet."

"He believed all right, but he also believed it was merely a movie...he was always in a monster movie. He believed that we were all shadows of sound and fury from God's projection bulb, the movie screen being the only material reality. He believed the movie he was in was always being edited and was full of bad acting and fake sets. He thought that special effects would be spliced in later. If he didn't see a ghost and he wanted to, he just said it would be spliced in later after it was photographed again through a soft filter so that it looked just right, and the editing would put it in as a double exposure. He told us all to pretend to see things so it would be easier to edit it in and look real. He would get very technical about it. He's dreamy and lost. He thinks the world goes blank at the end of time when God breaks—that's when the projector bulb burns out. He never fully recovered."

Joan asked, "Recovered?"

"He was in the mental ward for a short while. After he went three years without talking, as a boy. Maybe between the ages of eleven to fourteen, or so, he clammed up and nobody heard him say a thing except for a few times he only said, 'diddle diddle diddle,' in a most infantile way. His father tried to beat some sense into him but that didn't work. His father said he would not have a weird boy, and beat him within an inch of his life to try to fix him. One day his father disappeared. We still have no idea what happened to him. If it was gambling debts then why not sell the racehorses? He had a whole barn of racehorses and they were on a losing streak. All those were sold off anyway. The family fell on hard times after he left. Or was bumped off—there were probably debts to the mafia. Roderick Stuart took that badly, too."

"The poor boy! To be abandoned!"

"In those days Roderick Stuart spent most of his time on the back lot of Bray Studios stomping about like he was a monster. A boy Frankenstein monster, or something. It's natural for boys to play what they're seeing in the movies, but with him also not talking, that was very odd. He gave us all the creeps."

Joan asked, "Did the hospital help him?"

"They gave him shock treatments and it seemed to make him talk properly again. He called himself *Monster*, for a while. He wouldn't respond to us unless we addressed him *Monster*. He seemed to outgrow that but he's always been nervous since then."

"The poor boy."

Mary frowned. "And I'm sure he's even more disturbed now that Vanessa is dead."

"He told me he didn't know her enough to know those things about her."

"What? Your driver is her cousin. I think. I'm pretty sure of it. They're cousins although their ages are so different."

Joan furrowed her forehead. "He's not that old. Why did he lie to me about that? He is cagey. So proper one minute, like an aristocrat. So vulgar the next."

Mary shrugged. "Vanessa is dead. He probably doesn't want to talk about it. It's none of our business how he mourns. Mourning is ultimately very personal. I'm sure he's very disturbed about it all right now in some way. Some people cry a week after a funeral. It hits them when it hits them."

"Of course. Bless you for pointing that out. I had no right to pry, especially at a time like this. I'll try to be extra careful that I don't rub salt into his wounds. Not anymore than I have already."

Mary asked, "Has he hit you up for money yet? A lot of money? He has me, twice by now. But that's only been a recent thing, some recent trouble he's in, I suppose."

"Yes, and I told him *no*. I don't give anybody that kind of money. He'll just spend it on drugs, anyway. I'm sure of it. Or at the pub on beer. Easy come easy go."

Mary's face grew hard. "You didn't have him fired after that? I bet it made you very angry. He often infuriates me! How can you put up with him?"

"It isn't about me at all, not really. If he needs that kind of money then he needs a job. If he's a driver then he might not be good at much else. I'm not going to deprive a young man of the only job he can do. As it is, he seems torn between being a cash poor aristocrat and a hippy that thinks he doesn't need any money. Having a job is good for him. As long as he doesn't drive me into a ditch or gets lost then why should I complain at all? In fact he was an expert at finding an old beauty parlor for me, he knew all the numbers on the street. So that would be unfair for me to get angry at him as my driver. And I don't get angry so fast anymore. I've mellowed. It took awhile but I've learned that anybody can become angry. That's easy. But to be angry with the right person and to the right degree and at the right time and for the right purpose and in the right way…that isn't within everybody's power and isn't easy. That takes wisdom."

Mary made herself smile. "You're so correct, and so kind for thinking about him. You're far more charitable than I am. I don't think he has anybody who cares about him in his life right now."

"I know men. They need to feel useful or they feel worthless and go bad. Hell, it works like that for *everybody*. If I'm not juggling Pepsi bottles, while doing TV game shows and charities, spending hours on the phone getting acting work for my friends and family, magazine interviews, showing up now and again on a few TV westerns, movies like *Trog*, while watching daytime soaps to see who's up-and-coming so I can write them letters of support, and knit things for people, I feel like a slug. I think I'll knit a tea cozy for you, too. You have been most kind and helpful. I feel like we're friends now. I'll make you a blue one. Blue is the color of hope."

Mary said, "Love, you're too busy to do all that…and too busy to just stand around here. I'll give you a ride home. I don't think you should wait any longer for him. He probably thinks he's in a movie right now and who knows what the scene is."

Joan shook her head sadly. "The movies they see these days give them such bad ideas."

"He told me John Lennon had told him about God being a movie projector. And I got so mad at Lennon for saying something like that but then I found out that's not the quote at all. John Lennon had said that we are the light bulbs and God is the electricity."

Joan looked puzzled. "I thought John Lennon said he was God. It got all the conservatives into such an uproar."

Mary explained, "Not exactly. He said we were all God because Jesus had said that the kingdom of God was in all of us. I don't know how we can be both the bulb and the light but rock stars say all kinds of contradictory things from magazine to magazine, now don't they?"

Joan thought about how the things said and done by *all* stars were usually taken out of context. The best movie star quotes were when you weren't trying to say anything too serious and it was mere wit.

Mary put her hand out. "Wait here for me while I get my keys. I'll drive you home. We've waited here long enough."

Joan stood and looked out the door. "No. Here he comes. Maybe he's right on time. Our séance was interrupted, after all. Thank you for the offer, though. That was very kind and thoughtful. I do appreciate it."

Mary glared at the arriving car. "You're so good to people."

"Bless you. I try not to pick battles. The ones that pick me keep me busy enough, since I insist on always winning at all costs." Joan got in the car and leaned forward to her driver's ear. "Get me out of here now. I wasn't here. I can't be found here. I require good press and bad press, any kind of press, but not *this* kind of press. Horror press! The tabloids will just take it wrong and associate me with nothing but horror from now on and then I'm only thought of as second rate and washed up!"

"What happened?"

"The ceiling fell in and made such a mess, and there was blood, so gruesome, and at a séance of all things. What would people say? The tabloids would just take it wrong no matter what." Joan sat back and thought back to her real life horror in 1963 when she and her husband were in Dallas plotting how to get their Cuban sugar plantation back. Then just outside, Kennedy was shot dead in a most gruesome spectacle. She wondered how many people thought she was the one on the grassy knoll. She'd shot so many people in so many movies by then and people always confused her life with her movies. "A man was hit in the head! There was blood! Blood down his whole face. It was terrible looking. But he'll be okay. But still, I'm so upset." She shook her head.

"Did Vanessa say who frigging did it?"

"No. She just knocked…and knocked the ceiling down and that's all. A poor man was in the way and he was hurt…but not by too much, I hope. It just all looked so awful. Blood always looks so awful. Like he was shot in the head. But it made no sense. Words seemed to escape Vanessa entirely."

"Sooo…you don't know who did it?"

"No idea. It all seems like a dream now. What an odd long long day…I'm so tired now I can't think at all."

Roderick Stuart grinned as if he'd won something as he returned her to her hotel.

Chapter thirteen

Joan woke up and as she drew on her lipstick all she could only think about was if the queen of England was safe, if she had destroyed the wicked mummy in time. She called the front desk and asked for a paper. After she saw that there was no news about Queen Elizabeth she called Gloria Swanson up on the phone. "Can a mummy be brought back to life? If she was a queen could she take the body of the queen to do it? A soul transference? What's a soul transference?"

"Nonsense. It's dead. Its soul has moved on. That door has closed behind the poor dead dear. The dead are off to more fantastic things."

"It just dawned on me. If Queen Elizabeth was attacked by the soul of a long dead mummy then she wouldn't be dead or hurt from it. She'd simply be the victim of a body snatcher and we might never ever know that had happened! I hope I saved the queen in time! How would I know? How would I know who is the real queen?"

"Joan? *Hellooo*. That was a fifties movie. They were space aliens. Movies are not real."

"No. But this mummy was real. And the queen is real. What about those who think the soul can be saved with the body that has been preserved like a mummy's has...to last. But it doesn't really last, and so when the mummy is disturbed with spells then the soul goes into a new body. Like a body snatcher!"

Gloria said, "Then hold onto your hat when you die, with the way they embalm everybody today. And even before we die we embalm ourselves with all the preservatives we eat in our food. Or what you call it over there, your *nosh*! Who knows how long we might hang around, and who we might later...body snatch with?"

"Yeah. Snatch!"

Gloria wearily moaned. "Then we might have all been body snatched, already. The way you're going on we could *all* be taken over by the dead wanting new bodies. There has to be a lot more dead people wanting one then there are living people on earth right now today. They might all be fighting over us and we go through three a week. Do you see how silly that sounds?"

"Then I want to be cremated," Joan said.

"I think you've done too many horror films, Joanie, and they've given you nightmares."

"I don't do horror. I do serious films that have...moments. Like your serious drama *Sunset Boulevard*...it was a bit...odd."

Gloria laughed. "That was a black comedy. I was off my rocker and a dead man narrated the whole thing."

"People are going to start thinking I'm weird, aren't they. They're going to think of me as the queen of horror, and not the glamour queen of MGM or the film noir queen of Warner Brothers."

"I think you became the instant queen of horror when you did *Baby Jane*. That film had such an impact on the horror genre, and modern movies. I saw it in your stars. Remember I called you and told you that you had a hit because the planets were so happy."

Joan slowly nodded. "People didn't think less of me for doing it. In fact I got so much praise. But that film wasn't really horror. It was a drama about two sisters looking back on their troubled lives. Bette didn't seem to take any of it seriously but I did!"

Gloria insisted. "They sell it as horror."

"Well, when I first bought the film rights to the novel it said right on the cover, 'A novel of suspense' and not 'A horror novel' so I beg to differ."

Gloria asked, "Why should anybody think less of anybody for doing horror. It's a job. It can even put you on top. I was nominated for an Academy Award for *Sunset Boulevard*. You do it well and people like it."

Joan asked, "Are you sure the horoscope can do all that, say all that, about all that? Are you sure the horoscopes haven't been made into too much?"

Gloria gasped. "Bite your tongue! Everybody peeks at their horoscope in the morning paper and they don't think they're so terrible for doing that. So I study the topic a little farther than that. So what. Does that turn a harmless thing into a dangerous thing—to go into depth?"

Joan said, "I don't know about horoscopes like you do. But I do know things can get out of hand with the occult. I don't know how far this, that, or the other can be pushed, but it's dangerous to push it too far. I do know that much. I've seen it. There are things that shouldn't be messed with at all. It's out of our control. Leave it to the angels!"

"I won't argue with you there. Anything can go too far and you become obsessed, if nothing else. Life should have variety. We have to live everyday with the simple things of life and try to keep them simple." Gloria laughed. "Of course people think that's impossible with me. They think I really am Norma Desmond. They didn't realize that when I agreed to that role Hollywood was far behind me and I was having a great life with love, family, my own businesses and Broadway. It was fun to make the movie and poke fun at all those old memories again, but enough was enough."

In *Sunset Boulevard* Eric von Stroheim played her butler. In real life in 1928 he'd directed her epic unfinished debacle *Queen Kelly*. A clip from that movie, of Gloria's young face, was finally shown in *Sunset Boulevard* making it the most expensive close-up in history. Other old-timers were in the movie, too, playing themselves. Cecil B. DeMille, Hedda Hopper, Buster Keaton, and others. Gloria had begged Bill Haines to be in her card game scene but he refused.

Joan said, "England has really spooked me this time. I think I just need to get back to my old routines in New York again and then I'll feel like Joan Crawford again. Maybe my trouble is that it's hard for me to feel completely like Joan Crawford here."

"Nonsense. You've traveled the world for Pepsi as Joan Crawford. You managed to bring her with you wherever you went. *Trog* will not be thought of as a British movie. It'll be thought of as a Joan Crawford movie."

"Bless you."

"If you really want to bless me, mind the time change when you call from halfway around the world."

Joan scoffed. "Oh time, what is time."

Gloria chided, "I'm serious. And the next time you call me from where you are, please be a dear and remember that not only is there a currency difference but there is a time difference, too, and it is most important. I was just dreaming that I had pulled Valentino's pants down, and we were so young." She hung up.

"Oh, sorry. Bless you."

* * * * *

In the dressing room, Joan pulled her cheeks back tighter with her hands. "Damn you Billy Haines!"

Frenchy ordered her, "Put your hands down. You're just making yourself look funny that way."

"Bill says I look funny anyway. Damn him, he makes me so upset when he says things like that. It only bothers me when *he* says it, too. I don't care what anybody else says. After a professional life with Bette Davis I've got alligator skin." She pulled her cheeks up tight again. "Damn you Bill Haines! I'll show you how good I can look!"

Frenchy pushed Joan's hands away from her face. "He's like family and that's why he can get your goat. Only family has the power to upset us like that so very deeply."

"Yes, he's become more than a good friend. By now he's my family. He became the big brother I always wanted, since my real one was such a dirty rat. That's what gives him such power over me. What upsets me more is that he sounds so unhappy. Because he's family then I worry about him in a more special way, too. He's one of the kids. Kids are there for us to worry about. I'm worried sick that he's so unhappy. He only makes fun of my looks and of the passage of time when he's so very unhappy. When he's unhappy he lashes out."

"Maybe you're just catching him at a bad time."

Joan frowned. "That could be it. I have to keep remembering the time change and stop calling people when it's three in the morning for them, or during their nap at three in the afternoon, or whatever time I'm calling them, to find them at their best mood. I'm not even keeping track of when I'm calling from here. Maybe I'm the one in a bad mood! I'm just too busy to keep track of everything properly.

Frenchy nodded. "Time change is scary."

Joan nodded with her. "Time travel is scary."

Frenchy stopped nodding. "They're the same thing?"

"Sure. I traveled and the time went all to hell." Joan pulled her cheeks back again with her hands. "Damn you Billy Haines. If only I could just wrap my whole face up with a scarf like Katherine Hepburn got to do in *Lion in Winter*. And it got her another Academy Award. They would've never given her the award if she'd shown them her old turkey neck."

"That was a fine performance." Frenchy pulled up on Joan's hair.

"Of course it was. She's a most impressive actress with great presence. It's a shame she can be impersonated so easily but then she isn't as varied and subtle as I am. But she's great. She had a face! She still has a face—she just has to hide that neck. How can I do more to hide my neck? In *Berserk* they always put a strip of shadow over it. You try walking around yelling at people and always finding your mark on the floor so the shadow doesn't end up across your nose. You try it!"

Frenchy twisted Joan's hair. "That was such a grand movie, though, from such a clever play."

"*Berserk?*"

"No, Joanie, I'm thinking about Kate right now."

"Yes, *Lion in Winter* deserved its award for best screenplay, I'm sure. Did it get that? I don't remember offhand—I just remember the acting awards most. It sure had great lines. But for best acting they have to toss a coin. How can you really judge the best? All the nominees are the best. And there's great stuff that never even got included. Don't think for a second it means the Academy is fair. Where's one for Marlene Dietrich's horny gypsy or horny Russian countess or horny queen of Bagdad. Oh, and she played a horny German really well, too! Look at how all my MGM years were ignored by the awards. Look at how Judy Garland was ignored. Look at how Gloria Swanson was ignored."

Frenchy blinked away tears. "Poor Judy. It just breaks me up the way she was treated."

Joan added. "The one who's really been ignored is Lon Chaney Jr. You just can't ignore a star as big as he is as much as he is. Everybody has typecast him as a monster. That's fine in Pasadena to think that way, but Hollywood knows better. Hollywood knows what a fine actor he is and how many serious roles he's played. I remember when director Stanley Kramer once said that whenever a role came by that was too difficult for other actors he would call Chaney to do it. But no Academy Award, not even a nomination. No star on Hollywood's walk of fame even. He's treated like a monster. They probably didn't even think to give him the part of Trog because it would add too much to the budget to have another star. Now that he's all broken down and really is only good to play a monster he's now ignored for monster parts. That's what happens when you do horror. You become marginalized and cheapened. You're not taken seriously by anybody at casting. You end up kicked into the corner like Bela Lugosi." Joan frowned. "The likes of Gregory Peck, Richard Burton or Laurence Olivier would never be in a horror movie, for sure." Joan made fists.

Frenchy wanted to lighten the mood. "Poor Chaney. If he'd played Trog then you'd be the last of Mrs. Cheyney."

Joan busted into a peel of laughter at the silly joke—*The Last of Mrs. Cheyney* was one of the top movies of 1937 starring her. When Joan became serious again, she added, "But one thing Katherine Hepburn has taught us all is that you can still get another award after all these years. I'm going to try for one more award. If she can do it, I can do it. I'm still healthy and popular. I'll get an important script again, I know it! This movie will be ignored by the Academy because it's a British picture. They snub those. But wait and see, I'll get something again that was on Broadway first, to wake up the snobs, and the Academy will notice."

"Good luck."

Joan pounded a cigarette on the countertop as if it needed its tobacco packed. "They should give best actor awards to those who did the best in lackluster scripts. That's the very hardest to act.

Anybody can look good in a good movie. Try looking best in a blah movie. That should be the test!"

"Then you'd win for this one?"

Joan made a sour face. "I just wish something more had come of Ibsen's *A Doll House*." Basil Rathbone and Joan did an acclaimed production of it for live radio in 1938. "If that had been made into a movie it would have been the best woman's picture ever made—and of course that's a Joan Crawford movie. And doing a movie from such a great author would have given me more respect."

"And another Academy Award."

Joan gave a nod. "That's what they award."

"MGM should have done it!"

Joan laughed sadly. "If MGM had done that then it would have had a happy ending slapped on it...maybe it would have just been presented as a silly spoiled housewife's dream. Clark Gable can walk out on Vivien Leigh, sure. But the conservatives would have never allowed the wife to slam the door on her husband. They say that door slam at the end of that play rocked the world, they say it was the beginning of feminism. *Warner Brothers* might have done it up well, they didn't care what the bluenoses and German market thought, not like MGM did."

There was a knock on the door and the assistant to the director said through it, "Miss Crawford, we're ready to shoot the next scene."

"Bless you!"

Frenchy asked Joan, "What's the scene?"

Joan glanced over at her script. "I find the humanity in Trog. How am I going to look like I'm doing that?"

"Trog is human?"

Joan grabbed the script. "I'm an optimist. That's all I know. I'm the good guy. I give Trog a nice doll of a blonde girl and I should sing 'It's a Small World After All' while I do it. That's what the movie is really about, isn't it. We're all human in a small world. We should all try harder to understand each other. We should be kind and gentle. That's how I'll do it." Joan still looked uncertain.

Frenchy reminded her. "And then Trog kidnaps the real girl and runs off to the cave to get shot a hundred times by the army."

Joan flippantly shrugged at the fatalism, blew her nose, redid her makeup where the tissue had wiped it off, then marched out of the room on tall heels.

* * * * *

When the scene was filmed and Joan returned to her dressing room, she raised her Pepsi bottle in the air and gave out a holler. "Oh I was marvelous. The scene went marvelous! I feel so wonderful now! I was worried how I'd pull such an odd scene off but I think I made it all look normal and natural. I can't imagine any other actress pulling a scene like that off so well, let alone with a straight face at all. And no, I didn't sing to Trog that it's a small world after all although that would have made it all so much easier. I did so well because as Freddy yelled *action* I just remembered that the scene isn't really all about me. People are really waiting to see how Trog reacts to me as much as how I react to him. It's about Trog as much as it is about the doctor. I should get the Academy Award for pulling that off! Can you image Bette Davis and her cackle, or a horny Marlene Dietrich handing a doll to a trog and the audience not howling? I made it real! And the press have said my legs rival Dietrich's. I sat on the floor in this dress. My legs looked great. I hadn't realized before I'd get at least one good legs shot in this picture!" She smiled exuberantly.

"Gloria called," Frenchy reported.

"Can you image Norma Desmond handing Trog a doll?"

"She wants you to call back."

Joan continued, "It's hard to enough to act a scene with all those distractions going on beside the camera but for this movie it's really crazy sometimes!"

Frenchy added, "Gloria Swanson has been trying to get a hold of you. She says to call her when you can, but mind the time change."

Joan looked close in the mirror to make sure her eyelashes were still glued down in their proper curve. She winked at herself. "I'll call her now and tell her how well the scene went and let her figure out that math." Joan left the mirror, still winking but now to no one, lit another cigarette, and dialed. "What's going on? Bless you, dear. I hope you're okay. I hope you didn't poison yourself with twigs and leaves in that press-pot." Joan waved Frenchy out of the room.

Gloria sounded stressed. "No, dear, it's about Bette Davis!"

Joan was in a mood to joke. "There was a car crash? She's been decapitated but she's still cackling? She was never very original.

With me she was the same old song. Insult, demean, put-down, and try to ruin my parts and even rip me off out of my parts. The only thing she's never done is actually steal any one of my parts."

"No, no, not that. Oh Joan! *Oh Joan*! I sent my psychic masseuse Slicky Stars to Bette, as a gift, as you said to. It worked. It worked too well! She took it. He did the full astro-project massage with past lives regression for her…while he was doing nude yoga and body painting. The whole therapy hypnosis with her on the floor and he pushing on her at all the push points. He says she took to it very well and thinks that might be because of all the booze and pills she was on at the time. And the great cosmic alignment…there's a great cosmic alignment…so it amplified."

"So what happened?"

"Oh Joan! She is barking mad. She's barking!"

"Barking?"

"Like a dog."

"How do you know?" Joan asked.

Gloria answered, "I was told on the telephone."

Joan scowled. "You can't always trust what you're told on the telephone. People exaggerate."

Gloria got shrill. "Well how else am I going to be told? Skywriting? Pony express? What do you trust most? Slicky Stars is worried now about all kinds of things snowballing into disaster."

"Like what."

"Like atavism!"

Joan scowled. "She might fly away?"

"Maybe swim away, given enough time. He said we all have a map in us of when animal life on earth was still nothing but fishes. Then developments were added onto the map of life as animals became the little lizards on land, and then mice creatures and then monkey creatures and then trogs and then finally us modern humans. Her earlier primitive map of how a body should grow might start kicking in and she could grow a tail, for real. Her body could become confused in this state and she could grow into a throwback!"

Joan looked at the back of her marvelous human hand with lovely manicure. "Is that possible? We still have that in us? What's that word again?"

"Atavism." Gloria explained, "Did you know that if a human baby is small enough in the mother's womb it has a tail and gills?

Even in this life we start as a fish and then grow out of that phase right away to grow into a human, right away in the womb."

Joan said hesitantly, "Atavism?"

"You got it."

"*Hmmm.* I wonder why the script to *Trog* doesn't mention that? That is amazing. Where is Bette Davis now? Is she in a clinic? If there's a hundred tubes in her now I suppose I should send her flowers just to give her something to throw across the room…for exercise. You know how she's always thrown away the flowers I give her so for awhile I just sent her one flower at a time and then she called me a lesbian."

"He has her locked in a room now in her basement. It was a coal room before the house got a modern heater. He's trying to bring her out of it but that's complicated since she doesn't seem to understand words anymore. I'd have thought it would have worn off with the booze and pills but it didn't. And now she's growing fur."

"Are you sure? She always was untidy." Joan grinned wickedly. "Is she all full of coal dust? Oh, I shouldn't be so mean. But if you knew all that she's done to me. Remember when my dressing room had coal outside the door one Christmas? I wondered if that was her—it was when we were both at Warner Brothers."

"No. She's not full of coal dust. The room hasn't been a coal room for decades."

"Maybe she just hasn't taken the time to shave. She's been such a lazy drunk since she got fat and nobody will hire her—since she's been a has-been. Catch her in the right light with all that old lady fuzz and she might look like a trog by now just from that!"

Gloria said, "Joan, it's serious! I'm not joking. Stop joking! This is serious! It's terrible! It's hair that wasn't there before. All over her face and arms and back. Her leg hair might have already been there. I'm not sure. Poor Bette!"

Joan still doubted such a thing. "That's what Slicky Stars said? Is he used to old lady hair from women who've let themselves go and given up on a man's touch ever again?"

"It's more than just hair, Joan! He said he's never seen anybody regress back to pre-language. He's trying to think how to reach her at all."

Joan kicked out of her heels. "Did he sound very upset about it?"

Gloria answered, "Yes, yes, yes! He was in a state of panic!"

"They say if you shave it just grows back thicker. Maybe she shaved more than we all realized back when she was trying to be a movie star. She should be growing yarn by now, enough yard for me to knit a scarf all the way from here to Malibu!"

Gloria argued, "No, it's not true that it grows back thicker if you shave, otherwise we'd all be growing our own yarn by now. And I don't think this is mere peach fuzz. I really do think she's growing new hair. Her entire body is reacting to the past life regression and she is growing the hair of something primitive and ghastly! She's turning into a monkey monster! A real one! One that looks just like one!"

"Oh dear." Joan frowned. "That *has* gone too far. Has this ever happened to anybody before?"

Gloria said, "It's happened at Berkley in an isolation tank."

"What's that?"

Gloria explained, "They put a grad student in a tank of water and cut off all outside stimulation for hours, with lots of ketamine and LSD, until he went into an altered state of consciousness until he went into an altered state of form until he regressed back into a trog creature."

"Why would they even think to do a thing like that?" Joan asked. "Aren't the kids getting stoned enough as it is without finding new ways to do it?"

"It was for schizophrenia research."

"Oh yeah, the kids all have a problem with that these days, too." Joan blew her smoke away from the phone as if that would keep it off Gloria. "Wait a minute. That all sounds hard to believe. How many trogs are out there? My movie isn't about the first one? Are you sure?"

"Slicky Stars said so. He said he was at the symposium at Berkley."

That made Joan doubt even further. "What is he doing at a place like that? Trying to milk money out of the horny professor's wives?"

"I'm sure he did that too after he gave a talk on the spirituality of human development. But he said everybody was drinking too much by then to hear anything. That's what he said. He said three men were so gone on scotch and soda that they couldn't find the door."

Joan asked, "And where's this trog student now?"

"As soon as he came out of the tank into the modern world and the drugs wore off he began to behave like a modern human again. But they said they're going to put in the book that he ran down the alley and woke up in a zoo. That's so it can be made into a movie and it will have an exciting scene. The book will be called *Altered States* when it's written. Look for it, I will, I want to know what just happened here."

"Do you really believe all that?"

"It doesn't matter what I believe about that. That's Berkley's problem. I'm only worried about Bette Davis gone wild and all because we did it to her. It's all our fault. Slicky Stars thinks he might of unwittingly duplicated the isolation tank experiment—the same end result of it anyway."

Joan made a pained face. "If she's regressed back to where she's a troglodyte and she stays that way then what are we going to do with her? She has to snap out of this someday somehow. Until she snaps out of it feed her snakes and lizards! Just throw them down the coal chute if you're afraid of getting close to her. Trogs are dangerous! I don't care what I say about them in my movie."

"The coal chute was removed decades ago." Gloria moaned. "What if she never snaps out of it? What if she keeps growing hair and stays this way for the rest of her life?"

"Oh no. Now I feel guilty. I hope this doesn't last too long or else we have a complete disaster on our hands, and it's all my fault. All because I couldn't forgive her for her last dirty trick on me. And I was going to try and do better. I bet that if you feed her lizards and snakes she'll snap out of it. She'll find it disgusting, I hope, and finally remember that she's really a wrinkled has-been movie star. Toss her a lipstick. Maybe the smell of that will snap her back into her advanced modern form. Blow cigarette smoke her way. Maybe what she really needs is TV dinners! Maybe the smells of advanced living will snap her out of it. Put her on Astro Turf. Pipe in supermarket music. Put Tang in her water. Throw her some Lucite jewelry to play with. Put up a big Pepsi sign! Make her watch the late movie…it's always a Joan Crawford movie!"

"Good ideas! I'll have Slicky Stars try all that. I'm blaming him."

"That's clever of you. Always put the blame on a man."

Gloria moaned. "He feels terrible. I feel terrible! You should feel bad, too. We didn't mean our joke on her to go this far!"

"Nonsense! Not after how she stole that part from you and drove you from Hollywood? No wonder her forehead now looks like an old casting couch."

Gloria moaned louder. "Oh *that*! That was Harry Cohen who really gets the blame for all that. Really. Blame the man."

Joan insisted, "That bitch!"

Cohen was going to make a movie for Gloria in 1939 that she really wanted to make. She had a reading for him and both were in tears at the end, the story had such a great death scene for Gloria. But then the next day Cohen called Gloria on the phone to tell her some nonsense that if MGM wanted to sell it to him to do at Columbia then it must not be too good. Gloria had waited all morning for his call, all on needles and pins and knowing it was such a great story. When he told her *no* she went into a rage, swearing at him and telling him how much Columbia was the Tin Pan Alley of Hollywood and they wouldn't know a good story if it bit them. Gloria swore and screamed until she finally realized she'd been walking around with the phone plug pulled out of the wall and it was a thirty-five foot phone cord. The next day Gloria cancelled her contract and threw everything she could into her biggest car and drove to New York. She was moving away. She realized she'd stayed too long at the fair, she decided she was finished with movies. Gloria was getting too old for the good parts—she was almost forty and hadn't had a good part in a decade. And then Bette Davis got the movie and it was a huge hit. It was *Dark Victory*. And Gloria almost would have starred in it if Larry Cohen hadn't been so stupid to drop the story for the bone-headed reason he did.

Gloria asked, "Larry Cohen?"

"No, Bette Davis! See? She needs punished! She stole the part from you, and she stole it from Tallulah Bankhead too. *Dark Victory* was first a Broadway show and Tallulah did it first but then she didn't get the movie role. If I ever find out she stole it from me, too, I'll let her have it!" Joan made a fist.

Gloria said, "It was good I got out of Hollywood when I did. I got so rich in New York." Gloria had started to read every science journal and magazine she could, learning everything she could about patents. She snuck scientists out of Germany to save them from the Nazis and started Multiprises, Incorporated. Gloria saved lives, contributed to science, outsmarted Hitler and made more money than She'd even made in Hollywood before the income tax. "But in all those years of doing science I never thought I'd have a trog on my hands *that I helped cause!*"

Joan had calmed. "You've been a huge inspiration to me in business. From your producing in Hollywood to your many businesses in New York and your work for the UN, you've been a movie star pioneer. You've even done more than Lucille Ball."

"America seemed to grow up when the movies grew up and I was right there in the thick of it all. I am the icon of the century."

"No, me," Joan insisted. "Ever since I had that line of hats for Sears, Roebuck and Company Incorporated—that's what they called it back in 1927. I knew then that I'd be the ultimate pop culture icon of Hollywood, fashion, medical charities and business. I've been the icon every decade. And now I'm starting the seventies with a modern new look." Joan turned to the mirror. "Oh wait. I have to go now. Damn look at what happened to me!" Joan frowned in the mirror. She had gotten too excited. While on the phone she popped all eight of her silk face tapes on both sides of her head that pulled her neck, cheeks and jowls back, and eyes up. She thought she looked like a snake shedding its skin. "And I have such a big night!" Joan slammed the phone down and swore at the snake in the mirror. "Bette Davis turning into an animal? For real? Get out! That Gloria Swanson is pulling my leg!"

Chapter fourteen

Joan nimbly redid all her makeup, added a bigger taller hairpiece, square earrings, and went to nearby London to the BBC studios to tape an interview. After great applause, she briefly mentioned her current project. Then the host quickly changed the subject and started talking about war. Joan hated war movies and thought they were an insult to women's pictures, and so were an insult to her career. The rise of the war movie was the fall of the woman's picture. Soon women did not see themselves represented on the screen much at all except as mere soldier's sidekicks and whores, at best. Joan paid a fortune to buy herself out of her MGM contract when she was signed on to play one war movie too many. She was glad she did. It freed her up to go to Warner Brothers and led to the best woman's picture ever made…*Mildred Peirce*.

As the host talked on and on, Joan decided she hated the tone of his voice. She wished the whole interview was in sign language. She then realized she was too rusty for that and had not been completely conversational in it in the first place. After she had signed in her film *The Story of Esther Costello* a fan wrote her to tell her he could have sworn she had said, with her hands, "I have sex with the teacart under the ice skates." That had baffled her and she still wondered which one of her lines of dialogue could have possible looked like that to anybody. She looked down at her own hands. She glanced up and noticed the camera was still on him so she quickly signed in her lap, "God I need a cigarette."

Then he turned to her. The cue light on the camera that was aimed at her lit up. "And Joan, here is somebody you haven't seen in awhile. He's now back from the Soviet Union where *Waterloo* was filmed. Joan do you have any idea who that could be?"

Joan smiled big. "I have no idea."

"You have no idea?"

"I'm very good at the game shows. I need more clues."

"We invited him to join us since you were in a picture together once, and you both now have *new* pictures coming out. How exciting! We thought you would have a lot of catching up and comparing to do!"

Joan smiled big again. "Who could that be?"

"You were in a picture with him at MGM in 1953."

"That would have been *Torch Song*. Could it be…Michael Wilding?"

Michael Wilding stepped into the studio lights and walked over to the empty chair next to hers. Everyone in the studio audience applauded. Michael said, "That was a very nice introduction, Joan. Thank you."

Joan affectionately squeezed his arm. "I'm so taken by surprise. I haven't seen you since 1953."

"I haven't seen you since 1953 either."

The audience laughed. Joan laughed with them, then said, "After that, your wife took you away. I used to call her *the child actress*, I admit. She is certainly not a child actress anymore—she has far too many accomplishments for me to call her that anymore. I'll just have to call her by her name, Elizabeth Taylor. A lovely actress."

The audience applauded. Michael smiled tensely. "We haven't been married for a while, now. But I will say...that was a nicer introduction from you just now than I got from you on the set of *Torch Song*."

The audience laughed. Joan did not laugh. Joan looked confused as she said, "Why would I introduce you on the set, there? I was just one of the actors. I was just an MGM employee. I will forever have MGM tattooed on my backside."

"One of the actors? You're Joan Crawford, Miss Hollywood. I was the odd Brit out and standing alone on the set with no introduction."

Joan laughed nervously. "Don't make me try to remember every detail of something that happened in 1953 but I do remember *Torch Song* well. I remember you standing alone on the set and I didn't think anything of it. I was just trying to concentrate on my own part. I assumed you were out there doing the same...not waiting for a party."

"An introduction is not a party."

Joan smiled tensely. "I'm sorry our director didn't think to introduce us but I imagine he was very busy, too. Directing."

The host interrupted. "I guess you don't need introductions in America." The audience laughed.

Michael said, "It is nice to know who everybody is."

Joan looked amazed. "You didn't know who Joan Crawford was?" The audience laughed once more.

The host interrupted again. "Michael, tell us about your latest picture?"

"It's about Napoleon, called *Waterloo*. Directed by Sergei Bondarchuk. I play Major-General The Honorable Sir William Ponsonby."

Everybody clapped. Even Joan.

The host said, "And I hear you almost didn't make it."

"Well, no. My character dies in the battle of Waterloo and I almost did, too. We were filming in the Ukraine and I had a terrible epileptic fit. I told my co-star Christopher Plummer that I might not make it and he took such good care of me."

The host said, "How nice. It's a shame they couldn't have put that in the story. That could have gotten you an Academy Award!"

Michael continued, "They ran nine Panavision cameras at once when we did the massive battle scenes but none seemed to catch my seizures so I can't prove it." He chuckled sadly.

The host excitedly said, "They say the battle scenes involved one of the world's largest armies...and it was just a movie army."

Michael nodded. "The film included over 16,000 Soviet foot soldiers and 5,000 cavalrymen. Hundreds of circus stunt riders were used to perform the dangerous horse falls. They were split into three armies. They wore French, British or Prussian uniforms. They had to learn 1815 drill and battle formations, learn to fire cannons, sword fight, and load muskets."

"That is amazing!" The host turned to Joan and asked her, "What do you think of that!"

Joan gave a crooked grin. "That's a lot of men!" Everybody laughed.

The host asked Michael, "Where was this filmed? In the Soviet Union?"

Michael nodded. "In addition to the battlefield in Ukraine, filming also took place on location in Caserta. Interior scenes were filmed at the De Laurentiis Studios in Rome. We were in the largest soundstages in the world."

"That is incredible!"

Michael grinned big. "So far it's by far the most expensive movie ever made! And if the Soviet Union hadn't let us film there and hadn't chipped in, it would have cost three times even more!"

"Holy cow!"

Joan quickly injected, "But they're commies so they won't buy Pepsi."

The men excitedly talked about the war movie for awhile longer and then the interview was over. As the audience left, Joan hung out in the lobby, thanked everybody she could for coming, and pose for snapshots and signed autographs for everybody who wanted one. Herman Cohen had driven Joan to London. After they had dinner together at the Goring Dining Room he drove her back to Windsor. She sat in the front seat next to him.

Joan patted her stomach. "MGM paid us to starve ourselves. I always feel guilty after such a meal."

"I didn't bring your breakfast because you didn't eat your din-din!"

Joan let out a guffaw. Herman had just said a line from *Whatever Happened to Baby Jane*. Then she said, "I was serious. I suppose you were too."

"We waste too much of our lives feeling guilty about odd stuff."

Joan put her hand on her slim stomach again. "At least I didn't eat the whole thing. That steak and kidney pie was overcooked. You cook meat too much and there's no vitamins left in it. Then…what's the point?"

Herman chuckled. "It wasn't beans on toast, that's for sure. London can sure be snobby at a place like that. It was started in Edwardian times and is so close to Buckingham Palace."

"I'm not afraid of snobs. By now I'm completely immune to snobs. I used to tremble around Mary Pickford—she'd act as if she was better than I was and I was dumb enough to believe her. That was nice of you to take me to such a nice place. I'm not complaining. I'm grateful for such a lovely outing into London's finest. Snobs don't bother me. If the snobs are really awful to me then I have my revenge. Remember my Pepsi sign?" She grinned. When she had first moved to New York to be closer to Pepsi's business she tried to move into a nice apartment building with a spectacular view of the river. She soon found that it was a snobby building full of Babbitty Republican bigots, and everyone already living there voted not to allow her in. They didn't want a Joan Crawford Hollywood person who would have parties that would allow homosexuals, Negros, Jews, businesswomen, artists, Russian friends, French friends like Maurice Chevalier who they accused of collaborating with the Nazis while also being communist, and other colorful people into their socially sanitary building. She had her revenge. Across the river at its bank, in the middle of their spectacular river view, she had the world's largest Pepsi sign put up. It lit up their New York night.

Herman said, "I owe you many thanks for saving our Trog mask. You saved the whole film."

"You just have to know men's weaknesses. A peek up my skirt and his heart starts pounding. Once his heart starts pounding he drinks too fast. Men."

"You were showing him up your skirt?"

"Only enough. Do you want to see, too? Jealous?"

He kept his eyes on the road.

Joan continued. "Be glad Joan Crawford is a femme fatale or we'd be filming with that other mask now and the whole film would have to be set in heavy fog at midnight. That's what I told the director, Freddy, the instant I laid eyes on it. With modern color film you just can't show masks like that, clearly. They show up *clearly*! The Trog mask looks great no matter how close you get to it."

"Every Cinemascope frame of *2001: A Space Odyssey* looked great."

Joan gave a pert nod. "And now your film will too."

"I'm sorry the interview didn't go well. The war movie hogged it."

Joan looked out the side window and frowned. "I've already forgotten about it. I've done so many interviews so far and I have so many more to give. It went okay for just being one of many. My next interview I'll be all by myself again."

"You're a tough cookie."

"Of course. I have to be tough or be crushed. I always have to look ahead. Next! Herman, what's our next movie going to be? We have become quite a team by now. I'm so glad my dear friend Leo Jaffe at Colombia Pictures introduced us! We've had two wins so far, since. This one will be a winner, too!"

Herman smiled. "Yes, it will, no doubt."

"I wish I could still do romantic pictures but these days all they do is war and horror...and sex movies with lots of unmade beds and skin and nipples. In the olden days everybody knew we were having sex all the time but we weren't rubbing our skin in their faces. We kept it classy and so it ended up far more romantic and exciting. So, what's next?"

Herman frowned. "Joan. I have to confess that there isn't anything lined up yet after this. It's getting harder and harder for me to get new projects started. I was the king of the fifties. Those days are long gone."

Joan pounded her fist on her thigh. "Just tell the bastards that you got Joan Crawford and you'll be fine. Maybe by now Hollywood has learned not to underestimate me! When Warner Brothers did *Baby Jane* they had no idea how big a hit it would be. They gave us their smallest possible budget. They wouldn't even let us film it in their studios, they were so embarrassed by it. We filmed in a tiny barn where z-grade Westerns were filmed for television. But the movie became the biggest hit of the year and suddenly

Warner Brothers was proud of it. It was already a hit before Warners decided to start promoting it at all. Otherwise we were on our own and we made it and sold it ourselves! I hit up all the talk shows and I wouldn't shut up about it. Finally it got big enough that Bette even crawled out of her hole to try and take credit for it all. Well lucky her. You need work and talent and luck, not just a lot of money, to make a movie that sells. I don't have to be the lead in your next movie. I can play a smaller part if that allows you more flexibility. I can be in it just long enough to allow my name big on the movie poster to satisfy the theater owners. I can play something like the schoolteacher who helps the teenage boy who…who turns into a…a werewolf. A bit part but still a star part."

"A werewolf?"

Joan nodded. "Sure, hell, why not. You made yourself famous for that in the first place! I haven't played a schoolteacher before. I can play the P.E. teacher…to show off my legs. I want to blow a whistle. Get Michael Landon back. He can play his father. Remake your first big hit. 1970 is ready for a teenage werewolf again. It'll be so important if done carefully, the kids today are worse than ever and it needs exposed! Tell the banks that you got Joan Crawford and you'll get far in getting it off the ground!"

"*I Was a Hippy Werewolf?*"

Joan made an awful face. "The youth are troubled in these times more than ever, so it must be serious, as if the werewolf isn't really a monster but is something serious, is really a poetic metaphor…for all that is wrong with kids and their world today. It won't be a horror movie, not really, I don't do formula horror movies since I'm a serious actress, but it's a serious film about psychology with moments of terror and suspense. That's the kids of today."

He grinned as he daydreamed.

Joan thought about how Herman Cohen still had potential and she wanted to help him some more. He was worth it, he was an ambitious self-made man. He had started as an usher at a movie theater in Detroit when was only twelve years old and by eighteen he was managing Detroit's largest movie theater, the Fox Theatre. After being in the Marines he became a sales manager for Columbia Pictures in the 1940s. In the fiftes he started producing, first as an assistant producer for *Bela Lugosi Meets a Brooklyn Gorilla*, then *Bride of the Gorilla* with Lon Chaney Jr.

Herman struck gold in the mid fifties writing and producing *I Was a Teenage Werewolf* for American International. The film cost $100,000 to make and earned more than two million. It made Michael Landon a star. Herman followed that success with more B movie horror that did well at the box office. His last two movies were financed because of Joan Crawford's name and Joan hoped a winning business team was born. She missed being in a man and woman team so much since her last husband died.

* * * * *

The next morning, Joan rang Bill Haines up while she was still in bed having her coffee. "Billy, bless you, tittle-tattle time! I just saw Michael Wilding last night in London! We were on TV together. It was a surprise. I hate TV surprises but this was so sweet since we hadn't seen each other since *Torch Song*. He looks terrible. He was crabby. Rude even. He was just in the Ukraine filming *Waterloo*, a big Dino De Laurentiis movie filmed all over the place in several different countries. He said he almost died while there. And not from the trots. He had a terrible seizure, for real, in the battlefield and Christopher Plummer took care of him, the dear, put him in his own bed and nursed him. I must send Christopher a thank you card. Michael said Russia was hot. I never think of that place as hot. How odd. The interview started out very rocky and ended so boring with the men acting so chauvinistic again as men always do when they gang up in a conversation and act all smart and superior. Everybody thinks war movies are better. And it was all very snobby—*Waterloo* VS *Trog*. But I was lovely, gracious and kind. And I was grateful for the interview, who knows who will be watching and I met fans afterwards. After working with MGM and Pepsi I know how to roll with the punches, or just sit and smile. I can find my serenity in the storm. I know storms don't last. I know better. And I looked better. But I thought Michael was rude. But I can't be sure. And then I ate a steak and kidney pie that was overcooked. I missed you. You should have been there—at the restaurant. It was right up your alley. Classy and expensive with handsome waiters. I would have paid for it, of course. I'm rich. Or you could have paid. You're rich." She laughed.

Bill finally said, "How was Michael rude? Maybe he was just tired from filming in Russia."

"No, I'm not sure exactly but he was angry at me for something that happened long ago. Michael has a chip on his shoulder about something from *Torch Song*. He thinks he should have been introduced on the set. He thinks *I* should have done it. I admit that it was the farthest thing from my mind at the time. I was just thinking about my part and my lines. I didn't know I had to take care of him too. Was I rude? Back then? Do the British really all require introductions? And why did he expect *me* to do it? Wasn't that for the director or producer to do?"

"The letter of the law probably says no but the spirit of the law probably says that you should have introduced him to everyone since you were really the one in charge on that set."

"Now I feel guilty. Damn, I feel like I just dropped the teapot on the queen. I felt bad all last night and I could hardly sleep. I tossed and turned. I really do think they were making a comparison between *Waterloo* and *Trog*. I think they were putting me down because his movie cost more. But I can't be sure. He and Elizabeth Taylor were so snobby to me back then because they were younger. That's how I felt. It all seemed so snobby against me, again. Treating me like a washerwoman's daughter. I'm surprised they didn't just tell me to scrub the BBC floor! The bastards!" Joan let out a sob. "Bill they made fun of me! They didn't mention that anything I did in my movie could help make it a box office hit! They only praised him and his movie!"

Bill said, "Are you worried now about being in a silly monster movie? Are you finally worried it'll just be silly? Are you worried about how people will think of you because you did a movie like this? It's a bit late now. You better make sure your next movie is a huge distraction. Maybe you need to team up with Bette Davis again. That'll get the press clucking."

Joan replied, "Bite your tongue. I'm not a Satanist. And look at you, Mr. High Horse! Are you worried about repeating yourself? Are you worried about having negative thoughts? Are you worried about being grumpy and cantankerous about everything?"

"I worry about *you*, Cranberry!"

"Bill, is anything wrong? How's Jimmy? Are you two still as happy as ever? Gloria and I worry about you. Is anything wrong?"

"Joan do you ever pay attention to the time zones? Do you pay attention to anything anymore? Do you ever pay attention to your scripts anymore? Are you on drugs? Are you nuts?"

"Bill, there's no shame in being a lady scientist and speaking out for science. I have several little speeches in the movie where I defend Trog from the mean people who don't care about science at all. Trog is just a silly monster, sure, movie monsters all are, but this one means something a lot more. It's symbolic. Trog is symbolic for all our science. And Michael Gough's character represents the business interests that too often get in the way of science. And business causes extinction of wildlife, like trogs…and buffalo and dodo birds. It's really all very logical when you think about it as a scientist. It's really a very deep and important movie…when you see the metaphors. And it's about kindness. The world needs love sweet love."

"Business causes extinction? Be careful. They're going to call you a commie."

"Me?" Joan loudly scoffed. "After how angry I got at Castro? After the things I called him and would have told him on the phone if communists had proper long distance service? I don't think so. But don't get me thinking about those days again. Those were such horrible times. I learned a bitter lesson from those days. You work hard for a lot. But the more you have the more you can lose. I thought I lost a lot when I lost the sugarcane fields of Cuba. But then I lost JFK and then my own wonderful husband." Joan let out a sob. "But don't get me started down that path again. It still feels too raw. Thank you for being there so I could cry on your shoulder through all that, even though you probably thought I was the one on the grassy knoll with the gun. You probably still think it, deep down. You're so bad. You're so wicked to me." She tried to laugh.

"You're a bad girl if I ever met one. If I'd been in Dallas at that time I probably would have shot you. I probably would have been jealous of you two, shot you, and taken him."

"And Jimmy would have shot you. All of us shooting each other in a turkey shoot."

"It would have been hard to blame it all on just one bullet then."

Joan shivered. "I shouldn't joke about such things. I just felt such a black cloud come over me, the same one from back then. It was so horrible to lose a friend that way. I don't think I've known anybody else who was shot. And since he was the President it was all over the news for years so it was impossible to shake the feelings from it."

"You did take it hard."

Joan felt herself tear up again. "Thank you for being there for me. I've cried on your shoulder since the 1920s. You were the first one to be nice to me when I first came to Hollywood. We had such fun. And we're still here. Damn, you're a good friend! You're true family!"

Bill asked, "Since when were you ever a spokeswoman for science?"

"Since I played a lady scientist...just now. For years now I've always spoken out for all sorts of medical charities for cancer and children's health, and heart disease. Science is what'll fix all that. So I've always been speaking out for science! It isn't just for men. Gloria Swanson got heavily involved in science. I can too."

He yelled, "To a trog! Ridiculous!"

She yelled back, "I'm sixty-six and I'm not going to be ashamed of playing a scientist at that age, damn you." She sighed and began to talk sadly. "When I did *Torch Song* back in 1953 I was sweating bullets. 1953, valium was still ten years off. I was forty-nine and had to look twenty-five and dance and sing perfectly like a teenager, all while looking cool as a cucumber. I was worried my high notes were too wispy and then when they dubbed me I worried that I sounded far more ridiculous. But when it was all done people came to the theaters to see a grand Joan Crawford show, and nobody found me ridiculous for doing it. *Torch Song* wasn't a nail in my coffin as I feared it might be. I have gone on and on. And after this movie I'll continue with all sorts of new parts. My singing and dancing days are over. Good! I don't have to push it anymore. I don't have to push anything. I can easily play scientists and countesses and boss ladies and tea pouring sleuths...all the many roles a mature actress plays. Those roles are easy and dignified. My true glory days are just beginning! I still have the body of a girl, anyway." Joan just wished she could keep her face tight.

"I bet scientists aren't much to look at, in real life."

"Bless you. What? Oh, sour grapes. I'm a Joan Crawford lady scientist. If you want the lady scientist next door, go next door. And Herman Cohen and I have the best idea for our next picture. I'll play the part of the high school teacher who helps the boy who turns into a werewolf, done as a serious drama with moments of suspense. I play the P.E. teacher to show off my legs and I blow a whistle. We hope to get Michael Landon back and he can play his father, or the policeman who catches him in the end."

"And call it all, *Joan Crawford's Monster*?"

"No, silly. Herman wants to remake his first big hit, *I Was a Teenage Werewolf* for the seventies. It would keep that same title, I suppose. It's a remake. That would give it such great press. There's a lot of different things I can do next that'll get super sensational press!"

In a condescending tone, Bill said, "Cranberry, listen to yourself."

"Who knows, I might play the troubled boy's psychologist. That sounds smarter, doesn't it? But then you don't see my marvelous legs. I will play both!"

"You're an egomaniac."

"I know I, at least, have the legs. I have more confidence now that I'm not expected to be the ultimate perfect love goddess, not for the 1970s, and I don't worry about being an egomaniac anymore, anyway. I now realize that *all* performers need to trick their ego to find their bravery. Performing always takes bravery. Every time. For every performer. You always have to throw a lot of fire on your ego to get your best performance out of yourself—no time for self doubt. I'm not just some washerwoman's whore daughter to hide in the backroom waiting to scrub the floor after all the men have finished pissing on it. Balls! I thinks it's best if the psychologist is also the gym teacher. I do both! That would work just fine and force more scenes! That would get my legs back in a movie. It worked so well for the circus movie."

"Now you're daydreaming."

"That's how all movies start, all art. Dreams. Bill, I don't care how crabby you've gotten. I know you love me. You and I go back before all my husbands. And for all the yelling and fistfights and divorces, if I'm going to still love all them for all time then I'm still going to love you for all time, too. And when I get back to the States I think it's time you redecorated my apartment again. It needs a new seventies look. The Hollywood Regency look you created will never age. Just give it a new modern twist, I know you can, and that will be all the rage in the magazines and everybody will want the brand new Bill Haines seventies Hollywood Regency! I'll show it off in *Homes and Gardens*. And we can sit on a brand new grand chesterfield done up in some sort of new seventies color and we can talk about all sorts of chairs, and how almost all the new stars are dirty slobs and brats, and that'll make us happy again."

"I'll talk to you then."

* * * * *

The morning sun was still low in the sky, lighting up the wings of bugs in the grass. Joan Crawford walked across the patch of lawn between Bray and the Thames to Herman Cohen. He was standing on the banks of the river, his back to her. She called out. "There you are. Doing nothing but dreaming. Plotting your next movie, I hope. We both have a spare minute so I want to ask a favor of you."

"What."

She asked, "Where did you rent the car from—the one that Roderick Stuart drove me around in?"

"A petro station in the village. Why."

"Drive me there. I want to see something."

"Have Roderick Stuart drive you. That's what we pay him for."

"This has to stay a secret from him."

Herman looked angry. "Why, what's he done now?"

She put her hand up. "It'll either prove nothing or little at all."

"What do you mean?"

"Just drive me there and we'll see if there's anything to see."

"Why?"

Joan shrugged. "It's just a thought I have. It might be cockamamie. Maybe not. I'll explain one way or the other when we are there. It'll be easier then." They got into his car. As they rode, she asked, him, "And how are you going to make sure this picture does even better than the last one? We worked so hard to make that circus picture fun. It had animals, a well-hung hunk in silver pants, stunts, and murder. What else could the fans have wanted? We gave it our all."

Herman said, "I now realize monsters are where it's at. If only that circus had a monster. A dinosaur! Or a werewolf! Why didn't I give the circus a werewolf." He laughed. "We've got a star *and* a monster, now. This movie is on a firm foundation. It's a winning formula for the youth crowd. *Trog* will do even better, I'm sure, and that'll lead to another picture. I can't stop thinking about what good timing it is to remake *I Was a Teenage Werewolf*. You're genius to suggest it."

Joan nodded. "That's what I've been thinking about this picture too. We can't go wrong this time. And that's good. You're only as good as your last picture in this business. Luckily your circus movie had my legs and that's all anybody remembers of it." She smiled down at her legs.

When they arrived at the petro station, he asked her, "What are you looking for here? A Pepsi machine? Will you write them a ticket if they don't have one?"

There was a Coca-Cola sign in the window but she pointed the other way at four cars parked in a row. "I want to look in those cars over there. In their back seats."

As they walked over to the cars, he asked, "Why?"

"The car I was first chauffeured in is not the car I'm chauffeured in now. These look like they might be one of the first cars."

A big black dog ran at them barking. Joan crouched down to it.

"Joan, run! It's a mean ole junkyard dog!"

"Nonsense. He just wants love, like all dogs."

The dog stopped in front of her and barked viciously.

She put her hands out. "Here pooch. Look at the baby. Come to mommy."

The dog started wagging his tail as he barked.

"That's right, you just want mommy to give you lovies."

The dog put his head down and walked into Joan's arms. Joan petted him.

Herman asked, "How did you do that?"

"I'm a pet person. I've always had pets. I bet he smells them all over me."

The dog gave Herman a dirty look, barked at him once, and then ran off behind the petro station.

Joan got up and walked to the first car. She opened the backdoor. "Look!"

"Blood?"

She tapped at it. She leaned forward and sniffed at it. "*That's what smelled like fingernail polish! Red spray paint! It leaked out onto the floor. He must have tossed the can in here and it leaked. And so he had to switch cars. I bet that's what happened. I'm sure of it!*"

Herman gasped. "Roderick Stuart? Did he spray paint your trailer in the moors? That was him? He *is* wonky! Is this a clue to something? Why would he put *MONSTER* on your trailer?"

"I have a clue. But I need more."

"Joan, what have you been up to?"

Joan made a determined face. "I'm not sure. I'll have to ask him. I'll have to see what he's been up to. But I'll have to be careful how I ask him. If you just come out and ask a person what they don't want you to know then they'll just lie to you, and then you have worse than nothing. I have to trick him somehow. How does a person get clues? What are clues? How does a person figure things like this out? How does Sherlock Holmes do it?"

Herman shrugged. "I just make movies with monsters. Don't ask me."

Joan tapped her finger on her cheek, and pondered, "Who to ask."

They returned to the studio.

Chapter fifteen

Back at her dressing room at Bray, Joan had an urgent message to call Mary Winklehorn of the Helen Duncan of Windsor Castle Spiritualist Society.

She decided to call Agatha Christie first. It took awhile with the operator since Joan didn't know the number, but after getting it from Gloria Swanson who had gotten it from Marlene Dietrich who had related it in a heavy cockney accent, Joan found the famous murder mystery writer. She was at Winterbrook House north of Cholsey Parish in the county of Oxfordshire.

"Agatha, I'm here in England filming my 81st movie! That doesn't include TV and industrial films of course—I've long ago lost count of all those productions."

Agatha Christie perked up. "Really, love? How tickety-boo! This year celebrates my 81st novel! *Passenger to Frankfurt*. Our stars are aligned this year, it seems."

"I called to ask how you write murder mystery novels. How do you know what a clue means? How do you find clues and add them all up until they mean something?"

"Are you going to become a writer now?"

"Oh no. That sounds fascinating and I *would* like to take classes to learn to write novels someday. But for now I'm a movie star. I ask because I think I might have a real life murder mystery right under my own feet. But I'm not sure. I might just be over imaginative. Artists are."

"Hold on. Before you say another word, let me get my pencil. I never know where my next idea for my next novel might come from."

"Oh this would never be a clever Agatha Christie novel. What's happening here in this village isn't so clever and convoluted. There's only one body that I know of and the police say it's a suicide."

"Oh. The coppers are usually correct on these matters. But not always. Of course I know that coppers can be fooled. What are your clues so far?"

"I don't know if I have any that point to murder. How do I find clues?"

Agatha said, "Just nose around. And talk to the people who you suspect, talk to them all that you can. Make an excuse to spend some time with them and see what falls out of their mouth and into your lap. And don't let them on to you. Don't let them think for a second that you know anything. Play stupid so they give you the easy clues. When people are off their guard they do that. Get their guard down! Get them talking. At least in my novels that works for Miss Marple. Good luck. And if something interesting happens call me back. I never know where my next novel will come from. I can always add murders to it to get it so it has more than one."

"It may not be easy for me." Joan moaned. "You get to put it all together so tidily in fiction and I'm stuck out here in the real world and the clues just aren't so grand. And I really am in a movie called…Joan Crawford really is in a movie called *Trog*. For real. *Oh my god*!" Joan began to weep at the sudden horror that she was really making a movie called *Trog*. She suddenly felt ashamed admitting it to the likes of Agatha Christie.

Agatha asked, "Did you hear what Bette Davis said about you recently? She said you should commit suicide because you are making this movie. She's spreading the rumor that you had to change clothes in an old car in the bog, you didn't get a caravan on location because the show is so cheap and despicable. That gave me an idea for a new book. I love it when movie stars give me ideas for books."

"Called *The Joan Crawford Murders*? Your books aren't considered horror so they are taken seriously."

"I won't use your real name, of course. Like I didn't use Gene Tierney's real name in *The Mirror Crack'd from Side to Side*."

Joan grumbled, "That Bette. I hope she's the one who's found poisoned by her tea and crumpets, in your story. I'm so tired of her comments and antics against me and my work all the time. All the actresses who have caused me so much grief are all such monsters. She's the worse. She wants people to think I'm ridiculous. She spends all her time badmouthing me."

"Hollywood is full of monsters—actresses and actors who are so vain and self absorbed that they can only destroy to get ahead."

Joan whistled in the phone, "*Phew*! I heard you there. I'm glad I can make friends easily and that most the actresses in Hollywood have been good friends with me for decades and decades by now. And of course the actors, too." Joan chortled. "But those bad apples are just monsters, for sure. They only cause trouble the second they're on the set, making everything about them and them alone. That's not me. I'm a team player. I know it takes everybody working their best to make a good movie. Some people are just monsters. They get ahead as they do only because they fascinate people. Monsters are fascinating."

Agatha said, "Psychopaths are fascinating! That's the clinical word for what they are."

"I've met my share. To them, everything is *me me me*. They don't even give me respect for being a top star since they're only thinking about how to get to where I am. They hate me because they're not where I am. And I didn't decide I was a top star because I decided that while looking in the mirror. The fans decide that. Luckily the mean actresses out there are few compared to those who are my friends. There are many lovely actresses in Hollywood who know that standing out isn't all about putting others down."

"You *are* the Hollywood star! And it's a title you have worked long and hard for over and over again," Agatha kindly said. "Love, when they make their next movie from one of my books I'll make sure you get a part."

"Bless you!" Joan started to cough. "Sorry. I've had a cold. I need to smoke more, it'll break up this congestion."

Agatha said, "I'm the only one in England who doesn't smoke. I tried it once. It's the most vile thing I've ever tried." Joan finished her chat with Agatha, ending with Agatha trying her utmost to impress Joan with her most dramatic recitation of all twenty stanzas of the poem The Lady of Shalott… "Out flew the web and floated wide—the mirror crack'd from side to side. 'The curse is come upon me,' cried the Lady of Shalott."

"Cheerio." Joan hung up and made a new drink and then called Mary Winklehorn. Mary explained, "I did a tarot card reading today and it said a famous person I knew would be in great danger as if a curse was upon them. They can only see the world from a mirror's reflection and once they turn away from the mirror there is no turning back. The mirror cracks from side to side."

"It said all that? About the mirror, too?"

Mary admitted, "Well…I've also been thinking about the poem The Lady of Shalott."

Joan gasped. "How uncanny! So have I! So has Agatha Christie! Everybody's thinking about it right now. Why now? Do you think it has something to do with the stars aligning?"

"I didn't realize."

Joan insisted, "That's all I keep hearing about, as if it's what's going on in the world right now—that we're lost in a mirror image of life instead of seeing the real thing…or something."

"The poem seems to be more about movie stars than Camelot, to me. It reminds me of you, the ultimate movie star. It's too easy to see life from the screen, and not from real life anymore."

"Nonsense," Joan argued. "That sounds like some fans, though. But I see plenty of real life and I don't ever confuse it with a movie, I see all the backstage when I do a movie. I've seen all the grimy underbelly of the movie industry, to fall for any of that. I know what's behind the tinsel. And I'm not afraid to look away from the mirror. I'm not cursed like the Lady of Shalott. When I look away from the mirror it doesn't crack. I'm not lost. I just see all the many wonderful things in my real world! I see so many wonderful people. I only look in the mirror to get my freckles covered, it's required for work."

Mary nervously tried to say something but it just came out nonsense.

Joan assumed, "You now think *I'm* cursed? Is that what you're trying to say? *I'm* the famous person you see as in danger? I try not to worry about myself so much like that anymore. It's easy to do that too much when you're famous and everything seems to revolve around you all the time. One time back in Hollywood I just had my hair and face done for a children's hospital charity and I was running to the car and it started to rain and I yelled, 'God why did you do this to me!' And then I realized the rain had nothing to do with me. Everything isn't always all about me. Sometimes it just rains. And I always don't have to pray to God about me. I don't always have to think God is just doing things to me. I can pray for others. I drove to that children's hospital praying for those children, although I thought my hair looked like hell. And then when I saw pictures of it all later my hair looked just fine. A miracle of God? No. I was just worried about myself, too much."

Mary said in a worried tone, "Joan, I'd think that it was *you* who was in great danger…but…but I did an automatic writing and it spelled *Cranberry*. I'm so baffled now. Who could it be? Was your name ever Cranberry?"

For a moment Joan felt dizzy. "That was my name before MGM gave me this name I have now! My good friend Bill Haines from the silent days still sometimes calls me Cranberry. He called me that first thing because of my red hair. That's what it was when it was natural. Oh, no. What do I do? I can't let *Trog* be my last movie. I am still young enough to play all sorts of parts! All the obituaries will say *Joan Crawford of Trog*. I need more serious pictures to end on, when that far off time comes. Will I die on a boat like in the poem? Or will my ashes be spooned off a boat?" She shuddered. "Hey! What do I do?"

"I knew you'd ask that so I asked my tealeaves. They said that something would come to a resolution."

"That could be a good or bad resolution."

"I think it means justice. Are you guilty of anything?" Mary asked.

"Not that I know of. I once stole some dance costumes in Kansas City. I feel so rotten about that even though it was in 1923. I wasn't even a Hollywood star yet, I was so desperate. I wasn't even in New York yet. I wasn't anywhere yet. I was still a kid! Will I forever be punished by God for that?"

Mary said, "I'm asking not because I want to frighten you but because if you're innocent then the justice won't fall on your head but somebody else's."

"Nobody is innocent. And I can't really regret anything, not really. Everything I did in life made me Joan Crawford. If I hadn't stolen those dance costumes then I would have had nothing when I went to New York. And then I wouldn't have made it to Hollywood.

How accurate are those tealeaves? Are you sure they didn't slosh more then they should have in the cup and they really tried to mean something else?"

"They go where the fates tell them."

"I don't understand." Joan asked, "How do tealeaves work? They make pictures? Were they pictures of those damn dance costumes? Am I still to be punished?"

"It's called tasseomancy. You drink the tea until just a very small amount is left and then you swirl the cup. You carefully pour off what is left. The pictures that are left are interpreted with traditional standards of symbolism. I have a dictionary here of symbolism. They're all to be interpreted intuitively, too. What you feel about what you see is as import as what any dictionary reads. It takes a lot of practice to not make a mess sloshing tea and then learning to see symbols from tealeaves. Novices just see a tea jumble and nothing more. I prefer the fine cut. I have no idea how anybody can deal with whole leaf. Fine cut gives you more caffeine from the leaf."

"What did you see in the tea leaves that told you there would be a resolution with justice?"

Mary explained, "The traditional symbols of flying birds and a candle flame. Resolution and justice...for somebody."

"I'll just have to see what that all ends up meaning, won't I? We'll just have to see what I get, in the end."

"You sound so calm."

Joan stated, "I learned long ago that serenity is not freedom from the storm but peace in the course of the storm...and heaven knows there are *always* storms. Oh, I have to go now, bless you for thinking about me, I'm so behind in my calls." Joan hung up and immediately dialed Gloria Swanson. "Gloria! I'm so glad you called. You did call, didn't you, and I'm returning your call? I've lost track of my phone calls. I have it so organized in New York but this has been crazy!"

"Yes, I left a message at the only line in the studio I could get through on. Your line in your dressing room is always so busy."

"Well, anyway, you must have felt me. Agatha Christie said I could have a part in the next Agatha Christie movie that's made! She said she'll insist. And I just can't shake the feeling something bad happened to Lon Chaney Jr. Is he still alive? Did he die last night?"

"He's still alive from all I can tell. I'm sure if he'd died it would be on the radio. Why are you worried about that right now?"

"I always worry about what old star will die next, not that you and I are old, I'm not talking about us, we still have sooo much kick in us…but when people like Peter Lorre, Harpo Marx, Tallulah Bankhead and Ramon Navarro and Kay Francis and Franchot Tone start having funerals you just have to wonder who's next."

Gloria added, "And Vivian Leigh. And Basil Rathbone. And Stan Laurel. And Spencer Tracy. And Buster Keaton. Oh god. And Clara Bow. The greats. Oh god, the list is so big, anymore. But don't get me started on thinking about that!"

"And last night I dreamt that Lon Chaney Jr. was playing Trog and he pulled the mask off and took my vodka bottle and then it was gone. I didn't have my vodka bottle! I went into a panic! How could I live without my vodka, with all the stress I'm always under? They say dreams mean things. You said that. You said they scream at us to pay attention to them! What could this have meant. I tell you what it means. It means that I need to keep a good eye on my vodka bottles or else the drunks around here are going to run off with them!"

"Joan, I called you to call me because I have news."

"Now what."

"Bette is fine again," Gloria said.

Joan swore.

"Bette called Agnes Moorehead who called Debbie Reynolds who called me right up to tell me that she dreamed she didn't remember being a troglodyte at all. She was the queen of Khemet, whatever the hell that is. Isn't it uncanny that when everybody has a past life memory it's always something so grand like that. Everybody has to be the queen of someplace! Even little Khemet gets one!"

Joan said, "She was a trog and that is all."

"The odd thing is that she remembers she had six fingers on her left hand. And when she died they tied her hands down with strong metal bracelets and chains so she wouldn't be able to still strangle her nemeses. I wonder who that would have been?"

Joan felt her face go white as he stammered. "S-six fingers? And did you say Khemet? That's Egypt!"

"How dumb," Gloria said. "All those fingers. But then that would make her a freak. And she said she tried to steal your soul by stealing your part."

"She steals everybody's part but she'll never steal one of mine! Over my dead body!"

Gloria continued, "She was stealing your next part but then she was set on fire and destroyed forever…and there was a black cat…and there was death on the Nile. There was a boat going down the Nile and somebody was murdered. Where have I heard that tale before? Why is it coming to us again from somebody Slicky Stars worked on, and worked on good? Why is Bette saying she kills you to steal your part…and if she plays a character you were supposed to play is that really body snatching? She said it was on a boat on the Nile!"

"Agatha Christie says I get the part!" Joan quickly excused herself, hung up, and then ran off to throw up.

When Joan returned to her dressing room, Mary was there. Joan asked why she hadn't called first since it's so easy to just talk on the phone.

"Your phone doesn't work. Why can't they fix your phone?"

"Yeah, yeah, it's been busy."

"No," Mary corrected. "I just hear terrible sounds. Buzzing. Like bees. A whole swarm of bees!"

Joan picked it up. "Of course it works. Listen. A dial tone."

"When I tried calling I only got the bees and angry sounding garbles. I wanted to tell you about Vanessa's childhood home because many odd things were happening there. May I take you there to see it for yourself?"

"I have to film in a few hours."

Mary insisted, "It won't take that long. We won't be driving far."

"Let my driver drive us. That's his job."

"I would rather drive us. I would rather that boy stay away from that house. I fear he's the danger that we've been warned about. I think we'll be safe in the haunted house if he's not there. If he's with us then all hell could break loose!"

Joan took a step backwards. "Haunted house?"

Mary urgently gestured for her to come. "See for yourself." After Joan downed a stiff drink to calm her stomach, and then made another one for the road, they walked out to Mary's car and she drove Joan toward Vanessa's childhood home. "Sorry to keep you so busy when you have so much to do."

Joan sucked nervously on her cigarette. "We're going to a haunted house? Really? Is that safe?"

"I want you to see this for yourself. Don't be so scared. I will be there with you."

"I suppose it will be clues. I need clues. I suppose getting clues is always dangerous." As the car sped down the road, Joan nervously chattered, "I've been so busy lately. A haunted house will be nice variety. How fun!" Joan smiled big but didn't look convinced. "It's amazing Joan Crawford can fit a haunted house into her busy schedule—who would have thought. I'm so busy these days! Are you sure it's haunted? How haunted? Do they come in degrees of haunted?"

"Don't be so frightened, Joan. I will be there too! Tell me about what you've been busy with."

Joan told her about a new autobiography she was starting when she got back to New York. "And I'll make sure I put a recent picture in it from *Trog*. That'll show how proud I am of it, completely. That'll show a science picture isn't beneath me. I'm not a snob. I like to work, and science is a serious theme of many modern pictures. I've done everything, but a haunted house is unusual for me. Are you sure it's really haunted?" As they pulled up to the house Joan noticed a huge black mess off to one side of it. "A fire?"

Mary nodded and pulled to a stop between stone lions in the driveway. "Just one wing of the house burned. Just two rooms. An upstairs and downstairs, only. The upstairs room was Mary's bedroom. The ground floor room, a study. The rest of the house wasn't touched."

They got out and walked up the rest of the driveway to where it looped in front of the mansion. Joan asked, "But if her room burned away then what is there to see?"

"Something very bold and odd on the other side of the wall from it."

Joan looked about at the house and grounds. "She lived in this nice place? She was once a princess."

"Only as a child," Mary explained. "We have found that manifestations often occur where a person has been a child, if they have lived many places when alive. Vanessa told us that she first became interested in spiritualism as a child when she had a toy horse that she insisted talked to her. She said it was somebody who had died who was channeling through the toy. So she has always had strong psychic abilities."

"Was the toy horse burned in this fire?"

Mary said, "I imagine all those toys are long gone, long before this."

Stepping over the threshold of the front door, Joan clawed at the air in front of her face.

Mary said, "There's no spider webs here."

"I feel them on my face. And... I smell flowers! I smell an entire flower shop." Joan looked around and didn't see any bouquets. "Do you smell it too? Where's it coming from?"

"No. I just smell *burnt*. Maybe you smell the ghost."

"We can *smell* ghosts?"

Mary nodded. "They engage our senses however they can."

Up the stairs and in the hallway they opened the door to her bedroom, now opening to the outdoors. Joan looked down at the burnt rubble. "What is there to see?"

"In here. Look at what's on this wall. Look at the burn marks in the wallpaper. The other side of this wall was her bedroom."

"I see something, yes. Does it say something?"

"Oh yes." Mary nodded. "You can't see it clearly just by looking at it, but look at it in the mirror."

Joan turned her back to the hallway wall and held up her compact. In it, she looked at the wallpaper. In the reflection, in reverse, she saw *MONSTER* burned on it, looking like spray paint letters. In the same instant she spotted that, her mirror and her cocktail glass broke. Her vodka was already gone but the ice cube slid all the way across the floor and rested against the far wall. "Is the floor tilted?"

Mary gasped. "The floor? Glass broke! Your mirror!"

Joan shivered. "Yes. Uncanny. Terrifying!"

"And didn't you see it? *MONSTER*! It isn't Vanessa's word for herself but a word to accuse another. Roderick has been putting that word on walls around town. It was on this side of the wall backwards, somehow burned through from the other side. She wrote it from beyond the grave from her bedroom. That's why the letters are backwards to us here in the hall. It's a clue from Vanessa to us about Roderick."

Joan rubbed her lip in thought. "How do you know he's been doing this vandalism? What evidence do you have? Have you *seen* him do it? What do you know? I have my own suspicions but I want to know why you think that."

Mary put her hands up to feel the air. "*I just know*! And I just know Roderick killed Vanessa." She folded her hands. "And I once saw him buying a can of red spray paint at the do-it-yourself shop. The hardware shop. He looked so guilty. He had *vandal* written all over him. They should refuse to sell spray paint to shifty young people that look like him. I asked him what it was for, I was so suspicious. He had to think and then he finally said he was painting a bike. I've never seen him with a red bike, or any bike."

"Are we sure?"

She gestured to the hallway wall. "Don't you see it here?"

Joan looked around at the hallway. Her eyebrows knitted together. "I see the words on the wall clear as day, especially when in the mirror. *MONSTER*. That, I see. And yes, it all seems to suggest Roderick Stuart. Now if there's nothing else to see here, get me back to the studio before I'm missed."

Chapter sixteen

After the last day's shooting ended, Roderick Stuart held the car door for Joan. She was dressed in a black and white plaid dress with a red plaid Scottish tam that had a red pompom on top. She bragged, *Trog* and *Berserk* both came in on schedule and under budget. Herman Cohen and I are sure to be the next big team!"

He congratulated her.

She asked if there was any place in town to get fish and chips.

Roderick Stuart nodded. "At the frigging pub. Sure they got nosh."

"Nosh. Right. And ale!"

"Of course there's that, there, too."

"Oh wonderful. Drive me there. I won't get fat in one day, and even if I do it doesn't matter. All the shots are in the can. I want to have some fish and chips, and some ale before I go back to New York. You can get all that in New York, too, sure. But it's not the same as having it here."

He drove her into the village. When he stopped, she said, "I can take a cab home from here. No need to wait for me. I'm sure you have other plans tonight—better ones than babysitting a movie star on the town."

He insisted that he had no other plans.

Joan looked at him sadly. "Bela Lugosi once told me, 'I guess I'm pretty much a lone wolf. I don't say I don't like people at all but, to tell you the truth, I only like them if I have a chance to look deep into their hearts and their minds."

"Wow, man, you knew Bela Lugosi? He's my very favorite!"

"Of course I did. He made movies. I made movies. We're both movie people."

Roderick Stuart stood firm. "I'm like Bela Lugosi! I only like people I get to know. I've gotten to know you. I want to stay and drive you home. And until then buy me a blooming beer."

"Very well. But just one. I don't want you driving me into a ditch." As they walked up to the Werewolf Inn, Joan asked, "Was this named that because back in medieval times there were terrible wolf attacks?"

"No. It was named this in 1960 when Hammer Films came out with *Curse of the Werewolf*. Otherwise, before then, it was just called The Acorn. Not as exciting for tourists who have come in to see Windsor Castle."

He held the door for her as she asked, "Did Freddie Frances direct it?"

"No. Terence Fisher. He's a great Hammer director, too." On the wall facing the door was a large framed movie poster of *Curse of the Werewolf* and it had been autographed by its star Oliver Reed. Roderick Stuart shouted, "Presenting Joan Crawford in town to shoot at my Bray Studios!"

Everybody was gobsmacked at the sight of Joan Crawford but then after he repeated it there was finally applause and whistles.

Joan put a cigarette between her lips as she turned to Roderick Stuart and said, "Bless you, and I'm sure everybody in the pub thinks of Bray as their own, too. Now light me up, handsome."

He did. They sat at a table and Joan asked for two orders of fish and chips and a pitcher of ale. Then she got up, mingled, and signed autographs to greet everyone in the bar, and put them at ease. "I'm delighted to visit your werewolf pub. Now I want to see the movie."

"Oliver Reed was okay," a man said, "but it should have starred Margaret Rutherford."

Joan asked why.

He said through laughter, "Then they wouldn't have needed any makeup for when she's the werewolf." Some others laughed. Some groaned.

One woman grew angry. "Margaret Rutherford is a national treasure!"

Roderick Stuart laughed. "When she's wearing a tie she looks just like a lezzy."

Joan grabbed Roderick Stuart's arm and steered him to their table. A pitcher of ale was already there waiting for them. As Joan poured the pitcher, she said, "That's enough fun at another actress' expense. Especially one who is so good at acting. If you want to mock someone, mock a woman who is worthy of it. Bette Davis."

Roderick Stuart asked Joan. "Is she a lezzy?"

"She's a werewolf. That I'm sure of."

A young woman walked up to Joan with a blank piece of typing paper. "May I have your autograph?"

"Bless you. For you, dear?"

"For Mum. It'll make a nice birthday present. Could you write on there *happy birthday Mumsie, from Jane*? And then your name real big right there. She used to go to your movies all the time, being an old timer."

Before Joan wrote anything, she looked hard in the young woman's eyes. "I suppose you already think your mother is an *old folk* and she probably isn't even forty yet. You probably think she hasn't kept up with the times so you just tune the *old folks* out. This is a crises for any thinking woman that I call *the late-thirties syndrome*. Kids always take mother for granted. Kids think they're smarter than Mom once they go to school and learn anything, as if we *old folk* went to caveman school and only learned old fashioned things that don't matter anymore, it being so long ago. You think that all us mothers worry about is if you dress correctly and say all your prayers before meals and bed—and you think you're too modern to dress up or pray…or be nice about anything at all."

"I'm not putting Mum down. I'm thinking about her now. This'll give her such a thrill!"

Joan wrote on the paper and then took off her earrings and handed them to her. "These don't match my outfit anyway. Give these to your mother from Joan Crawford, also. She loves you very much and deserves a special day that's all about her."

"But…but…that's too much!" The young woman ran off with the gift. Their fish and chips arrive. Joan nibbled on one of each.

Roderick Stuart said, "That was so nice of you to give your earrings away like that. Now you don't have any earrings on."

Joan shrugged. "If anybody takes a photo of me now do you think I'll look any less for it? Look at me." She resituated her loud hat. Then she rummaged through her purse, found two other earrings to clip on, and then took out her cigarette lighter. She put it on the table and slid it to Roderick Stuart. "Try not to hock it right away."

He looked amazed at the lighter.

"Yes, take it. It's silver. And my name is engraved on it so there's no doubt it's all Joan Crawford. Don't lose it and you'll have something to show your grandkids as you tell them the tale of Roderick Stuart and the movie star." She took a book of matches from the table and tossed them in her purse.

He thanked her profusely.

A man walked up to the table and said with an Irish accent, "I know this is just a pub and not a cowboy tavern but could you say something from *Johnny Guitar*? I love that movie. I can't say I love cowboy movies but that was such a treat that *you* did one. There's no cowboy movie like it."

Roderick Stuart grinned to encourage her. He added, "Nobody would care about it today if it wasn't a Joan Crawford movie!"

"I almost got killed in that one. Boy did they pick on me in that movie."

The Irish man asked, "For real? On the set?"

Joan chuckled. "No. My character, of course. Otherwise the movie was one long picnic with my children. But here's a good line for you, for this place." Joan stood up, held a butter knife out at him, and gave him the evil eye. "Down there I sell whiskey and cards. All you can buy up here is a bullet in the head. Now what do you want?"

Everybody clapped. Joan smiled, bowed, and then sat. The Irish man asked her, "You're such a sport. It's such an honor to have a star as big as Joan Crawford in our club. Would you like to join our werewolf club? Then you can sign your name in our special pub book."

Joan grinned. "Bless you! It would be such an honor. I'd love to! How thrilling to be asked to join a club! I'm so excited! How do I join? This is a sign, I'm sure, that I'll make another picture with my wonderful producer. We'll be the next new team!" She grabbed for her purse. "How much?"

"No fee. All you have to do is tell a werewolf story for us all to hear. It doesn't have to be a corker. Just something. Last night your producer Herman Cohen joined our club. He told us all about his first big hit, the one that made him a big producer. He told us all about *I Was a Teenage Werewolf*. Out in 1957. He said it made over two million in its first run. Wow. Who would have thought you could add a monster to *Rebel Without A Cause* and make so much money?"

Joan nodded as she winked. "He thought it! He's a clever chap. And a little birdie told me he might remake it for the seventies." She looked around. "Look at how popular this kind of thing is, and I'm always up with the times." She put her finger over her lips. "But it's not official yet so don't go telling everybody yet. And I might play the part of the understanding high school P.E. teacher who is also the school psychologist. So I can show my legs *and* be smart! And I also hope I have a scene in my kitchen at home where I'm making sandwiches for the kids and talking about kind and gentle things. That's what a monster movie really needs to be all about, in the end…that we all need to be more kind and gentle to each other. People take their friends for granted too much anymore. The kids just don't realize today could be their last. Put a werewolf in their lives and that'll wake them up!"

The Irish man said, "He says he'll send up a movie poster of the original movie. He's going to get Michael Landon to sign it too. That will be the bee's knees up on our wall next to Oliver Reed!"

Joan looked at the wall with everybody else. "Yes, it'll be lovely for a werewolf inn." She imagined a new color poster next to it with her screaming face on it that read *Joan Crawford in Teenage Werewolf 1970*.

"Will you become a member too? It'd be so thrilling to have your name in our book too."

"I don't know if I know any werewolf stories. I haven't read the script yet. The remake hasn't been written yet!" Joan looked lost.

He said, "Just make something up. Anything."

"Anything? Oh dear." Joan looked off in thought, and then took a big gulp of her ale. "The only werewolf I know is Bette Davis. Or maybe she's a trog bitch. Maybe she's just a mutt. A junkyard dog."

Roderick Stuart encouraged her. "Tell any blooming story you like! Tell us about that old wound up dishrag."

Joan stood. "This monster tale is from far far away. This is the tale of the Hollywood Werewolf. Baby Jane. I was a fool and felt sorry for Bette Davis and thought she was a good actress and nothing more. Little did I know I'd been confusing good acting with crazy antics and mannerisms. And never confuse good acting with vulgar behavior. I bought the film rights to the novel *Whatever Happened to Baby Jane* and asked Bette to be in it with me, since her career had tanked by then and mine was going strong. I felt sorry for her. That's the only reason she agreed to do it—she badly needed work. She was broke. She hadn't had any work in quite some time. Hollywood was through with her and had already forgotten about her. I was supposed to play Baby Jane. So the first thing she did to throw me for a loop was insist we switch parts. I did it because I didn't know yet that if you give her an inch she takes a mile. But in spite of Bette's antics behind the scenes, the *Baby Jane* movie did very well and her head swelled up like you wouldn't believe, and she took all the credit."

There was applause.

Joan put her hand up for silence. "This monster tale has a part two. *Baby Jane* was so popular that everybody insisted we do another movie together right away. When another story starring the both of us was agreed upon that had the right mix of drama and suspense, she had decided from the start that she would get rid of me and then make the film all her own. That's how ungrateful she was that I'd saved her career by giving her that comeback. As we filmed *Whatever Happened to Cousin Charlotte*, its original title to remind everybody of our earlier success, she did everything she could to sabotage me. She came back with even more antics. She had the script rewritten to steal my scenes. She made rude noises during my takes, and then she'd always say to me afterwards, in a shrill voice, '*Is that how you're going to play it?*' I'm a sensitive actress and I absorbed all her hate and anger. I became a nervous wreck. It became nearly impossible for me to face the camera with her sneering at me right in front of the cue cards. One day when I was hunting down empties to return I found a Pepsi bottle full of pee. You just don't know how much money Pepsi loses when bottles are not returned. I blamed Bette for that pee stunt, of course. I finally fell sick. Then Bette Davis swooped in like a raven of death. She called

Olivia de Havilland and arranged to have her replace me. While I lay in the hospital bed with a high fever, while listening to a radio interview with Bette Davis, I heard her say that I was fired and replaced. That's how I first heard the news. I was devastated. She had my three Pepsi machines on the set sent to the town dump and then she paraded around the set with Coca-Cola as if she owned that company. I should have been immune to that sort of mean and nasty nonsense—I fought Norma Sheerer all the time back in the thirties at MGM and she always won since she was married to the head of production. But it felt like a kick in the gut just the same." Joan wiped a tear. "That is the true story of the Werewolf of Hollywood. Thank you and please choose Pepsi and give generously to the March of Dimes. Now, Roderick Stuart, can you please be a dear and have this pitcher refilled." When he got up she took a compact out of her purse and redid her lipstick.

* * * * *

The next morning, Joan sat in the back seat of the car holding a funeral bouquet of orange and yellow gladiolus, carnations, and Peruvian lilies. "Careful around the turns in the road, today. My head is spinning. With those extra pitchers of ale, on top of everything else, I'm rather hung over this morning. What am I doing up? God it's early. What time is it really? It can't possible be what the clock says it is."

Roderick Stuart said, "Thou art so fat-witted, with drinking of old sack and unbuttoning thee after supper and sleeping upon benches after noon, that thou hast forgotten to demand that truly which thou wouldst truly know. What a devil hast thou to do with the time of the day? Unless hours were cups of sack and minutes capons and clocks the tongues of bawds and dials the signs of leaping-houses and the blessed sun himself a fair hot wench in flame-coloured taffeta, I see no reason why thou shouldst be so superfluous to demand the time of the day."

"Was that insolence?"

"Shakespeare. If you've made yourself ill at the tavern always consol yourself with Shakespeare. Shakespeare said everything first. England is best." Roderick added, "That was fun last night, wasn't it? You were pretty gassed. On the way home you were so out of it you kept saying that there was a little bit of trog in all of us."

"Oh that's right! That's the word I couldn't remember. It was right on the tip of my tongue. Atavism. Yes, we do all have a trog in us. It's called atavism! And if you're naughty you might grow your tail back, too."

"You need to go the pub more often."

"I hadn't danced those dances since the 1920s…oh my aching back."

"If you need to honk just let me know so I can stop the car."

"Honk?"

"Puke. You sure have a lot of great stories about old Hollywood."

"Yes I do. And there's a very naughty one I forgot." She leaned forward and told Roderick Stuart her bawdy Tallulah Bankhead story.

He replied, "I didn't know she was a lezzy."

"A what?"

Roderick Stuart repeated, "A lezzy."

Joan asked, "As in…*lesbian*?"

"Yeah." He shook his head in dismay. "*Sheesh.*"

Joan took her pencil and pad out of her purse and tapped it on his shoulder. "Could you spell that for me? I want to write that story down for posterity."

"Write what?"

"Write the word lesbian down for me. Just do it."

He took it and wrote while driving, "L. E. Z. B. I. A. N."

Joan took it back and clasped her hands as if in prayer. "Thank you Agatha."

"What was that? Who?"

"Agatha Christie."

"You know her too?"

"Yes, we just talked on the phone not too long ago and she promised me a part in her next movie from one of her novels. Now…I may not be as clever as Miss Marple…but…" Joan clenched her jaw. "…you killed Vanessa. Didn't you."

Roderick Stuart jolted. "W-what? Why would you say that?"

"It isn't spelled with a Z."

"Time to slam on the anchors!" He hit the brakes hard and turned the car around in the road in a violent spin, almost hitting a red phone booth at a crossroads.

Joan fell sideways onto the seat, almost sliding to the floor, as she yelled at him and cursed.

Roderick Stuart yelled back, "Man, you've been snooping around where you shouldn't have been. Man, you really did it now!"

Joan put her hand on the door handle. "Drive me back to my hotel immediately. I'm through with you young man!"

He pushed down harder on the gas. The car roared and bounced violently down narrow gravel back roads until he came to his own house, a small unkempt cottage with a small weedy front yard. He grabbed her arm and forced her inside. Finally sitting on a chair in the small kitchen in the front of the house, she asked him, "Are you going to rape me?"

He grabbed an extension chord and tied her hands behind the chair. All the while he grumbled and cursed while reciting mad bits of Shakespeare.

Joan screamed for him to stop it.

Roderick Stuart smiled oddly, showing all his teeth. "Don't worry, not really, it's all just a movie. Life is just a movie. Shadows full of sound and fury. And after I kill you in the killer movie, you will star in another movie! But in this movie you don't touch me. I touch you. I touch you…tomorrow and tomorrow and tomorrow, creeps in this petty pace from day to day…"

"Don't touch me!"

"To the last syllable of recorded time!" He finished tying her up and stepped back.

Joan asked, "Now that I know you killed Vanessa, why? Why?"

"Told by an idiot! Sound and fury!"

"Why! Why!"

He stomped his foot. "The studio, you idiot. She didn't want to sell. I needed to sell to make some money. I need some money fast."

Joan looked at him cockeyed. "But…but Hammer owns it."

"No. Granddad owned it and he died. He put in his will a list of relatives that needed to all agree on what to do with his estate. And agree unanimously. It was owned by a Winklehorn. Vanessa is my cousin and she didn't want to sell."

"That's why you killed her? Are you on drugs? Where did you get this information? Was there actually a reading of the will, in the real world, that spelled all this out? Was it legal? It's absurd! Hammer Studios owns it and bought it in 1951. Now Hammer has it up for sale. Everybody knows that!"

"I don't know about all that with Hammer. I just know granddad really did own it. It's a Winklehorn manner house. A Winklehorn Studio! We had it first! We have it forever…until I sell it!"

"Who told you that? Did Vanessa tell you that?"

"She just told me that we were in her movie. And then she later told me that she hoped Hammer never sold Bray. I always told her it was mine. I grew up there. Grandpa had it and he grew up there! I played there at the back lot. I knew all the secret ways to get inside and all the secret rooms in the main house. It was mine! It's mine! It was *my* movie, not hers! And everybody has to give it to me! I need to sell it! I need the money! It's all mine."

"Is that why you spray painted across my dressing room trailer, and the back lot, and wherever else you might have put your name? *MONSTER*. You thought you were putting your name on it all?"

"Monster! Monster! Monster!"

Joan winced sadly. "You're insane. At what age did you start doing drugs? You are on drugs, aren't you?"

"I've never done drugs…no way…uh uh…except the mental ones they gave me at the hospital. And it's all Vanessa's fault anyway. She needed to die anyway."

"For being a lesbian?"

"I don't think she was one of those. Not really."

"Then why make it seem like she was? That was cruel to her memory. Now that's what the police think of her. Luckily they didn't make that suicide note common knowledge. It's fake!"

"I should have exposed her for what she really was but I thought it would look worse to make it seem as if she was a lesbian. Then everybody would believe that she needed to kill herself."

"What do you think is worse?"

He sobbed. "When I was little she molested me. She diddled me in the night. I would wake up to her diddling and diddling!" He started to scream. "Diddling and diddling! Diddling about! Diddling about!"

"But she was just a girl. Was it so bad?"

"She said it wasn't real because it was night—to pretend it was only a movie. I was her little monster and she was the princess. She was weird. She scared me. She said I had to do what she wanted because I was in her movie. Everything was only her movie. She did weird things to me in the night when she stayed over in the summer. Diddling and diddling! Pulling on me like that! Pulling and diddling and kissing and licking and sucking like I was soon to be eaten down like crumpets! And the way you looked at me in the rearview mirror as I drove you back and forth! Making me blush. Wanting to diddle me! Diddling and diddling and diddling! *Diddle diddle diddle*! Everything a movie! Making me think about diddling and diddling…and terrifying me! Don't touch me!"

"I am tied up. No one can touch you now, so now calm down, Roderick Stuart. You've had a terrible shock in your life as a tender boy or at least some confusion you never sorted out for some reason. Vanessa playing a nighttime game of princess and monster should not have done all this to you. Children play doctor with each other all the time and as naughty as that might get it usually doesn't lead to such shock. There is something deeper. Talking about it is the first part of getting well. And shock treatments work, too. They worked for you once and they'll work for you again. They did for Cliff Robertson in *Autumn Leaves*. I stood by him, I'll stand by you. I'm sure they've improved shock treatments since you've last had them. Let me take you to a hospital that can get you proper care. I'll pay for your bed and I know a doctor who will treat you for free. I've been doing this for people for many decades now. It's one of my charities, paying for hospital beds for those who can't afford it. Sometimes that goes for mental healthcare, too. Let me help you! I want to help you! Oh wait…you already get that provided for you in England, anyway. It's all yours, all the care in the world. Here there is healthcare for all! Take it!"

"Father tried to help me! He beat me saying it would toughen me up! He smashed my models kits, telling me they were a bad influence. They were glow-in-the-dark Universal Monsters! I made sure he sunk to the bottom of the Thames one fishing trip! He wanted me to be normal and fish. I made sure he was in a movie where the sea monster drowns the stupid drunk fisherman. I made a movie where the fisherman became fish food. And he never came back!" Roderick Stuart laughed joyously.

"You need help!"

"Just give me the cash! Give me the cash now! I need money now! I need it now or it's a gangster movie and I'm dead!"

Joan stubbornly shook her head. "No, you'll just spend it on the wrong kind of drugs. I don't blame you for doing drugs. You were just trying to medicate yourself. But you need a doctor's care and treatments that will work for you."

Roderick Stuart picked up a heavy cast iron frying pan and screamed, "I will smash in your head! The monster is on the loose and the villagers are screaming in the streets with pitchforks and torches and angry faces and angry minds! Everybody is killed and stomped on and smashed away for all time! Everything burns down! The windmill burns down! The dam breaks! The monsters are washed away in a great deluge!" He growled. "You can't look at me, then! You can't touch me then! You can't diddle me and diddle me and diddle me! And the studio will stay mine and I will sell it and make the money I need! I will make my money! My money!" He started screaming. "The mummy movie will make a lot of money for me!"

A middle-aged thug with a Welsh hat walked in from the back of the house with a gun pointed at him.

Roderick Stuart dropped the frying pan and stopped screaming. He said, "Bloody hell. How did you get here?"

"I broke your bedroom window and you didn't even hear me, you stupid cabbage." He went to the front door and opened it. Three more men stepped in with guns drawn. The kitchen became crowded.

The thug with a Welsh hat said to Roderick Stuart, "You better have the money or you're in deep trouble." He looked at Joan. "What's with the little old lady. Is she rich? Did you kidnap her? You bloody idiot."

"I am Joan Crawford."

He looked at her closely. "Really? Hey boys! That used to be Joan Crawford!"

They all came close and talked all at the same time:

"I love your movies!"

"I love it when you shoot people!"

"*This Woman is Dangerous* was such a great movie!"

"*Sudden Fear* was best!"

"*The Damned Don't Cry* is my favorite movie!"

"You made the best crime movies!"

"The very best gangster movies were Joan Crawford movies!"

The thug with the Welsh hat started to untie her, "Why are you all tied up like that? What's this stupid cabbage been doing to you?"

Joan rubbed her wrists. "Anybody have a cigarette?"

They all said, with gusto, "Abso-bloody-lootely!"

"I'm dying for one right now." Joan looked pained.

They all rushed to give her one of theirs. The thug with the Welsh hat gave her his and lit it humbly.

Joan Crawford struck a subtle aristocratic Joan Crawford pose out of *Humoresque*. "Thank you, boys."

A thug asked, "Why did he tie you up? Are you kidnapped? What a bloody idiot!"

Roderick Stuart started to scream again. He was punched in the face. He fell silent.

The thug with the Welsh hat said, "He owes us money. A lot. In London he was doing heroin it turns out he nicked. It was during the All Monster Film Festival he was supposed to be helping out on. So don't worry about him. Funny how everybody thinks his father got done in by thugs. Well, like father like son. But before we let him take a swim in the Thames, before we go, before we can let you just *go*…can I have your autograph?"

They all insisted on an autograph and then they dragged Roderick Stuart to the door. Roderick said, "Wait a minute. May I say one last thing to Joan Crawford?"

"No."

Joan said, not looking at him, "Let him explain himself to me. He owes me that. That was very rude what he just did to me. And he once said he had fallen in love with me. It's always troubling when a fan turns on the star they loved with such hate."

"Well…okay…I guess just this once…since you're Joan Crawford, and all." The thug kicked Roderick in his leg. "Say goodbye to the lady."

"Shakespeare. He was the best…because he was British."

"Stop stalling!" The thug kicked him in the leg again.

"When in disgrace with fortune and men's eyes, I all alone beweep my outcast state, and trouble deaf heaven with my bootless cries, and look upon myself, and curse my fate, wishing me like to one more rich in hope, featured like him, like him with friends possessed, desiring this man's art, and that man's scope, with what I most enjoy contented least. Yet in these thoughts myself almost despising, haply I think on thee, and then my state…like to the lark at break of day arising from sullen earth…sings hymns at heaven's gate, for thy sweet love remembered such wealth brings that then I scorn to change my state with kings."

Joan blinked tears away from her eyes and said to the thugs. "Be kind to him. Don't let his fate be too harsh. He *is* a troubled young man. And he did recite so very beautifully. What a lovely accent. That means a lot."

"Yes, I am a great movie!" Roderick said.

The thugs grunted and nodded as if they were only humoring her and then dragged Roderick out and drove away.

Joan got in Roderick Stuart's car and drove until she stopped at the red phone booth at the crossroads. "Hello? Police? I mean constables. Is Bobby the Copper in?"

"Bobby is a Copper."

"Yes, Bobby. May I speak with him?"

"There's no one here named Bobby. Coppers are bobbies."

"I am confused. But at the moment I'm confused about everything. I just realize that I have no idea what just happened but I'm pretty sure it's crazy. Roderick Stuart my driver is being taken to the Thames and they say he's going to go swimming. But I fear they have other plans. I fear they'll drown him!"

"Who?"

"Terrible mean thugs."

"We'll keep an eye on the river. Where are you at?"

Joan sucked hard on the last of her cigarette and tried to think. "At a crossroads. Near the town of Bray. And Windsor at Berkshire. And I'm at Charring Cross and the River Thames, too. Hell I don't know. We're also filming at an estate that looks like a grand castle called Oakley Court just around the corner from Bray. And I think I heard there's a place nearby called New Lodge at Winklehorn. But they could take him anywhere along the river. And maybe they'll just push him in to teach him a lesson. But I don't know. I don't know what's going on! I once met a man called Bobby the Copper. Can you just ask if anybody there remembered filming with Joan Crawford? He filmed with her! Me! That's the Bobby I'm asking for!"

"Miss Crawford, we have a large department for this sized village, with Windsor Castle here and all. All the tourists everyday. Thousands of them every hour. I really can't help you too much with the information you've just given me. If you'd just come into the station we have people who are good at sorting out information. If you could just come in and make a report. We could show you pictures of our bobbies until you see the one you're looking for."

She hung up the phone, then added, "Bless you and I'll ask for Bobby later after I realize how anybody could be so stupid to think they could sell Bray Studios owned by Hammer Films, just because they have a gambling or drug debt, or whatever that was. I'll make no sense if I try to tell this as a story. Stories are supposed to make sense."

Then she drove on the wrong side of the road again until she could ask for directions and was also told to get on the right side of the road. She headed back to Windsor Cemetery and walked through all the pine trees and tombstones until she was at the far corner. She found Vanessa's new stone Star of David grave marker. She put the funeral bouquet in front of it. Joan gasped. It said that the woman had been born 1919.

Surprised, Joan said aloud to the grave, "You were fifty-one years old! And here all this time I'd imagined you were almost a girl. I had *decided*. How funny I did that. How odd that I did that to somebody that I have felt so close to these past weeks. Look at that. You are somebody I haven't known at all, and now I feel so silly. I suppose that's how it is with everybody. There's all sorts of things we don't know about a person that would change everything about them if we found out. I'm sure it's that way for everybody. May you rest in peace." Joan put the flowers on the grave, said some Shakespeare from Hamlet, "And flights of angels sing thee to thy rest", and she left.

Joan suddenly felt completely lost. She couldn't wait to get back to New York and sign on to another movie and be Joan Crawford again.

Epilogue

Roderick Stuart was never seen again, the village assumed he had gone back to London to be a hippy.

Trog was released in 1970 and 1973 as part of double bills and though it made a profit it was Joan Crawford's last big screen movie. Pepsi retired Joan Crawford after *Trog*, wanting a younger image. She appeared three more times on television in excellent hour episodes of *The Virginian, The Tim Conway Comedy Hour*, and *The Sixth Sense (*which was also re-cut as a half hour *Night Gallery* episode*)*. After 1972 she never worked again except for charity spots. She stayed Steven Spielberg's "Hollywood Guardian Angel" calling on her army of industry friends to help him all they could, until he made *JAWS* and then he didn't need her help anymore, but they stayed friends. In 1976 Joan was asked to appear in *Airport 77* but she had become feeble and reclusive so made excuses why she couldn't do it. Olivia de Havilland replaced her again. It would have been her third film with Maidie Norman as her sidekick. Joan Crawford died in 1977 after wasting away from stomach, pancreatic or liver cancer, possibly from having eaten so much lipstick her whole life. She never went to a doctor and refused all medicine even though she had given so much money to hospitals and medical charities in her life. She died at home with a few friends at her bedside. She had stopped smoking and drinking, cold turkey, three years before after falling in her apartment and hitting her head on the coffee table. She would have been offered the role of "Ma" Kent in the 1978 all-star *Superman* if she had lived.

Hammer Films sold the Bray Studio in November 1970 to a team of private investors in London and for the next few years filmed at Elstree Studios before it made its last horror movie in 1976. In 1975 *The Rocky Horror Picture Show* was filmed at Bray Studios and Oakley Court making the place famous all over again (too many people forgot that the French Resistance had famously operated out of there in World War Two).

Lon Chaney Jr. died in 1973 of a heart attack and his liver and lungs were put in jars to show the damage caused by smoking and drinking. Medical students dissected his entire body. To this day he has no grave nor star on the Hollywood Walk of Fame. The epic memoir he wrote about his and his father's career was never published.

Bill Haines died of cancer in 1973 and Jimmy committed suicide soon after. William Haines Designs remains in operation with main offices in West Hollywood and showrooms in New York Denver and Dallas.

Agatha Christie died in 1976 of pneumonia. When Bette Davis was in the 1978 Agatha Christie movie *Death on the Nile* she remarked to Mia Farrow, while on the boat, that she stole Joan Crawford's part "over her dead body". Bette died in 1989 of cancer. Bette's last words, "The best time I ever had with Joan Crawford was pushing her down the stairs" (referring to when filming *Whatever Happened to Baby Jane*).

Frenchy was stabbed to death in 1978 by a Joan Crawford drag queen. Michael Wilding died in 1979 after he hit his head from another seizure. Joan Blondell went on to appear in nineteen more movies, including *Grease*, after Joan saved her career by keeping her insurable. She died of leukemia on Christmas Day 1979. Gloria Swanson died in 1984 of a heart attack. Lucille Ball died in 1989 of heart disease. Vincent Price died from emphysema in 1993. Stanley Kubrick died of a heart attack in 1999. Freddie Francis died from a stroke in 2007. Elizabeth Taylor died of congestive heart failure in 2011. Herman Cohen died of throat cancer in 2002. May everybody rest in peace.

Have you read *The Joan Crawford Murders*? Available on Kindle and in paperback at Amazon.

Printed in Great Britain
by Amazon.co.uk, Ltd.,
Marston Gate.